CW00553051

'This novel does not shy away from blis[...]
identity, but rather leans into them . . . T[...]
capital "C" culture can be both all-defining in life and also a mere detail . . .
His greatest skill is in describing the simple pleasures that sustain us.'

Esi Edugyan, *New York Times*

'Talty's writing feels to me like a gift of many lifetimes. Forgiveness,
Morgan shows us, is also the work of a lifetime. The people to whom
we feel closest can somehow be right beside us in the kitchen and
simultaneously on some unreachably distant planet. People rotate away
from each other for days or seasons at a time, and it's miraculous when
they return to find each other again, turning towards each other instead
of away. It's a treacherous thing, to love another person in this world that
mixes so much beauty with so much sorrow. Thank you for reminding
us, Morgan, that it is the necessary thing.'

Karen Russell

'Talty is a beautiful craftsman . . . His narrator made me care most about
his story's most vulnerable person.'

Dan Shapiro, *Washington Post*

'Soulful and assured.'

Hamilton Cain, *Minneapolis Star Tribune*

'It's Talty's commitment to the hungover, anti-lyrical nature of fiction that
gives the cathartic moments in *Fire Exit* their beauty and communicative
power. At the end of the day, that's what the book's realism moves us
toward . . . a desire to show us a reality that we recognize, and in so
showing give us something to share—something we can have in common.
Its picture of suffering is one we know, because it echoes disasters that
we have seen and failures we have lived through. In this way, the healing
message that it's sending turns out to be addressed to us, whether we
like it or not.'

Josh Billings, *Los Angeles Review of Books*

Fire Exit

Morgan Talty

SHEFFIELD – LONDON – NEW YORK

First published in the UK in 2024 by And Other Stories
Sheffield – London – New York
www.andotherstories.org

1 3 5 7 9 8 6 4 2

ISBN: 9781916751040
eBook ISBN: 9781916751057

Typesetter: Tetragon, London; Typefaces: Albertan Pro and Linotype Syntax
(interior) and Stellage (cover); Series Cover Design: Elisa von Randow,
Alles Blau Studio, Brazil, after a concept by And Other Stories.

And Other Stories books are printed and bound in the UK on FSC-
certified paper by the CPI Group (UK) Ltd, Croydon. The covers are of
299gsm Vanguard card, containing a minimum of 30% upcycled fibre,
and are made in the Lake District at the environmentally friendly James
Cropper paper mill. They are embossed with biodegradable foils.

A catalogue record for this book is available from the British Library.

And Other Stories gratefully acknowledge that our work is
supported using public funding by Arts Council England.

For our children
And their children,
and their children,
and their children

I wanted the girl to know the truth. I wanted her to know who I was—who I really was—instead of a white man who had lived across from her all her life and watched her grow up from this side of the river.

It was late spring. I sat outside drinking coffee and not smoking because my lighter had run out of gas. Fog rolled off the water that divided the Penobscot Nation from the rest of the state of Maine. I was waiting, as I usually did. Soon, across the river and on the reservation, my girl—a woman by that point—came out of the house and got in her car to go to work. I didn't know how many times I'd been through this same routine, but that morning, something took hold of me. Something was different this time.

She started her car and backed out of the driveway, and then, as usual, she was out of sight. I got up and drank the rest of my coffee and thought about calling Louise, my mother, but decided she was probably sleeping, so I went inside to make breakfast, not because I was hungry but because I needed something to do so I could think about what had come over me. Maybe the change had come about because I'd stopped working in the woods so much and had more time to think, but the fact was that I'd gone along for too long with Mary's plan to lie and say that the girl was another man's, an enrolled Native man's, so that she, our daughter, could be on the census—Mary's Penobscot blood plus Roger's—giving Elizabeth exactly what she needed to be enrolled. But that morning I wanted our daughter to know the truth. I was tired of holding that secret.

I was going to make eggs and some seasoned hash and think about all this, but when I cut up the washed potato, I nicked the tip of my thumb real good with the knife and got blood all over my hand and said forget it. I went to the couch and sat down, and I wrapped a paper towel around my thumb and watched the blood seep through and then there was no denying what I wanted. I did want the truth to be known. The blood that came out of me was blood that ran through her veins. It's strange: all blood looks the same, yet it's different, we're told, in so many various ways and for so many various reasons. But one thing is for certain, I thought: you are who you are, even if you don't know it.

I didn't know much about her, except what her mother used to tell me—which was years ago now, maybe twenty-three or twenty-four—when she'd come to check up on me, to give me a little news about her and to see if I was drinking. I was, but told her I wasn't, that it had been four days, eight days, twelve days. But I'll get to that, the lying—mine and hers.

Her name is Elizabeth Eunice Francis, and her maternal grandparents were Eunice and Philip. She was born in January 1991. I'm afraid to say I don't know the exact date, but I think it was the fifteenth, sixteenth, or seventeenth. Those were the days her house was empty and I waited anxiously across the river for her to be brought home.

She knew my house. She'd seen it, both from over there at Roger and Mary's—her parents—and once, when she was young, on my road with her mother. But she'd never been inside, and there was no reason to believe her mother had told her what it looked like. My father, Fredrick, and I built the house in 1983 (thirty-five years goes by fast, faster than the Penobscot River in spring with all that water and ice). I don't know if I can call it a house—it's only five hundred square feet—but this place, while small on the outside, feels big on the inside: there's the living room and kitchen, which are connected and form one room, and then there's a small hallway, just wide enough an entry to turn around in and go into the bathroom or bedroom. The doors to those rooms open inward, but if you open the door to the hallway closet too wide it will catch the lightbulb hanging above that space. Over the years it filled with boxes whose contents I'd forgotten and the gun—a pump .22 Fredrick gave me when I was a boy.

Fredrick and I built the small house three years after the Maine Indian Claims Settlement Act was passed. Fredrick was strongly against the act and spent a great deal of time with the tribal council trying to persuade them to go after a better deal as well as a great amount of time laying out his frustrations for my mother and me during dinner. The act, when passed by Congress, had restored to the tribe its inherent sovereignty, so they could make and pass laws. While the white folks who had owned land prior to the act could remain, as well as those who had married in, one of the first laws the tribe passed concerned non-Natives: anyone who wasn't Native at all had no right to live on the reservation. And since Fredrick was my stepfather, I wasn't Native, and so I couldn't remain on the reservation when I came of age. My mother, a non-Native, could stay, of course, since she had married in.

Around that time Fredrick's father, Joseph, was dying, and the bills were adding up—and what little money I was making working in the woods wouldn't be enough for me to buy a place of my own off the reservation. When the time came to pay for his father's funeral—Joseph died, not peacefully, in the summer of 1982—Fredrick sold his father's camp and land, which got a lot of money. The place was densely forested and far from any town, and bear trappers stay out there now and take people out to hunt. Fredrick still owned his land, which was not very far from his father's, and after settling the medical bills he used the rest of the money to pay for my land and the building supplies. Since the settlement gave the tribe some land outside the reservation or the option to buy some at a low cost, Fredrick was able to buy from the tribe a lot cheaper than the state would have sold it. It was purely coincidental that the land we bought was across the river from Roger's house. I had no idea how important that place would be to me, or the role it would play in my being able to see her.

Fredrick and I spent all summer building the house. And it was a hot summer. My boss at the woodyard let me borrow the buncher—and so we were able to clear the land very quickly, just enough for a road and a yard. We laid the cement and put up all the walls with a good-quality chipboard, and we stuffed the walls with insulation, which we stapled, and we laid all the floors with a cheap linoleum, except in the bedroom, which is carpeted.

It took over four months to build the place. We measured and cut and swore and sweated and got dust and flakes of wood in our eyes, and we built each day after work and even more so on the weekends until it was finished. Louise, my mother, kept us fed during that time, when she was well enough, which was not most of the time. She suffered terrible bouts of depression, which she always would. It was three and a half decades since we'd built the house

11

and I had yet to put trim up or even hang a picture. Who did I have to frame? I'd stopped saying I'd get to it.

As soon as it was built, Fredrick signed the land over to me, and for a number of years until he died, I gave him as much money as I could spare to help pay for what he'd put into this place, what he had given me. I insisted each and every time, but he always tried not to take the money, always said this is what fathers are supposed to do.

We met once when she was three. For a few years after she was born, her mother used to visit me. It was always the same routine: park way down the dirt road and walk through the woods to the back of my house and crawl in through the window. She used to give me news about our child, the only one Mary would ever have, but sometimes she just showed up and gave me nothing but her company for an hour or so. Once she was inside, she would visit like a neighbor would, and we'd have coffee at my kitchen table. We'd smoke a few cigarettes and she'd ask after my mother and after my work and after my drinking and would tell me I should do something to the place, like get some decorations. "At least get a painting or something," she'd say.

It was during a late spring Saturday when Mary asked, "Do you think it would be a good idea if you met her?" She drank her coffee and smoked, lounging, taking her time because Roger was not home; he had taken Elizabeth ice fishing. I don't know who it was Mary felt bad for: Elizabeth or me. Maybe both of us?

"Of course I want to meet her," I said.

"But is it a good idea?" She held her hands together on the table.

"I don't know," I said.

"Neither do I. Get me a coin. A quarter, dime, whatever."

I got her a penny.

"Heads you meet her, tails we forget I asked."

The coin landed on tails.

"Two out of three?" I said.

The next one landed on heads. And so too did the next one.

And that was it. Mary left through the window and every so often a branch would snap and echo in the woods. A car door slammed shut and the engine revved and faded until everything but my breathing quieted.

The week after Mary's visit, I went to the grocery store. I bought two Lunchables. I didn't know which she liked, or even if she liked them at all or if Mary ever bought them for her. I got one with crackers and squares of ham and cheese and another with chips made for tiny fingers and nacho cheese and salsa. I bought a two-liter of Sprite and a big bottle of apple juice and a small tub of red powdered Kool-Aid. As I went to check out, I remembered Mary.

I went back to the deli and got slices of ham and roast beef and turkey and American cheese and a loaf of white bread. In the produce section, on my way back to the checkout, I grabbed a tomato and a head of lettuce that looked like it was dying.

I left the grocery store and drove up to the strip mall across the way from the on-ramp to I-95. I smoked a cigarette before I went into the dollar store. They had two aisles of toys, and a lot of stuff was for the summer, plastic buckets and shovels for sand and crinkly bags stocked with water balloons and mesh bags bulging with colored blocks for building. The bottom shelves were filled with stuffed animals, and I crouched down and pawed through them, holding and turning them over in my hands, petting them for their softness, squeezing them to see if any made noise. Buried deep in one metal bin was an elephant, upside down. I squeezed its soft center and out came the most realistic elephant trumpet I'd heard, and I started laughing, this slow, low laugh that took me over, and I kept squeezing and squeezing the elephant and laughing and laughing and shaking until my face was wet, until the noise coming out of me was so unclear that a worker, a man in a green vest whose name was written in unreadable cursive on the sewed-on name tag, stood over me and asked if I was all right.

*

On the day Mary decided she'd bring our child by, I waited all morning outside, sipping coffee and smoking. I watched their house across the river. Roger had left about seven, and Mary's car remained. It must have been about eleven or twelve when I saw them come out of the house. Mary helped her into the car. Then she got in, started it, and backed out.

About halfway down my dirt road, I waited. But Mary didn't show up. I went back to the house and saw across the river that Mary had returned, her car parked and nobody in it. I sat again, waiting and waiting and waiting. Finally, she came out of the house again with our child. It was about two in the afternoon. Again her car started, backed up, and disappeared from view.

I went back to that same spot on the dirt road. Cars drove by at the end, and each vroom made me more and more nervous. Then came a car that slowed, a green Elantra that eventually became Elizabeth's, and it turned toward me. I started walking back to the house a bit. I had this feeling I had to move. But then I turned and watched Mary park her car where she always did.

Did she remember this day? Did she remember it at all? Or was she too young, as Mary hoped, to remember? Did she know this history—this story—her body held secret from her?

She was here, on this road.

Mary took her from the back seat, and her feet touched the dirt. Mary said something and pointed down the road.

She started to run-wobble in my direction, but Mary chased after and held her by the hand. She pulled her back, told her to wait. Mary was getting something from the back seat. Elizabeth waited, holding back an eagerness in herself to get to me, to get to the end of this road.

And when Mary started for me, not through the woods and through my window but directly for me, she followed. But then she saw something and stopped moving. She grabbed her mother's leg. No amount of ushering her along could get her to move from that spot. I realized, right then, that she hadn't seen me, but now she had, and once she did, the sight of this man down the dirt road frightened her.

Mary picked her up and carried her down the road, with her face buried in Mary's hair and neck, and right as she got close she started to scream, started to yell so loud it echoed, the noise carrying every which way. Mary walked her back to the car, stopped, put her down, and waved me over.

She didn't look at me and held Mary's leg. I couldn't get over how full her face was, her cheeks more precious than air.

"She's just shy," Mary said. We leaned on the hood of the car and watched.

"Is she hungry? I bought her lunch. And you too, if you want."

"We're fine," Mary said. "What did you buy?"

I told her.

"She doesn't like the ham. She likes the cheese and crackers, but that's it. She's never tried any of the others."

We were quiet. Some birds chirped and bounced from branches. Elizabeth kicked at the hard dirt and waved a long piece of grass. Then she smelled it.

"Keep that away from your mouth," Mary said. "Come over here and say hello."

I thought it was funny that she didn't listen, that she stayed right where she was, sniffing that piece of grass.

"Hey," Mary said. "Doosis. I'm talking to you."

I turned to face her by the brush. "You want to see something?" I asked.

She didn't look at me and kept on swinging the grass.

"I'll be right back," I said to Mary, and I walked down the dirt road to the house and inside I got the elephant. I held it behind my back as I returned.

"You want to see something?" I repeated.

She looked at her mother, who looked at what I held behind my back.

"You didn't need to," Mary whispered.

"Well I did," I said.

Mary looked at her. "Wait until you see this," she said. "You'll like it."

The long piece of grass fell to the ground. She lifted her little hand and extended her even littler finger. She pointed, and her nails—on that one hand, anyway—were painted pink. The gesture, the first time recognizing me, how could I forget it? And to have it followed by her voice, the first intelligible words I heard her speak, so near, the only time I've regretted the wind, wished it away, that slight breeze that carried her breath away from me.

How terribly did I want to know her.

"What is it?" she said. She spat out her hair that was in her mouth. She reached for it, the animal I'd forgotten I held behind my back. I held it out for her.

"What do you say?" Mary said.

"Wikawɑt." Please.

Together, we held the elephant between us. She didn't try to take it. She simply touched its gray soft ears and long trunk, squeezed its legs, and patted its head.

She called it a cow.

"It's an elephant," I said. She did not repeat my words, and she wouldn't take the stuffed animal from my hands. She kept touching it, feeling it, inspecting it for something unknown to everybody but herself.

"Here," I said. "You can have it."

She took the elephant and held it.

"Let me show you," I said.

My hands held her hands as she held the elephant.

I don't know if I should have prepared her for what was to come, should have said something else, like "Ready?" or "Listen to this!" but I didn't say anything besides "Let me show you." I gave her hands holding the elephant a squeeze, and out from the elephant came that loud, realistic trumpet. Her eyes widened and she let go.

"No, cow! No!" she said, and she started to cry and ran to Mary, who was laughing.

"No more," Mary said, either to me or to her, I don't know. She picked her up and put her in the back seat of the car.

"You're leaving?" I said, holding the elephant to my side.

"She's tired."

She was still crying, calling for her mother. Mary went to her, calmed her a little bit, but she started again the moment Mary left and came back to me.

From outside the car I waved to her, a hello and a good-bye. She kept on crying.

"I take it she won't want this," I said about the elephant.

"I have to go," Mary said.

"Should you bring her back here?" I said. "Another day?"

"Charles," Mary said.

"I'm just asking," I said.

There was nothing but her screaming.

Mary went to the car and dug around in the center console. She got out of the car but leaned back in.

"Heads another day, tails no more."

It landed on tails.

"Two out of three?" I asked, again.

But Mary said no, and it took me some time to realize that that would be the last time for a long, long while that we'd all be so close.

Now, more than twenty years later, I knew something Elizabeth didn't know, or something she didn't remember.

2

It was 1996 when I started AA, and I made it a point to reconnect with my mother. Maybe I felt enough years had gone by for us to move past what had happened.

I knew where she lived off reservation because I had helped her move in years before, not long after Fredrick died, but when I arrived, I found out from the landlord that she hadn't lived there for more than three years. I felt something like betrayal, but not quite so, that my mother would move without letting me know. She called every so often and would leave these long voicemails telling me about her day or week, and so I wondered why she hadn't told me she was moving or had moved.

The place my mother now rented was, as the landlord said, three streets over and at the bottom of a steep hill. I'll never forget it: I drove to the top of that high hill, and as I started descending, I saw something at the very bottom, right where the road leveled out. It looked like a hole—not a pothole—that stretched the width of the street, and it looked portal-like, and endless. The closer I got to it, the more frightened I became. But before it could swallow me and the truck, I splashed through it: a puddle.

I buzzed the buzzer that went to my mother's apartment, but my mother was not home. Her neighbor—a tall, skinny guy I learned Louise called "shovel man" because he was always outside shoveling snow or, when there wasn't snow, dirt, which he used to keep his dirt driveway flat—was outside, sitting on the bottom step, smoking and inspecting a worn nightstand, its wood chipped and flaking. He seemed to have a lot of garbage in his driveway, right at the end near his house. I felt him watching as I kept buzzing the buzzer to my mother's apartment next door, and when nobody answered I started for my truck, but thought maybe it was worth asking him about her.

And so I did, and he said to me, "I ain't selling anything right now."

"No, no," I said, looking at the nightstand and other junk he had there. "Louise. The lady that lives here. Do you know her?"

He set the nightstand aside and stood up. "Who are you looking for?" he said.

Again, I told him who. I still stood by my truck.

"Your mother?" he said. "What's your name?"

I told him that too.

He laughed. "I thought she was making you up," he said.

"What do you mean?"

He waved me over. "My throat's sore and I'm not going to yell."

He told me Louise had told him to tell me that she was going away, that she'd be back in a few days, and that I shouldn't worry. "She's been telling me to tell you that for years, every time she left. I thought she was crazy. But you are real."

I asked him if he knew where she'd gone, and he said he didn't know. "I told you all she told me."

"Do you have a phone I could use?"

"I don't," he said. "You got a cigarette?"

I gave him one, and he lit it.

"Hey what's that in your truck there?" he said, blowing smoke and pointing. "You throwing it out?"

He was talking about my fuel tank for work. And I told him as much.

"Fuel tank, huh?" he said.

I didn't find Louise that day and when she finally called I wasn't at home—I was at work up north clearing land—and I called her back in the evening. This was a few days after I'd gone looking for her. We talked for a bit. She sounded tired, like she wasn't up for talking, and so I didn't tell her anything about having gone to her old house and then to her new apartment. I just said I'd come by on Sunday, and it was then that she told me she'd moved and it was my turn to act surprised by it.

When that Sunday came, I almost didn't go. Elizabeth was outside, in her backyard, with her father. She was playing ring toss. I didn't know how big or small five-year-olds were, but she was so little and couldn't throw the rings very far. What she did was toss one, then take a step forward, reaching, and toss another, and so on until she was right over the pole, and she'd drop the last ring from her hand, and it wobbled in place.

I stayed watching until Roger looked at me, and then I walked to my truck.

Louise was outside when I showed up. I don't know what I expected when we saw each other. It had been at least three years since I'd seen her, but she acted as if she had just seen me the other day, as if I had just seen her. The only time she got close to acknowledging how long it had been since we'd seen each other came when she said, "You look good." That was it. My mother didn't care very much for discussing things in the past. I don't think she liked talking about the future, either, and she always, when I was young, changed the subject when Fredrick talked about the what-ifs of the Settlement Act, particularly my having to leave the reservation when I turned eighteen.

From that day I saw her on as many Sundays as possible, which was typically once a month. She gave me a key to her place—both the house door and her apartment door—and when I asked about the dead bolt, she said it didn't work so I didn't need to worry. She stopped telling shovel man to tell me she was leaving, and instead would call me and say, "I'll be out and about on Sunday, so don't come by." Out and about. I learned where she went eventually when I saw the medical bills on her kitchen sideboard. She went to the wellness center, where they gave her a bed and fed her and monitored her for a few days. She never told me though, and I don't know if she knew I knew. But when I heard her say "out and about," I came to know where she was.

When I began to visit her more often, I only ever asked her a few questions about her past. One was about my father, what his name was.

"His name?" Louise repeated. "Brian. Isn't that a boring fucking name? Brian." She stopped talking for a bit, and then said, "I wonder where he is."

She never said what happened to him, but I took it he left. You'd think men would come up with a better story, or a different one.

I came to realize, through my visits with her, that I didn't really know my mother. I started to think that Fredrick had understood her in a way nobody else could. It explained how well they worked together. But what exactly made them so close I never found out. I guess the simple answer is: Just because. That's how it happened. They fit together. Louise's mother, my grandmother, who Louise and I lived with when my birth father left, eventually disowned my mother for seeing Fredrick. And apparently she tried—and was successful, only for a bit—to get me taken away by telling the state that Fredrick beat me. I was almost four, but not old enough to remember.

"And when they saw you had no bruises," Louise said, "no swelling, nothing at all, they let us take you back. We were all in court, even my mother, who thought she was going to leave that day with my child. That's the last I saw or heard from her."

For days after hearing that story, I felt strange. There was this history I was a part of, a history my body had experienced and moved through, but I never knew it. It made me wonder how much I didn't know. We had that in common, Elizabeth and I. And I felt she should know her body was special, and she should know its history, especially the one it would not tell her and the one she could not see. And I decided to tell what I knew, because she deserved to know it.

For the first time in nearly two and a half decades, I spoke with Elizabeth's mother. I wasn't seeking her out—I just wanted to know about burial rights. After seeing my mother age, I'd started to think a great deal about how, like all mothers everywhere, mine would one day die, and I hadn't given any thought to what would become of her body. She had never said what she wanted done at the end. Maybe she didn't care, or maybe she was like me: afraid to talk about it. My guess was that she would like to be buried with Fredrick on the reservation and that was my business: to see if that was possible, since my mother was not Penobscot.

I didn't know who to speak with and so I went to the chief's office at the community building next to the school. I looked for Elizabeth's car, the green Elantra, the one Roger had kept alive over the years until Mary had passed it down, but didn't see it. Nobody was at the community building. Nobody at all. And all the lights were off. It was when I was leaving that I saw the printed pink sign on the door that said all offices had been moved across the street to the building behind the health center. I wasn't surprised the tribe was tearing down the community center; it had been there for so long that it must have needed to be taken down before it decided to do so on its own.

I walked across the street and took the small path behind the health center to the building where the pink sign said everyone was. Every room in that building was occupied, some doors open, some shut, but each with a sign: "Finance," "Department of Natural Resources," "Tribal Clerk," and so on, and I checked almost all the doors until I found the chief's office. The door was partly open, and so I pushed it open to find not the chief but instead Elizabeth's mother. Mary sat behind a large brown desk, a computer in front of her. She never wore glasses when I'd known her. At first, I did not recognize her. But when I did, I forgot what I wanted to know—about burying my mother—and I asked what she was doing there, and for a moment she stared at me, or maybe she wasn't staring but thinking about things shared and hidden, a thing that, no matter what, connected us.

"I work here," she said, and whatever wall had come down between us for those brief seconds was back up. "Can I help you?"

I asked her what I wanted to know—if my mother could be buried with Fredrick on the reservation—and if someone had asked me such a question about a person I had known and liked but hadn't seen or heard of for many, many years, and especially with no other context, I too would have reacted how she did. She stood up from the desk.

"Louise?" she said, that wall coming down again. "She passed away?"

"No, no, no," I said. "She hasn't died. But she's ill."

"With what?" She sat back down.

"Old age and what comes with it," I said.

She said she was sorry to hear it. She asked again what it was I wanted to know. She thought my mother could be buried with Fredrick, but she needed to call the funeral director of the church on the reservation to make sure. She called, and I don't know who she talked to, but it wasn't the director.

"He's going to call in a minute," Mary said, hanging up. "He's away for the moment."

She said I could have a seat. There were two chairs, one on each side of a small end table with a lamp that was turned on. I sat. Neither of us spoke while her keyboard clacked.

I could have said or asked a number of things in those moments while we waited for the call: "Louise asks about you," or "How's your family?" or "I've been sober for twenty-two years," or "How could you have done this?" or "I understand why you did this," or "What is she like?" or "Are you as lonely as I am?"—or, or, or. So many things I could have said, but I said nothing, asked nothing, and it was sadder than anything I could have said or asked. Here we were, Mary and I, in the same room, both at the same end of our lives' biggest secret.

The phone rang and Mary answered.

"Calling about what?" she said, and she took off her glasses as if that helped her understand whatever the person on the phone was saying to her, as if the voice needed to be seen to be understood.

"I did?" she said, and it must have been me in that room who reminded her why the person was returning her call, and it must have been me too in that room who had made her forget. "That's right, sorry, busy day."

When she got the answer, she hung up.

"Since they were married at the time of his death," Mary said, "Louise has the right to be buried next to him."

I said OK, and Mary coughed.

"But you have to buy the plot beside his," she said.

Dying isn't cheap and I didn't ask how much the plot was.

Before I left, I found the courage to ask, in a whisper, how Elizabeth was doing.

"She could be better, but she'll be OK," is what she said. It hurt me deeply to know that she was not well, and it hurt just as deeply not to know what was wrong, and it hurt more than both those things to know I couldn't do a damn thing to fix it. I couldn't help but feel that I had abandoned my daughter, and I was afraid to know if what I was feeling was the truth.

I hoped it would get better, whatever was going on with her. For the next several days, I speculated on why she could be unwell, and each time I arrived at the reason I most feared: that she was suffering in the same way my mother had all her life.

At home I was thinking about what Fredrick had told me when I was young, that the reservation used to be a burial ground. I must have been about ten or eleven when he told me the story. For a long while after I didn't dare walk in any of the woods, and I think that's what Fredrick wanted: this was about the time Roger's parents both drowned in the river and his cousin and her boyfriend moved in to take care of him. For years the tribe held donation gatherings on Sundays in the Kateri Center for those in need, and the people who could chipped in money and food and other necessities. Fredrick always donated some of the meat he'd gotten from hunts with Joseph, usually deer but sometimes moose and even rabbit.

Fredrick told me the story to keep me away from the woods and the river, since all the woods on that island, that reservation, lead to it.

I don't remember where we were when Fredrick told me the story. It wasn't even a story as much as it was a detail. Before his ancestors—and Elizabeth's—had given up much of the land, and had much, if not more of it, taken, they used the island as a place to bury the dead. "That's why there are large boulders everywhere," Fredrick said, "on all the paths, that stick out in awkward places and look to have been put there." I'd never noticed them before, never noticed all the rocks, some the size of basketballs, others the size of garden sheds. "They mark the dead," Fredrick said.

I wish I could say Fredrick told me more intimate details about the burials. How were they performed? Who attended them? I was eight when the last "traditional" burial occurred on the reservation, but for reasons I didn't know then I wasn't allowed to attend. When it was over, I sneaked out to where everyone had gathered, and I looked at the carved pole that's still out there today but has since toppled over. It was down by Joe Pease, that rocky-water part of the river by Rolling Thunder Drive. When I was a boy it looked as tall as any tree, and now it's as long as any fallen one.

Maybe Fredrick made the whole story up—maybe the whole reservation wasn't a burial ground. While he wasn't my real father, I always thought of him as such. I was two when he and my mother met, and I was three when I moved into that house with him. It was 1967. So I felt I belonged to Fredrick, and to his family: his father, Joseph, and his mother, Maxine. It didn't take time to grow into that feeling of being welcome. I was so young when we joined their family. My mother and I were not Penobscot, but I spent all my early years on the reservation and was taught at the school, the Kateri Center, which used to be right near the church, before they built the new school where Elizabeth went and where I figured out over the years she taught now. I was around the tribe day and night, and I felt it was where I belonged, who I was. Gizos, a boy my age and my only real friend on the reservation, certainly made it easier to feel this way.

Growing up, I should have asked Gizos about the boulders, but I never did. He might have had a different version, or maybe it would have been the same. For all the stories that Gizos told, only one dealt with the topic of death, but it equally told of creation.

He told a story about Gluskabe's attempt to create the first people. Rock people. I can't remember which attempt

Gluskabe was on, or how many attempts he would make before he got it right, but during one try he made people out of stone. Gizos said that Gluskabe tried to teach them, these tall rock pillars, but they were unteachable. They could not hear, they could not talk, and they could not see. They were brash, and they moved about the earth with their heavy bodies and stripped trees of their bark and crushed the animals. When they collided, they would fight and smash each other until all that remained of one was a pile of pebbles and sharp, pointed fragments and rock dust.

They were violent. Gluskabe thought he'd let them destroy one another until only one remained, and then Gluskabe would shatter it and start over. But, Gizos said, before they could finish one another off, something happened. Their joints of quartzite sparked and created fire that caught the grass and spread to the oak ferns and then to the shagbark hickory and birch bark and oaks until half the world was burning. Having thought that the stone people could not reason, Gluskabe was shocked to see one stone man point into the sky—to the sun—and point back at the earth, as if predicting that the earth, too, would become a ball of flames. Right then, Gluskabe set out to destroy all of them. But Gluskabe wouldn't get them all, Gizos said. While he destroyed many, some escaped to the mountains.

"They have no hearts," Gizos said, and then he said that maybe his father was part stone person. "They like to come down once in a while."

Even if Gizos's story were true, Fredrick's wouldn't be entirely wrong: the boulders are markers of the dead, of beings fallen and smashed before our time. And at the end of both these stories—Gizos's and my father's—the reservation is covered with bodies. While Gizos's story seems far from the truth, and my father's closer to it, the reality is that today four Catholic cemeteries dot the small reservation, and so in any case many people have been buried under the earth there. The reservation is a burial ground all right, just as the rest of the world is. Land is land, and one day, I knew, Louise would return to it.

3

I grew up just down the road from Roger's house. Ours was the big one on the corner, right by that stop sign that everybody rolls past. Fredrick had left the house to my mother, but she couldn't stand to live there anymore, especially since I stopped visiting her after he died, and so she sold the house, and the man who bought it from my mother planned to turn it into a little museum. Henry David Thoreau had stayed there with my father's great-grandfather for a day or two until Thoreau found someone in the tribe who would guide him through the woods. The buyer thought the house had enough history to warrant a museum, but it never came to fruition. I heard later that he ended up selling the house to the tribe, who planned to burn it for firefighter training. When I first heard about that, for weeks I kept watch from outside, looking for smoke, but I never saw any and the house kept standing.

The house was smaller indoors than it appeared on the outside. From the street you'd think there were many rooms upstairs given the several windows and thin curtains, but in fact there were no rooms—it was just an attic filled with junk. Louise had a curtain addiction, and many of the boxes were filled with curtains, which she kept clean and neatly folded in case she had to hang them up, which was never. The downstairs had a kitchen and a living room, and down the hallway were three rooms: mine, Fredrick and my mother's, and a spare where Fredrick's father, Joseph, lived until his death. Before its roof caved in, the garage was filled with a heavy ash-pounding machine, which I had never seen run at all during my time living there. The garage was also the place where Fredrick and his father used to store what they'd hunted at camp, usually deer and the occasional moose, and they had a freezer out there too, filled with meat. That place always smelled of the cold and sawdust and guts.

Going to AA makes you think a lot about the past and how it shapes you. And thinking about AA now makes me think of the future and the past all at once and about how I met Bobby. Bobby—a friend from way back—wanted to go away, and he asked if I'd go with him. He said Florida, but I wasn't sold on it. I didn't tell him that—I told him I needed to think about it. There was still time though. He was waiting to retire, though I was pretty sure he could have done it already. He'd owned his own plumbing and heating company for a number of years, of which he was the sole employee. He'd made good money doing it, or so he said. But I couldn't leave until Elizabeth knew the truth. That was all I wanted.

I met Bobby in AA in the spring of '96. Back then, Bobby had few people in his life, which is still the case today, I guess. He'd been divorced three times—no children—and he was going through that third divorce when we met. AA was held in the Elks Club on Main Street. Bobby had been attending for almost a year. I can't say he'd been clean for almost a year, because I came to learn he was still drinking some nights a week. When meetings were over, a lot of folks stuck around and smoked outdoors if the weather was fine enough. I had gone to four meetings so far and when that fourth one ended, I didn't want to go home. I felt a certain strength the more I was around the building and those people. And I don't mean a strength put toward not drinking but rather a general, spirited strength. Maybe to live, I guess.

We were all outside after the meeting and we stood in a circle under an orange streetlight, some of us smoking. Some were waiting for rides, some were waiting for those who were waiting for rides to leave, and some, like me, didn't know what they were waiting for. In time, everyone went home, one after the other, until it was just Bobby and me and this guy whose name, I think, was Melvin or Kelvin. He wasn't there too long before his ride showed up.

The quiet was sharp when he left. He'd been the one talking to us, keeping the conversation going.

Bobby, this non-Native, asked if I was waiting for a ride, and I told him no.

"I have a truck," I told him, and he said he did too, that his wife had dropped him off in it, and so he was waiting for her to pick him up.

"But she probably ain't coming," he said.

I had no idea then that he was on his third marriage, and I had no idea then either that that third marriage was unstable, like something stacked too high. I guess I should have known something wasn't right when she didn't show up. I ended up bringing him home, which was the beginning of me always bringing him home and picking him up for meetings.

He didn't live too far from the Elks Club. That night, however, he made me believe he did. For most of the drive he kept saying, "I appreciate this, I do," and "I can't thank you enough, really, I can't."

No problem, no problem, no problem, I told him over and over again, until finally I just said to him, "You don't got to thank me anymore. I don't mind."

He told me his house was three miles down a dark road with very few streetlights. It was out near the border of Overtown. "Just keep going straight," he told me. "I'll tell you when we're almost there."

"Take a left," he said. "Take a right." Bobby seemed nervous; he kept tapping his fingernails on the window.

"Take this left," he said. "I'll tell you when to turn again."

He tapped on that window.

He asked me three times if I had a cigarette he could bum. The first time I told him I was out. I said the same thing again when he asked the second time. I thought maybe he hadn't heard me. But when he asked that third time, I said to him, "What's the matter with you?"

He stopped tapping on the glass and he shook his head. "I'm fucked," he said, and he said it as quietly as somebody would say it who truly was fucked.

I stopped the truck on the side of the road. We'd been driving for twenty minutes.

I pointed up ahead at a stop sign. "It doesn't matter which way we turn," I said to him. "Both ways bring us to the same road we were just on. Where is your house?"

"We passed it," he said.

"We passed it?"

"Look, I'm sorry," he said.

I started to think that Bobby was a liar. I wondered about all sorts of things: Did he have a house? Did he have a wife? Had she dropped him off in his truck? Did he have a truck? Was he even an alcoholic?

"I can't go home," he told me.

"Then why are you making me drive you somewhere you can't go?"

"I'm sorry," he said again. "All right, it's up there. Just drop me at the curb. I can go there, really, I can."

He told me not to pull into the driveway but to park on the street. I did. He got out of the truck, and he didn't say anything to me. I watched him walk across the front lawn, the grass up to his shins. He was halfway to the front porch when he turned around and looked at me. He waved me off.

The front door of the house opened, and a woman—who was his wife, he'd tell me after, while on the way back to my place—screamed at him. I rolled down my window to listen, but I couldn't understand a word she was saying, not anything Bobby was saying when he spoke over her. It was all in French. But when I recognized what she threw at him—thick glass bottles—I didn't need to know what they were saying to know what was going on.

Bobby ducked and dodged as she threw the bottles, and he looked to be returning to my truck. But he wasn't. He searched the dark grass for a bottle, and when he found one, he pelted it in her direction on the front porch. It shattered against the house right above the porch, and glass sprinkled down on her. Only then did he run back to my truck, because she ran after him.

"Go, go, go!" he yelled, hitting the dashboard.

I could have decided not to be a part of his mess, especially after his wife hit my truck with a bottle. I could have decided to drop him back off at the Elks Club, could have told him to sort it all out himself, to leave me out of it. But I didn't. I told him he could stay the night at my place, and he said no, he couldn't do that. And then he asked if I could bring him to work in the morning, and I told him I could, but that he might get there earlier than he'd like, since I had to be out and on the road by 4:00 am.

I didn't sleep at all that night. When we got home, Bobby used my landline to call her. But he didn't speak to her for very long before he handed the phone to me. "She wants to talk to you," he said.

Her name was Heather or Gael. I can't remember which. I didn't have to talk to her—I could have hung up—but Bobby kept saying, "Tell her, just tell her," and I wasn't sure at first what he wanted me to say. But when she accused me of drinking with her husband, I knew what he wanted me to tell her.

"It's not like that," I told her. "If your husband's drinking, it ain't with me."

"He is drinking," she said.

"Well it ain't with me."

I don't know at what point she believed me, that I was telling her the truth—or if she didn't believe me but just got tired of asking—but eventually she stopped talking, stopped arguing, and I thought she hung up.

"Hello?" I said.

"What do I do?" she said. "What do I do?"

Right then, I realized I knew very little about Bobby, about this man who was sitting on my couch in my house. I saw him holding Elizabeth's stuffed elephant, the one

I bought and tried to give her when she visited with her mother that one and only time as a young child, and Bobby mouthed, "You have kids?"

"He won't stop," she said. "Why can't he stop?"

"Are you asking me?" I said.

"How did you stop? What made you stop?"

I wanted to say what had made me stop was myself. But that wasn't true, and I didn't know what had made me stop. Maybe it was fear; maybe it was what I wanted. Or maybe it was just time to stop, something unexplainable working below the surface of my being. Or maybe it was the guilt I felt about my father Fredrick's death, wanting to get clarity enough so I could finally tell my mother the truth about what had happened.

"Can you help him?" she said.

I told her I'd try, told her I'd see what I could do, which turned out to be very little. She asked to talk to Bobby again, and I was expecting those two to be on the phone for a long while. But they said barely anything. "I won't, won't," Bobby said quietly, and then they hung up.

I sat with him for a bit on the couch, and when he looked to be sleeping, sitting up, I started to leave.

"How do you do it?" he asked. "How do you not drink?"

"I just don't," I told him.

"You don't ever just want to?"

"Sure," I told him. It's been so long since then that I can't remember if that was true. We hear all the time that to quit something is to battle with the desire not to quit, but to be honest I don't think that's how it was with me. I wanted to drink once or twice, but that was it. Today, it would be just about impossible to convince me to drink.

"Look," Bobby said. He rubbed his eyes, and then he took out some cigarettes he'd found in his jacket. He held the pack up, and I told him he could smoke on the couch. I brought him a cup of water for an ashtray. He blew smoke and sat forward. "I just don't want to quit. I don't want to be sober."

And he didn't want to be. He tried, for whatever reason he tried—whether for her or for some small part of himself that wasn't sure what he wanted—and he stopped drinking only long enough to remember that he did not want sobriety. He didn't drink at work, but he oftentimes went in buzzed from the night before. That was when he drank the most, at night, even on the weekends. He avoided it all day until it got dark or close to dark. But he tried to quit; for three weeks while he stayed with me he didn't drink anything, or if he did, I knew nothing about it. When he finally went home, he stayed sober for a while, and then he was right back where he started, on my couch again while I talked to his wife, but she didn't ask for help. She said he could go back home when she left in a week. She was going to her parents' in Quebec. It's interesting: I never, not once, met her. I saw her silhouette that one time as she stood on the porch in the dark, chucking bottles at Bobby. But besides that one time I knew her only by the conversations we had on the phone, her body the shape of a voice on the other end of the line.

4

In the days after I saw Elizabeth, when I learned her mother
would never again bring her to my road, I got to thinking
about the word "dirt." Maybe it was the memory of her
little feet touching the ground that brought the word to my
attention. This is embarrassing, or maybe the better word
is dramatic. I was upset. And drunk. I took that elephant
and set it sitting upright on a blue plastic chair on my front
lawn, and I put the .22 to its head, the .22 that Fredrick
had given me. I didn't shoot the elephant. I held the gun
to its head, and before I pulled the trigger I lowered the
rifle and the bullet flew and shattered the leg of the blue
plastic chair, and pieces went flying all over the earth's dirt.
"Dirt," Middle English: "excrement, dung, feces, any foul or
filthy substance." If you look the word up, there's also a line
about it meaning "mud" or "loose earth." I guess I just don't
understand this, this one word for two different things.
Like Gizos: his name meant sun and moon. Is it indeci-
siveness? Is it neatness we're after, tidiness? Is it a desire to
make sense of a thing on the basis of another? Maybe all we
are is creation's translators, putting things like granite or

oak or elephant or corn in a language they want to be put in, to give them bodies made of sound so they're measurable. "Measurable" sounds like "miserable" when I pronounce it.

There's a story I want to tell, and it has to do with Gizos and his father, Lenno. To get it right, I thought I had to ask Bobby. We were at the bar, but I wasn't drinking. The story happened in the mid-'70s. Bobby grew up right off the reservation on French Island, and so he might have heard it, I thought. And when I asked him, he snapped his fingers and pointed at me.

"I know what you're talking about," he said, and he began.

According to Bobby, there were two guns and two men.

"I had an aunt. My dad's sister. She was living with this Lebritton on the reservation. She saw it happen. The two men are drunk. One is standing on his steps, looking down the barrel of his rifle at the other man, who is at the end of the driveway, right near the road, looking down the barrel of his own rifle at the man on the steps. She said they both were swearing and stumbling, telling the other to shoot. The men yelled it over and over again—'Go on, shoot! Come on!'—and they each walked closer and closer to the other."

Bobby took a drink of his fourth beer of the night and said, "I guess one of them—I think the guy who was standing on the steps, that's what my aunt said—was sleeping with the other's wife. If that were me, I would've already shot the bastard."

But neither man pulls the trigger, according to Bobby. They both yell and swear, slurring their words. The rifles are pointed at the other. The street is full of neighbors, all Indian except Bobby's aunt, all watching. Some are trying to approach, trying to take the guns, to defuse the situation. But the two men want nothing but the rifles between them, and so they point the guns at those trying to help until there's nobody left in their line of view but the other with a weapon.

"They got close enough that each of their guns was in the other's face," Bobby said. "'Do it! Do it!' they kept saying. 'You don't think I will!'"

Bobby was laughing. "When my aunt told me this—well, she was telling my father, who'd come down too, he needed to fix something in her house—anyway when she told us this, I didn't think neither one would do it."

There are two men and two guns, as Bobby said, each pointed at the other's head, and as they each tell the other to do it—two voices screaming—they each pull the trigger. For the briefest of time, an amount hard to measure, two bullets are between them. But then it's over, and the bullets are no longer between them but in each man's head.

"They died right then and there," Bobby said.

I laughed in his face. "Your aunt told you this story?"

"Yeah," he said.

"Well, she got that one way wrong."

"What do you mean?"

"They didn't die," I said. "I was there. I saw it. One of those men was Fredrick, my father."

Bobby asked the bartender for another drink.

"Remember you're driving," I told him.

"Yeah, yeah," he said. When the drink came, he took a tiny sip and set the glass down with a thud. "So then why did you ask me if I knew the story?"

"I just wanted to know what you knew about it, that's all."

"Well, there you go," he said.

I asked him if he wanted to hear the real version.

"Does one of them die?" he asked.

"No," I told him.

"Then I don't want to hear it."

But I told him anyway.

Bobby got some parts of the story right. There were two men, and there were people watching. There weren't two guns, though, just the one, that .22 I now owned and kept in my closet. Fredrick held it, aimed it at the other man, Gizos's father, Lenno, as he stood on his steps. Neither was drunk—well, maybe Lenno was, since he did drink a great deal, but Fredrick didn't drink.

But there were things Bobby couldn't have known. It was winter 1976, and I was thirteen. The day was bright and sunny, the sky blue, the white snow on the ground hard but melting. Fredrick and I had spent the better part of the day up at camp clearing Joseph's roof of snow while he made us lunch, and inside under a lantern at a wobbly table we ate it and then played a game of cribbage. When we came back home we did the same to the house, pushed the snow off the roof and then cleared the giant piles away from the foundation, and when the roof was clear and we were back inside, Fredrick made dinner. Louise had not felt well for the last few weeks. "I'm sorry," she would say to my father as he brought her food. "I need to sleep. I don't feel well today. Maybe I'll be better tomorrow." Fredrick cooked the blanched and frozen fiddleheads he'd collected in the fall, and we ate them with salted pork for most of our meals.

Whenever Louise was ill, Fredrick seemed to talk and talk. But that day I didn't listen to a word he said. My mind was elsewhere. I had this terrible feeling that something bad had happened to Gizos. For over a week he hadn't been in school, which for many of the kids wasn't abnormal. I sometimes missed that much. But for Gizos it was. And whenever I went to his house, nobody answered the door. He was home too: through the window, I'd seen his shoes neatly tucked on the floor against the wall.

When I finished eating what little I could that day, I told Fredrick I was going out to meet Gizos, and Fredrick asked why Gizos hadn't been by. "Did his father finally convince him that we're Goog'ooks?" he said, meaning evil spirits.

Gizos was usually the one to come and get me. I told Fredrick I didn't know why he hadn't been around, that we'd simply decided to meet by the river.

We'd gotten so much snow that the roads on the reservation were as narrow as wooded paths, and all the trees, heavy and bending with wet snow, leaned in as if listening. All the way to Gizos's I felt I was being watched.

Gizos's house was up on a small hill, where the road rose and then dipped back down. It was the highest point on the reservation, which wasn't spectacular because it wasn't that high a hill. The house, whose red siding was faded, had an upstairs, and above that an attic too, but what was up there, if anything, was a mystery to me. Lenno had grown up right there. It wasn't the same house though—before Gizos was born, Lenno, according to Fredrick, had ripped down the old home and had built in its place this red one. That was when his wife still lived there, before she left them. Gizos very rarely talked about her, his mother, not because he had some painful memories but because he didn't remember her.

The sun was setting, and with it what little warmth it offered. At the bottom of the hill to his house, a giant rock split the road in two, one branch going all the way through the reservation, past the lumberyard and continuing to the bridge to Overtown, and the other just a dead end, a cul-de-sac with a dense thicket of pines through which the river flowed. Lenno's gray truck was parked in the driveway, and so I waited at the rock, watching and hoping he'd leave.

But the sun set more and more, and with each inch of its sinking the cold grew deeper and deeper. I waited for as long as I could, and then I walked up that hill and down the driveway to the door. I took my glove off and knocked on the window in the door, the glass frigid on my knuckles.

Footsteps. They got louder and louder until the noise stopped right behind the door. The white curtains that hung over the glass parted, and Lenno looked at me. He gestured with his hand—leave—and the curtains fell back in place.

I went back to the rock and waited. But for what I didn't know. It was almost dark, the sky purple and pink on one horizon and the other, opposite, almost black, the sky a huge fruit starting to rot.

I sneaked around the house to Gizos's window. It was hard to keep quiet. The snow creaked, and every so often it collapsed under me and made a loud thump. There was no way to approach without making any sound, and so the best I could hope for was that Lenno wouldn't hear me. As I got to the back of the house, which was almost pitch-black because of the thick pines blocking what was left of the sun, a light from indoors shone through the window, Gizos's window. I went to it as quietly as I could and crouched down right below it. I stood up and looked inside.

It's hard to remember what, exactly, Gizos was doing. He was on the bed, I know that, sitting against the wall.

He may have been reading, I don't know. Even saying this seems impossible given his situation. When I looked, all my attention was drawn to his face: his forehead was swollen and protruded out, and his eyes, equally swollen, were small slits. He had dark skin, and so it was difficult to tell if his face was bruised, but his face was so deformed—so changed by violence—that he didn't even look like Gizos but instead like some alien, some extraterrestrial, that was waiting, wounded, for the mother ship.

A glass bottle shattered next to me. I looked up, and Lenno, hanging out the second-floor window, aimed another, and it would have hit me if I hadn't fallen backward. To a boy, he was a terrifying man. He had wide shoulders, and he just looked large. But up there he looked smaller. And so it must have been that that made me feel safe. I picked up half a broken glass bottle and hurled it in his direction. He ducked back inside as the bottle shattered near the top of the window and glass fell down on me. I picked up another, waiting and waiting for his head to pop out again, but it didn't. And in not very much time at all the front door opened and banged shut, and I heard the snow crunching loudly under his feet as he came around the corner. I felt that something depended on my staying right there, but whatever it was, it left the moment I saw he held an iron fireplace poker, the end curled like a finger. I ran as fast as I could, climbing over fallen trees until I got back to the road, and when I was on that road, I looked back to see him still behind me, coming out of the woods. I slowed, thinking those lines of trees were as far as he'd go, that he'd quit. But he ran for me, and I ran with all I had down the road, and I kept going, turning on one narrow road after the other until my legs were as heavy as the snow around me and I collapsed, breathing deep and long, a hunted animal. I looked back, and I was alone.

I don't remember the walk home, and before I knew it, I was inside. I was sweating, and I felt the sweat run cold when I took my jacket off and hung it by the woodstove. The lights were bright, and I had to squint, and I didn't see Fredrick.

"What happened to your hand?" he said.

I didn't know what he meant. "I lost it," I said, talking about my glove. "I'll find it tomorrow when there's light."

"No," he said. I could see him now. He was coming from down the hallway. He stood in the kitchen, facing me. He pointed. "Your hand," he said.

I looked at my hand. The blood was dried like mud.

"What happened to you?" he said. "You have no color in your face."

Maybe I was still afraid he'd get me, but I just blurted it out. "He tried to kill me," I said, and I told Fredrick what had happened, all of it, starting with how long it had been since I'd seen Gizos. He came to me and brought me to the sink and scrubbed the blood off my hand and was inspecting the cut, and as he turned my hand over in the light,

I saw there were multiple cuts, none of them deep. My hand felt swollen and the water and soap stung.

He didn't ask if I was sure. He didn't press me, didn't act as if what I was telling him was untrue. In fact, the only thing he said to me was, "Get in the truck."

I've had a long time to think about this incident, particularly Fredrick's wrath, his anger, that brought him to Lenno. If Gizos's father hadn't been the chief, if he hadn't been pushing the tribe so hard to accept what little the Settlement Act would give them—which was less than what Fredrick felt the tribe was owed and was a constant point of contention between the two—I wonder whether Fredrick would have done what he did. I've questioned the source of his desire to act, to stand up to something that was wrong: Was it what Lenno had done to Gizos? Was it what Lenno had done to me? Or was it what he planned to do to the tribe, to sell his people out for less than their suffering was worth? Maybe it was all three things working together that filled Fredrick with a rage I never saw again. He's been gone now for more than a quarter century, and regardless of how much thinking I've done on the matter— about where his anger came from that day—I remind myself and I will continue to remind myself that it's easy, too easy, even natural, to doubt the character of someone who is gone. Fredrick was a good person.

As he drove the narrow roads that night, Fredrick made me load the gun, the .22. It was hard to do so in the truck.

I had to roll down my window so there'd be enough room to pull out the loading rod, and my hands were shaking when I loaded it and slid it back in place. I tried to hand the gun to him.

"Keep holding it," he said.

I didn't want to hold the gun. The more I held it, the more responsible I felt, and if there was one thing I didn't want, it was to feel responsible.

"Can I set it down?" I asked. "Lean it against the seat?"

He answered with a grunt, and I wasn't sure what it meant. I kept holding it, and the steel grew warm in my hands.

We arrived at the house, and Fredrick parked in the driveway. He kept the truck running, and he put the high beams on. Fredrick grabbed the gun from me, but I didn't let go.

He pulled again, and again I didn't let go.

"What are you going to do?" I said. It was the first time Fredrick saw my fear. I was scared, frightened at how wrong this could go.

"I'm going to fix this," he said. "Now let go."

I didn't plan to, but when I heard Lenno's voice, heard and felt a bottle shatter over the windshield, I let go of the gun.

How fast Fredrick lifted the gun has never left me—it was one quick movement, the butt of the rifle to his shoulder, his eye peering down the scope.

"Where's your boy?" Fredrick said to Lenno, who came outside.

"You should be pointing that gun at your son for what he did," Lenno said.

"Your boy," Fredrick said. "Where is he?"

"He's a little faggot," he said, pointing to me. He spat and, ignoring the gun, took a step. "Go on," he said, yelling to me in the truck. "Tell your stepfather. Tell him what you did to my son when he wouldn't do what you wanted."

I felt Fredrick look at me, but only briefly.

Fredrick then yelled Gizos's name. "Come out here."

Lenno looked over his shoulder. "You stay in the fucking house," he said. He looked at Fredrick. "What do you want?"

"I want to know the boy is safe."

"'Safe,' says the man coming to my house and holding a rifle. Get out of here and take that gay son of yours with you."

Fredrick shot and cracked the ice sealing the concrete steps.

"Aim better," Lenno said.

Fredrick aimed the gun at him as he took a step toward him. I sat watching, as frozen as the world that held us. I had no idea what Lenno was talking about. Fredrick's gay son?

I don't remember how long this standoff lasted. Both Fredrick and Lenno grew more and more annoyed at the other, yet each did nothing. They were yelling, screaming, and I hoped somebody, anybody who was outside now, watching the two in each other's faces, would call the police. But I had to remind myself that nobody besides Native people cared about Native men going at it, however violent they were. I didn't know what to do, how I could end this. I was about to get out of the truck when Gizos appeared on the steps. His face, obviously, looked the same as it had. Both Fredrick and Lenno quieted.

"Did he do this to you?" Fredrick asked Gizos. Lenno said nothing. His people, his tribe, many of them gathered at the end of the driveway, were watching. I thought I heard Lenno tell Gizos to get back in the house, but his sentence was cut off by Gizos finally speaking up. Whatever emotion Gizos had, it did not show through his deformed face. He looked at his father, and then he looked at me. He nodded his head toward me: an accusation.

"He did it," Lenno said, and he raised his voice to be heard by everyone there, watching. It was as if he had rehearsed it: he said I had beaten Gizos, beaten him so badly when he refused what I wanted. I was out of the truck now, standing behind the open door, calling him a liar, saying he had done it. Fredrick looked at me, listening to Lenno. Gizos was no longer in the doorway. I would, of course, in my life, encounter deeper loneliness than this— much, much deeper, more pronounced—but right then I felt that that was the loneliest I could be.

"Liar!" I yelled, but Lenno spoke louder than me.

"That's the truth," he said, not addressing Fredrick or me but speaking to those who had gathered to watch, those who mattered to him: the ones who kept him in power.

Fredrick told me to get in the truck. As we backed out, Lenno walked in the headlights with us, almost pushing the truck. Those who were in the driveway parted for us, and they banged on the truck as we pulled away. Fredrick said nothing the entire drive home, and the gun lay in his lap, almost pointing at me.

Bobby set his mug down.

"Well, did you?" he asked.

And I said, "Did I what?"

"Beat him up when he wouldn't give you a blow job?"

A very old guy with no teeth sat not far from us, and he laughed with Bobby.

"I don't know whose version I liked better," Bobby said, "yours or my aunt's."

I wasn't really done telling him the story, but he was done listening, wanting to go home and drink some more. He paid, said he'd see me later as he laughed his way toward the door.

But there was more to the story.

We got home that night and Fredrick didn't get out of the truck. He sat there, hands on the wheel, gun across his lap, the barrel still pointed in my direction. When he made no move to leave, to shut off the truck or the lights, or even to speak, I said, "Are you going inside?"

I think he nodded, but maybe that's not right. He said nothing, I know that.

"It's not true," I told him. "What he said. What either of them said."

If I had felt betrayed by Gizos, I don't remember. Right then, I was too disoriented to feel anything but unsafe. I don't mean that in terms of being physically safe. I guess what I mean is that my situation on the reservation was already precarious, and this—this story—could snap what little thin line had held me in this place. Finally, Fredrick made a move. He opened his door and turned the gun around. He removed the loading rod and emptied the bullets into his lap. He dropped one and had to fish around for it on the floor of the truck. Then, when he'd given up looking for it, he pocketed the bullets and handed the gun to me.

"Keep this," he said.

I told him I didn't need it. What was I going to do with a gun?

"Exactly," Fredrick said. "It's safer with you."

He turned the truck off, and I followed him into the house.

Maybe I should have said nothing, should have let Gizos heal, let everything go back to normal. I drank three glasses of water at the sink. Fredrick was in his bedroom, and then he was in the bathroom, and then he was back in the bedroom. I didn't expect to see him again that night. He'd gotten ready for bed. But as I was drinking another glass of water, I heard him come down the hall.

"You should know I don't believe him," he said. "Not one bit of it."

I felt relieved for only a moment that he didn't believe the story. It wasn't the accusations, wasn't the story and its particulars that bothered me. I was more upset with the lie than what the lie said.

All relief I felt disappeared when he spoke again. "But it doesn't matter what I believe," he said. "It's what they will believe. And they will believe his story, believe the display in front of his house."

My mother coughed, and Fredrick looked down the hallway. If she was there, out of bed, I didn't know. I don't think she was—I didn't hear a door open or close. She must have still been in bed. In any other world, my mother would have come out, would have risen in this time to help in any way she could. But she didn't; she was sick.

"Good night," Fredrick said.

I said it back to him.

In the morning, Fredrick acted as if nothing had happened. He went on living. And this is important, because it's when, I think, I learned to carry on through an untrue story that pushes back, and this was the moment I thought of the most when I felt hopeless about Elizabeth and her mother, how I'd never see my child so close again.

After that incident, all the work Fredrick had put in with the tribal council was gone. People, he said, stopped listening to him, stopped caring. He used to stay late at council meetings, leaving Louise and me home alone to eat dinner together (or leaving me to eat by myself, when she didn't leave her room). He started coming home halfway through the meetings, and then he stopped going altogether. He spent time away, at camp, with Joseph, who was getting weaker and more careless, skipping meals and carrying too much wood as if he were still young.

It might be too easy to assume that Fredrick began to think about things that mattered more, like his family—Louise, me, his father—although maybe that's true. We can complicate things, offer explanations that are as grand as sculpted marble, but sometimes simplicity is best and truest. In its simplest, I think Fredrick was just plain tired, tired of fighting against something that so many wanted. And whether or not he was right—right to seek more for everyone, on the basis that he thought there was more to take—didn't matter: Who wouldn't want that, who wouldn't want more, not for the sake of having more but because it was owed?

With people believing the story Lenno let loose on the reservation—that Gizos's wounds were from me—he was able to go back to school. No questions were asked. It was known or believed I'd done it. But no students said a thing to me about it, maybe out of fear I'd do it to them, I don't know. Three days after—when a deep loneliness had taken hold of me—Gizos spoke to me. He didn't offer an apology, nothing like that. His face had started to look normal again, had started to reverse itself from how the violence had shaped it. It was during lunchtime, and he came by the table I was sitting at, and he said to meet him down by the river, the same place and time we usually met: 4:00 pm.

After school, I went home. Louise seemed to feel better and was moving around the house. She no longer lay in bed but sat in the living room, on the couch, reading and drinking tea, while Fredrick worked or was outside doing who knows what—he was always either chipping ice or trying to fix the ash-pounding machine. Louise didn't look up from her book as she asked how school was, and I didn't turn from the sink where I was washing a cup when I said it was fine. I usually ate something when I got home, but I wasn't hungry.

In my room, on the bed, I waited for four. Each second felt longer than the last, and with that I had more time to think. When it was time to leave and meet him, I took that .22 Fredrick had given me without the bullets. I was half-way down the driveway with it when I remembered that, that it wasn't loaded, and I felt weaker with that empty gun than I would have unarmed. And then it came to me: that one bullet Fredrick had dropped in the truck. In the daylight—or whatever of it remained—I found the small bullet the size of a carpenter ant, and I loaded it into the rod and snapped the rod back in place.

I was on the path, in the woods, heading for the bank of the river where we usually met, where Gizos told his stories. The gun grew cold in one of my hands, the other gloved, and so I took to holding the gun in that gloved hand. I turned the bend in the path and saw him down there, standing and looking my way, hands in his jacket pockets, and when I got to him, he said nothing about the gun. He looked at it once and only once.

"Here," he said, and from his pocket he took out my glove. It was an awkward exchange: I wouldn't let go of the gun, wouldn't set it down. When he saw I wouldn't let the gun go, he took the glove back and grabbed my cold hand and put the glove on for me. And then he wouldn't let go of my hand. Even when I pulled away, he held on, kept looking at the hand he'd just gloved, and I looked too, started to think he saw something there, on me, something of such great importance, and right when I accepted that there must have been something miraculous we were looking at, Gizos began to cry. Not a little, a lot. Since that day I've never seen a boy, or a man, cry that hard. Now I know such a thing could do the world good, not the crying, not simply the body and spirit's self-recognition of pain, but the publicness of it, the body and spirit's communicating to another's body and spirit in one and only one language—that of deep, deep emotion—between the flesh of two free bodies. I say "free" here because it's true—what is freer than that, freer than one body welcoming and receiving another's in a state or condition so unchanged since the very beginning of bodies, a state or condition that has continually been jailed time and time again since that very beginning?

If you had asked me at that age what I'd done while he cried, I would have said I'd watched him, watched him cry and cry and cry along the frozen river and below the bending branches covered in hard snow. But the truth is that I cried just as hard as he did until we both saw how ridiculous we each looked. And then we laughed, that type of heavy laughter that comes after an escape from some sort of danger.

Of course our moment had to end. When it did, we were both quiet, still, listening to the crackling of the ice and its echo upriver. Finally, he spoke.

"You want to hear a story?" he asked.

But the strange thing was this: I felt as if I had just heard one, and I told him that and said I didn't need another one.

"Not all stories are spoken," he said. "But your loss. It would have been a good one too."

I still wonder what it was he would have told me, and I regret not hearing it.

"Give me that gun," Gizos said, and I handed it to him. "We can't go home not having done nothing out here but cry like wimps. Is it loaded?"

"With one bullet."

He looked at me. "Psycho," he said. He took aim out over the river.

"What are you aiming at?" I asked him. It was almost dark, and the sky was that dim fading blue.

"I don't know," he said, but he looked to be aiming at something; he followed it with the barrel, whatever he saw out there. And then he pulled the trigger. A small pop.

"Got him," he said, and he handed me back the gun. He said we'd see each other the next day, which we did. On the way home that night, I wondered who, or what, Gizos had seen out there, at the end of that barrel. All I had seen was a cold dark over the ice. But what he'd seen could have been anything, anyone, including me.

5

When my mother and I came back together in 1996—years after Fredrick had died and when I joined AA—Louise was who she always had been: my mother who suffered from severe depression. But as the years went on, she began to change. Her memory started to fail her. At first, she mixed up details in a story or lost the words for things, words as simple as "chair" or "phone" or "cup," and would say, "You know what I mean." I thought it was just old age getting at her, but then it got worse, and by the fall of 2017 I knew it wasn't old age.

I went to visit her. It was Sunday, as usual, and I hadn't been by for about a month, as usual. And as usual her neighbor was outside, the snow melted mostly, and he spread dirt and leveled the soft ground near the junk he collected—a mangled metal bed frame was new. She must have heard me coming up the steps because when I went to unlock the door, Louise opened it and asked what I was doing there.

"Did something happen?" she asked. "What's the matter?"

I told her no, that I was there to visit for the afternoon.

"Why?" she said. "You were just here yesterday."

I asked her what she was talking about, but before she could answer me, something righted itself in her brain.

"Never mind, never mind," she said. "Just come in."

I shut the door behind me. I asked again what she was talking about, and that time she yelled at me.

"I said never mind! If you want to stay, stay; if you don't, leave."

I dropped it, but I paid close attention to how she behaved. Whatever version of her I saw at the door—the one that thought I was there the day before—did not show itself again while I was there that day. But it did show itself again the next time I visited, the following week.

She began to call me Fredrick.

Sometimes she owned the slip—"I mean Charles," she'd say. "Ha! Not Fredrick." Other times she would not—"Stop that!" she'd say when I corrected her. "You listen to me."

One Sunday I made the mistake of suggesting that we go to the doctor, and she kicked me—well, Fredrick—out of the house. If she hadn't rolled her ankle on a bunched-up rug by her bedroom door the next Sunday, I don't know how I would have convinced her to go to the doctor. Before I brought her in, I made it a point to tell the doctor that, yes, the visit was about her ankle, but it needed to be about her memory too. I had him all caught up.

Louise and I were in a room in the back of a local clinic, and the doctor tapped on the door and came in. "Let's see that ankle," he said, and if Louise suspected that the tests he was completing on her had nothing to do with the ankle, she said nothing about it. But he did not lie to her. He began to ask about her memory, and she caught on then.

"What is this?" she said. "What are you on about?" He was straightforward, but he knew not to aggravate her.

Everything but her memory of people and her occasional loss of words was fine. She wasn't forgetting how to care for herself, wasn't forgetting how to live—she could clean and cook, never forgetting to turn off a burner and always remembering not to put soap on the cast-iron skillet. She didn't forget to lock her door at night, and she didn't forget to turn off her candle wax burner.

"It will get worse," the doctor said when we were alone in the hallway. "It could happen quickly or slowly over a long period of time. Just pay attention to her."

And so I did. I paid close attention.

The doctor gave her Seroquel, and it helped her sleep and helped with her irritation and her depression. It alleviated the anxiety she didn't talk about but that I knew was there, especially when she thought I was Fredrick. It wasn't that often she called me by his name, but when she did, she became very fearful, not of me (or him) but of something else, something that was clear only to her. Maybe she remembered, or could sense, the memory: that for so long she and I had not faced the truth of what happened about his death.

Now when she got in these moods, when she thought I was Fredrick, I pretended I was. No revelations came, no hidden knowledge between Louise and Fredrick was ever revealed. She only talked about simple things: "How much wood do we have? Is it all chopped? I can help stack this afternoon. Don't forget to clean the chimney. Do you want me to check on Joseph this weekend? He should come home for a bit and have a real dinner instead of canned chili."

I told her we were all set with wood, that it was all chopped and stacked, and that I'd cleaned the chimney before I went and checked on my father, who was fine.

"But he needs a real meal," she said.

I told her I'd bring him something.

When I left her house that random day, she sent me home with meatloaf and mashed potatoes and green beans. It wasn't the first time she had done this, wasn't the first time she'd sent me off with food for a man who had not eaten on this earth for many, many years.

I never had the stomach to eat it.

Until very recently, I had thought her condition was worsening at a slow pace, if worsening at all. But earlier that spring, as we were watching TV—a show about a medical examiner, Dr. Something or other who solves crimes by looking at the body, the vessel, with a standard Y incision, as the narrator calls it—I felt her looking at me.

I had been Charles, her son, all day. I said her name.

When she didn't respond, I sat forward to get closer, and I said her name again.

"What are you doing here?" she said. "How are you here?"

She was terrified. She gripped her blankets and held them up to her neck, as if she were trying to hide.

"Mom," I said. "It's me, your son."

I rarely called her Mom; we had a mutual understanding that that was what we were: mother and son. All those years of silence after Fredrick died, that distance and separation we created between us because neither of us knew how to approach it.

I was no stranger to the great sadness I was filled with. Elizabeth comes to mind—knowing that your own blood doesn't know who you are, that you exist. But in Louise's bedroom that day as she became frightened, all I could feel was fear that she was passing a point we'd never come back to, that any chance of fixing ourselves, our relationship, was gone.

"Am I dead?" she asked me. "Where is he?"

"You're not dead," I said.

She got up from the bed.

"My ankle is sore," she said, limping out of the room.

I stood up, and when I tried to explain and follow her, she told me to sit, to stay away from her.

"Don't come near me," she said, and she began to walk around her apartment.

Doors opened and shut, and cabinets creaked and banged closed. When she came back to the bedroom, she held a rolling pin.

"Where is he?" she said again. "They took him, didn't they?"

I didn't move. I felt that any movement might make her worse or more fearful. I asked her who she was talking about.

"You know who," she said. "My son. Did Mother take him again?"

It's sharp, like cold air—that feeling of remembering your body knows something—that feeling of remembering that your body knows something about your past that you don't.

"Louise," I said. "He's at school."

"Don't you lie to me, Fredrick, don't you lie!"

"He's at school, I promise."

"I want to see him," she said. "Get him."

"I can't take him from school."

"Call there," she said. "I want to talk to him."

The first time Bobby met my mother, it was over the phone. I called him, and I told him what I could while Louise kept telling me to give her the phone ("the secretary is going to get him right now, you need to wait"). When Bobby understood what I was asking him to do, he laughed.

"Are you serious?" he said. "You're serious. All right, put my mother on the phone then."

I handed the phone to Louise.

"Charles," she said, her hand on her chest. "Are you all right?"

They weren't on the phone for very long, and I couldn't hear what Bobby said to her. I met him that night at the bar, and he told me that all he'd said was he was fine, that he was in class. He asked her if she was all right, which helped make sense of her constantly saying, when they'd hung up, "I think I worried him."

Louise saw a lot of Bobby that spring and summer, and aside from their phone introduction, she had yet to think that he was anybody but Bobby. I never asked Bobby to watch her, but he offered to do it when I couldn't, if I had a job somewhere, clear-cutting. And it wasn't like she didn't know him. A few days after the phone incident, I'd taken her out to lunch to meet Bobby. She was doing fine, was her old self as much as she could be. She didn't recognize Bobby's voice at all as the voice of the person on the phone and she rather liked him.

"You remind me of my cousin's ex-husband," she said, pointing at him with her fork.

"Maybe I am," he said.

That afternoon when I dropped Louise off at home, Bobby and I helped her upstairs. As I've said, her body was fine, and she could have gotten indoors with no help, but we went up anyway. We didn't stay long, and we didn't drink any of the coffee she offered. As I was driving Bobby to his car, which was back at the restaurant, he asked how fast my mother's condition would worsen.

"She doesn't seem that bad," he said.

I told him I didn't know, that the illness came and went as it pleased.

He asked if I was up there every day. I told him no, that I couldn't go every day, but that I called her every night. And that was when he asked if I needed any help, and he said he didn't mind going to check on her or even visiting with her when I couldn't.

I didn't know if Bobby thought my mother's illness might affect whether I would go to Florida with him, if he thought at all about it and if he believed at all that I would go with him, which I was still unsure about. I had nothing keeping me there, except Elizabeth, of course. Every so often Bobby would bring up leaving, and he had started to look up apartments and small houses in other states. Florida, California, North Carolina, all these places that were on the coast and had a beach. He'd never struck me as a beach person, but he'd even started to tell Louise about it, that he would be moving soon. "Sometime next year," he would say, which was what he'd been saying for a while.

6

Summer was turning to fall. Bobby planned to visit states and look for property for "our move," as he called it.

And so he left for about two weeks. He wanted me to go, but he knew my mother was unwell. Part of me wanted to go, wanted to get away with him and out of the normal rhythm of what life I lived, but another part of me knew I had to stay for Louise. Up until he left, Bobby had been requesting information on small houses and condos from all over the country, and the day after we last saw each other, he was heading to North Carolina to see about a place.

"I'll take some pictures and show you," he said.

I don't know why he wanted me to go with him so badly. I shouldn't say badly—it didn't come across that way. But how can someone's big plan that includes you not seem like that person wants it that way so badly?

He took the bus as close as it would get him, and then rented a car. I got a call from him a couple of days later, when he was supposed to arrive, but he was a day behind because he'd stopped off at the casino in Connecticut.

"Christ," he said. "Why can't our Indians up there have a casino like this?"

It was the first time I'd felt animosity toward him. I didn't say anything though. In fact, all I said was, "Hey, there's the Bingo Palace," but Bobby said, "Fuck the Bingo Palace. They need cards."

At first it was the "our" part of his sentence that bothered me, the way he laid claim. After we hung up and I had more time to think about it, I started to wonder about the possibility that I was just upset that he didn't say, "Why can't you Indians up there have a casino like this one?"

There's nothing strange about a white person wishing to be Indian. It's comical, if anything. And white people saying they're Indian happens all the time, and it's laughed at by Native people. "Oh yeah, your great-great-grandmother was an Indian princess? Boy, here's your per capita then." And I get it. I do. I'm not skeejin—not Native—and I can't say with any pride that I'm "Panawahpskewi" because I contain no blood connecting me to ancestors long gone. But I feel that I am, or that I have a stake in their experience. I don't feel this way because I grew up on a reservation. To think that the reservation is what makes an Indian an Indian is to massacre all over again the Natives who do not populate it. I could have grown up with my mother and Fredrick in a city, or in a country town, or, hell, in a dirty wet sewer, and I'd still feel this way. No place makes a Native a Native. It strengthens it, I'll say that, but it's not the deciding factor.

It was Fredrick's love that made me feel Native. He loved me so much that I was, and still am, convinced that I was from him, part of him, part of what he was part of. That was how I felt about Elizabeth—in truth, she was a descendant only from her mother's side, and if that were to come out and she were taken off the census, would she feel any less Native? I didn't think so. Blood matters only enough to keep us alive. She was Roger's daughter in the same way I was Fredrick's son, and I knew deep down he was as good to her as Fredrick had been to me.

And it seemed here, at least in my thinking, that to say blood doesn't matter was to let her go, to tell her that she was not mine, that we had no connection. And while all of that might have been true, it was all untrue, because I saw her as mine, as part of me. I guessed the only true thing I could be certain about—and this was really what had upset me about what Bobby had said—was that blood is messy, and it stains in ways that are hard to clean, especially if that stain can't be seen but we know it is there, a trail of red or dark red leading back to a time we cannot go to remove it. Or that red or dark red trail is our timeline, and if we could clean it away, then it would be some type of self-erasure, no different from the ways I've seen Native people erase their own kind. Mary has a story like that.

*

When the cattails swelled and bloomed like marshmallows, Mary and I used to snap them below the brown fuzz and together we'd slam them against the concrete to watch them explode. The cattails were the ones by the pond. Not on the side where the water flows under that small bridge out to the river but the other side by the light yellow service garage whose remnants are still there. We were teenagers then. Fourteen, fifteen. She was always coming to find me, and I think if she hadn't, I would have been the one looking for her. She had a walk about her—like the world could be falling down around her and she'd keep on going. It was such a different way of being from what I was used to at home, always seeing Louise fall away into that dark abyss of her mind. Mary was the joy that would get me leveled, that would set me right. I spent a great deal of time with her. If I wasn't with Gizos, and if I wasn't home or with Fredrick or Joseph or my mother, then I was with Mary. Like I said, I don't think I ever once sought her out to do something; it was always her coming up to my house and asking me outside.

Elizabeth is evidence enough of our bond, of where our relationship went, but that came later and was always secondary to our friendship.

One spring we were outside together, slowly making that side of the pond bald by plucking the cattails, the road littered with brown and white fluff. I don't remember the day, but it was near the weekend. The tribe was having a social at the community center. Two other drum groups were coming, one from the Point and the other from someplace else, some tribe I'd never heard of. There are so many of them.

We plucked most of the cattails. So few remained that we had to stand back and really try to find them among the tall spring-water grass. We were sharing a cigarette, searching, when Mary said, "I'm going to drum this weekend."

I've seen women drum since then. I watched Elizabeth drum when Roger taught her all the songs as a small girl. He set her up out back of their house on numerous occasions, and I always wished I could hear her. However in the late '70s, women weren't drummers. It wasn't "traditional." But Mary wanted to drum.

I asked her if she knew how. I didn't know how. I knew the songs and the footwork, and Mary and I danced once in a while. She said, "Of course I know how." After a pause, she laughed and said, "I asked Roger if I was doing it right."

"And?" I said to her.

"And what?"

I wanted to know more, since Roger had a thing for Mary. But I stayed the course. "Were you doing it right?"

"Duh," she said. "Want to see?"

Mary found another cattail, and she snapped it a foot below the top. With it in hand, she told me to follow her. We crossed the street and passed the service garage and went into the woods, where it was mostly swamp. River water flooded the area from the spring melt, and as we walked, we hugged the hillside. I didn't know where she was taking me, what she was looking for, and I didn't think she knew either until she said, "There's one."

It was a giant mushroom with a purple cap growing on the wet hill.

"This is the drum," she said. "Now sit and watch."

I sat right next to her, my shoulder almost touching hers, and she drummed and sang through a few songs: the welcome song, the honor song, and the snake dance. Whether she drummed them right, I'm not sure, because the cattail on the mushroom made little noise, just a small thump. But I'm thinking now that it isn't about the noise—it's part of it, sure—but rather it's the performance of it, the act of engaging with it, respecting it the way you respect anything that gives you life.

There in the woods with Mary, I listened, everything smelling of the spring dirt and wet leaves and cold, melted ice, until she finished singing. In my mind she'd sung and drummed perfectly, and when I went to tell her so, she said, "I fucked up like ten times." And then she crushed the mushroom with her boot and flung the cattail into the swamp.

"I'll get it right this weekend," she said. "You'll be there, right?"

Of course, I told her, even though I hadn't planned on going. I'd stopped attending them after Gizos's father had done what he did to Gizos and to me. Lenno was always at the socials. He organized them. But I knew I would go. I had to.

The location of the socials always changed and depended on the weather. If the ground wasn't wet and soggy, and if it wouldn't rain, they were usually held outside on the school's football field. We'd had such a wet spring—but not as wet as it would be eight years later in '86 when the spring melt and ice ripped the flat one-way bridge and took it away forever—and so the social was held indoors at the community building. This was before they got the basketball court and wood floors. It was smooth concrete back then—so many children cracked their teeth on that floor. I wonder, when they rebuild it across the street, if they'll have a good basketball court.

The building was full of people, everyone under the bright yellow lights high above. People mingled, paper plates of food in their hands. The whole place smelled like beef stew. The three drum groups were set up, and when one played, the other two listened. It was during those times that others—always boys, of course—would go over to the waiting drum group and ask if they could be part of the next song, and always some older Native would hand them his drumstick and move for them. Gizos drummed once in a while at other socials, but he wasn't there that day. He always said the older Natives teased him. Not just him, no, they teased all the young boys who drummed. Not in a way, Gizos said, where you felt embarrassed, but in a way that made you laugh too: "Jesum, gwus, last time you were here you had two whiskers, now it's three," and "I saw you with Alberta last week. You know she's your cousin, right?" But it wasn't always like that, the teasing, I mean. After Gizos's father had done what he did to him, I guess Ronnie, who was a distant cousin of Fredrick's and was as big as Gizos's father, told Gizos that he could always come to him if anything like that with his father happened again. Gizos liked to say that to be around the drum was to be ready for both the teasing and the seriousness, but that each was a source of strength in its own way.

I waited in the community building for Mary. I was near the stage, behind some tables where a few elder women sat over empty plates of food, talking to one another once in a while but for the most part sitting turned and watching the drummers and the children dance or run through with Hula-Hoops or basketballs until someone took them away. I thought Mary would find me, thought she'd come up to me and talk for a bit, and when our tribe's drum group was paused, their drumsticks resting on the drum in the shape of a snowflake, all of them waiting, turned in their seats, listening to another tribe's group, she would say, "Here I go," and she'd walk over to the group, tap on someone's shoulder, and he'd rise and give her his seat, and she'd drum the next song, and then the next.

But that's not how it happened, and I stopped looking for her. Lenno watched me closely, and I watched him talk to tribal member after tribal member as he kept on staring in my direction.

The drum group from the Point played an honor song. Lenno stared and stared and stared, and then his eyes caught something and he started to move toward it. He shouted. Or maybe somebody else shouted. A lot of people were shouting. I looked, and a wave of men—some from around our tribe's drum—were hurrying in one direction, not fast enough to suggest something terrible was happening and not slow enough not to catch the eye. The Point group didn't stop drumming, and they didn't stop singing. They were too focused, I think, to realize that anything else was happening.

Some of the men gave up on whatever they were pursuing, but others kept going through the double doors and outside. The older women sitting near me were really laughing at something, and as I went to ask them what had happened, a hand squeezed my shoulder.

"Where did she go?" Lenno said. I said nothing. I was too frightened. He put his other hand on my other shoulder and shook me. If people weren't watching, I wonder what he would have done. But he saw all their eyes on him. Then he let go and was gone. Maybe he saw the truth: that I had no idea what Mary planned to do.

The men eventually came back through those double doors and the social went on, and I left to find Mary. She was where we'd sat a few days before, right on the hillside deep in the swamp, near the large mushroom now crumbled and smooshed. In her hand she held several drumsticks, all ripped apart: the hide on each one torn open, all the beads and leather strips strewn on the wet ground, and the ones with feathers plucked, frayed, and bent.

"You're lucky," she said, looking at what she'd broken on the wet earth. "So lucky."

"I think if they had to choose between us, they'd let you drum over me."

She stuck a stripped drumstick into the ground. "That's not what I mean," she said.

"Then what?" I asked, but somebody was coming through the woods.

Mary and I looked back toward the noise, and when we both saw people, we ran. If Mary hadn't, I would have stayed, so I wasn't running away but following. My shoes and feet were soaked, and I tripped once over a hard root sticking out of the earth and got my knees wet. I kept following her through the woods and out of the woods on the road and then back into the woods until we were way away from that place and down by a fallen tree, sitting on it and breathing heavy.

"Fucking Native men," Mary said. "Fuck them."

"What happened?"

"They said no."

"I know that, but what happened?"

"You were there," she said. "You saw. I don't need to tell it."

"I didn't see," I said, and I told her how Gizos's father kept my attention, and I went on for too long, talking about how he grabbed me and shook me.

"I went up to the drum when they weren't playing," Mary said. "All of them were watching the Point group. I asked one person if I could have his seat, and he started to get up and was going to let me. But when he saw it was me—not even just me, but a girl—he sat right back down and told me to go. To go!"

"Who was it?" I said. "Henry?"

"So I asked the person next to him, and he said no too. It wasn't even that that made me mad. The first person I asked stood up and was saying, 'Go on, go on, you can't, go on, go on, it's bad medicine,' all the while flapping his hand at me like a dog."

"Who was it?"

"It doesn't matter who it was, they're all the same. But it was Henry."

"So you took the drumsticks because of that?"

"Let me finish. Henry sat back down, and he made eye contact with someone else drumming, and he pointed his thumb at me, and people laughed. That's what pissed me off. Their laughing."

She peeled piece after piece of bark off the log we sat on and flicked one after another.

"Bad medicine," she said. "Yeah, they got bad medicine all right. They all had their drumsticks resting on the drum, and I reached in and grabbed them and ran. The next thing I knew, you were here with me in the woods. How'd you find me?"

I didn't know how I'd found her.

"It doesn't matter," she said.

As we sat that day on that log, and before she went home, I told her about the women, the elders, how they'd laughed when Mary had done what she did.

"They're probably sick of it too," Mary said. She looked at me. "Were they all laughing?"

I didn't know, but I said they all were.

"Good," she said. "That's good."

I don't know if Mary's actions had anything to do with why women are now able to drum. And it's not like the next social or the one after featured an all-women's drum group. I guess what happened—how it worked out—was that she grew up, and so did the other women, and they made room for themselves at their own drums.

My mother thought what Mary had done was funny. I told her while we were eating dinner. Breakfast for dinner and the eggs ran thick and clung to toasted bread. While Louise thought it was spectacular, Fredrick was appalled.

"She shouldn't have done that," he said. "That's not right." He didn't mean that she shouldn't drum, no, he meant that she shouldn't have destroyed the drumsticks.

Louise had highs and lows, and she was at a high then. She laughed and laughed and laughed at how upset Fredrick was.

"It's not funny," he said. "Drumsticks should be revered."

"Revered!" Louise said, and she laughed and laughed.

It was always heartening to see my mother in such a mood, where she laughed at anything and everything. And while it was nice, it was also a reminder that just around the corner was that darkness, that deep, deep low that would put her to bed for weeks.

"Go ahead, laugh," Fredrick said. He looked at me, and I was laughing too. If he was upset about what Mary had done—and upset that we were both laughing about it—he didn't show it. He laughed too, and he shook his head. I think Fredrick knew how rare this moment was—Louise's laughter—and he'd give up anything, even all the reverence he held, to be part of it. Because what's more sacred than laughter at the dinner table?

7

When the doctor told me my mother's memory would get worse, I started to sleep less and less. I would sleep for about three or four hours a night. This would have been a problem if I were tired and simply could not sleep, but I wasn't tired. I wasn't sleeping much because it seemed I constantly had something to think about: Mary's cryptic answer to my question about how Elizabeth was doing, my mother's health, Bobby's plans, and the guilt I carried about Fredrick's death. It was like everything was piling on at once.

Maybe if my house were cleaner—or even decorated in a way that made it feel like a home—I would have slept better. My place wasn't dirty, but I hadn't been taking much care of it. The kitchen chairs around the table jutted out and away, and the rug under that table was bunched up. The sink was filled with dishes and glasses and mugs. The garbage wasn't full, but the plastic tub needed a wash. Coffee grounds littered the bottom. It used to smell only like cigarettes in here, but not since I'd started smoking outdoors. Now the place had a smell to it. Not foul-smelling, but there was a smell, and I won't be so delusional as to say it was a good one. The other rooms in the house weren't in too bad a shape. The bathroom smelled like toilet bowl cleaner. The tidiest thing in my house was my bed. Fredrick always said a made bed cleared the mind and helped with sleep. Maybe that's true, but I barely slept and when I did, it was on the couch.

And so I was awake the night of the fire. I saw from over here—and then from over there—what happened on the reservation. The news said it was arson and would later say it was that kid who'd done it, the young man who had robbed the tribal museum those years back.

It was a little past midnight. I sat on the couch with the TV on. I wasn't really watching it. I wasn't tired yet. I went outside to have a smoke and I sat facing the river. The good thing about having so few lights in the house is that when you go outside it does not take long for your eyes to adjust to the darkness. But maybe it wasn't that dark: the stars were out, and so too the moon. It was a dark blue night. A quiet one. I could faintly see the outline of Mary and Roger's house across the gurgling river. (I did miss seeing Elizabeth every day—she had moved at the end of that summer into a house she'd bought on the other side of the reservation.) Some people wouldn't consider silence a sound, but it is, and at night there's a certain silence emitted during the dark of night. Between the river's flow and the summer breeze rippling hard-to-see leaves and the sound my scraping shoe made on the porch, I heard night silence. I heard the workings of my inner body, the pump of my heart and the expanding of my lungs.

I smoked. When I finished, I smoked another. Something in me did not want to go back inside. But immediately as I sparked a third, I smelled something else burning. It was not my cigarette. I put it out and walked toward the river. I smelled fire smoke, and part of the sky above the trees across the river was graying like a storm cloud. At first that's what I thought it was: a storm, and that the fire smoke was just a coincidence, that somebody somewhere was awake around a flame. But when yellow light filled the gray clouds, I knew something wild was burning.

By the river I watched the sky grow brighter: a reddish-orange hue not quite unlike the soft chest of an eastern bluebird. Sirens wailed for a brief moment and then quieted, but that silence of night, the sound of myself, had been compromised: people, across the river somewhere, shouted.

Watching burn whatever burned, I wondered, What could it be over there on the island? The church, and mainly just houses. And then I thought of my old house, the one that the tribe had bought and planned to burn for training.

I should have known that they wouldn't have burned the old, crooked house that late at night, but I had watched day after day, night after night for smoke and fire. I'd never wondered about how I would feel when it was destroyed,

89

whittled down to its bones and ash. I'd only felt the waiting for knowing how I would feel. And so that night, when I saw the fire and thought of the old home, the waiting was over. I drove my truck over to the reservation. I was prepared to be stopped, prepared to be told I could not go that way, that the way was blocked, and while stopped I was prepared to see the house burning, flames flicking the smoke up.

But the house was not on fire. I kept on driving down that road, and I turned toward the pond. I was on the side where the pond water flows out into the Penobscot River. While I was the only person there in a vehicle, I wasn't alone. A few tribal members stood along the bent traffic barrier, watching across the pond as both the tribal fire department and Overtown's tried to subdue the flames, which grew higher and higher. I got out of my truck and watched with them.

I asked what was burning. Not to anybody in particular, but to the group of us there.

"I think it's the community garden," somebody said.

"No, can't be," somebody else said. "I think it's the garage."

"I can see the garage just fine," said somebody. "It ain't on fire."

"Well I can't see it."

"It's right there." A person pointed.

"I can't see it."

It was just the two of them talking.

"Well I can," said one, "and it's the garden that's on fire."

"Who would light the garden on fire?"

"Any one of those kids using drugs, that's who. Get your cousin to straighten this place out."

"He's trying."

"I didn't vote for him to try."

"Go to council then."

"They don't do nothing."

Someone asked me for a cigarette. In my hurry I hadn't brought them, and so I didn't have any to give.

"I got one," somebody said.

"Damn it's cold out."

We all kept watching the fire. I stepped back and then forward, and I could feel the fire's heat from across the pond. More people began to arrive.

People talked.

"I just texted my uncle," someone said. "He'll know what's burning."

"It's the garden," another said.

"I told him I think it's the garage."

"I just came from that way, it's the garden."

"You didn't come from that way. You live back over there. You didn't see anything."

I wanted to say I had thought it was my old house—and I was about to, when someone said, "Maybe they finally burned down Fredrick's old place."

"They ain't burning that down," somebody else said.

"Why not?" I said.

People looked at me. Even in the dark they knew who was who. That's how it is over here.

"Who are you?" somebody said.

"Who is this guy?"

Someone got in my face and then backed up. "I don't recognize him," she said, and she disappeared among the people.

"Charles," I said. "Fredrick's boy."

Those who remembered remembered, and those who didn't didn't care. I was recognized and placed.

"Jesum, gwus," someone said, laughing. "I heard you died. Your mom still around?"

I had no idea who was asking. I told her she was.

"That's good," she said. Then I saw how she was standing: bent over a bit and leaning on a cane. Her voice didn't sound old, but the sight of her showed she was.

Somebody asked if it was the garage on fire, and before anybody could say no—or yes—something across the way in the fire boomed and the flames curled and bloomed black into the sky.

"Christ, what kind of tomatoes they growing over there?"

Everyone laughed. A warmness from the blast rolled over me.

Soon the fire was under control, but not before it had spread to the garage.

"But it wasn't on fire before is what I'm saying," someone said as both fires were shrinking. "You thought it was on fire, not the garden, but the garden was on fire, and now the garage is."

"You think you know everything," somebody said.

I walked to my truck, feeling forgotten enough to leave.

8

We were on our way back from Home Depot, Bobby and me, having just bought an elbow pipe to fix my mother's sink—Bobby said he'd do it, "it's my trade"—when I called him on his bullshit. He'd been back from North Carolina for almost a week and he hadn't talked much at all about his trip.

"It wasn't good," he'd say, or "It's too humid there; I couldn't breathe by the end," or, a new one, "The piping was a mess." Every time I asked to see pictures of the place, he said, "Why do you want to see a place that's no good?" But that's Bobby: he almost never discusses things that aren't or weren't good. Maybe that's why I know so little about his childhood, his parents, his three marriages, his life before we met in AA.

But this time, I really wanted to know. It had nothing to do with my wanting or not wanting to go—I was just so damn curious. Bobby had been excited about the place. While he was there he had called and left voicemails, telling me what he was up to, the price of the place.

"If I sell my house and you sell yours," he'd said, "we can buy the place outright, including a strip of beach." It sounded good, truly it did, and his trip and what he'd told me through voicemail was in its own small way one of the reasons I'd been sleeping so little over the past few weeks. I won't lie: when he came back and kept deflecting, I felt a bit let down. When I did sleep, I had started to dream of a house that would never be mine, this small shack on a strip of beach under a dark blue sky. But that feeling lasted only so long as it could. Louise's illness reminded me why I could not leave. My mind still wasn't made up about going with him; some days I wanted to, some days I didn't. Who wouldn't want, at times, to get away from a life that seemed so empty? But one thing was certain: I wanted to know what had happened to him there in North Carolina.

And so we had just left Home Depot when I finally asked: "What really happened on your trip?"

He tried at first to say again what he'd been saying to me: too humid, the people weren't nice, it was overcast all the time.

"Really, though," I said, "what happened? I know you liked that place. I worried you wouldn't come home."

He took a corner too sharp and I was pushed into the passenger door. He braked hard at a red light. "I fucked it all up. That's what."

"How could you fuck it up?"

"I found the perfect place—" He waved his hands in the air like that described it. "Small gray cottage on the beach, two bedrooms, two baths, porch with a white wooden enclosure. The living room walls were painted light blue, and it was like you were in the ocean. It was just perfect. Perfect! Two neighbors, one on each side of the house, dry beach grass separating us from them."

"The light's green," I said.

"I know, I know," he said. He drove on. "And we could have afforded it, the both of us. Just down the beach—not even half a mile—was an outdoor bar. Indoors, too, but you could sit outside and drink and watch the ocean."

"So what happened?"

"I slept with the neighbor, that's what."

I really didn't see the big deal in it.

"Trust me," he said. "It's a big deal. She's married."

We were at another red light. Bobby inspected the elbow pipe. "Goddammit," he said. "Motherfucker. This is the wrong one. They need to organize those boxes better. I know I got this from the right box, but it was the wrong piece."

Instead of going back to Home Depot, Bobby drove us to Lowe's. I went in with him, and he went and found the right elbow pipe.

"She's married," I said. "So what? Just pretend it didn't happen, that's all."

We were headed to checkout, but he went to the service desk instead.

"I'm going to swap this," he said.

"You didn't buy that here," I said.

"They don't know that."

We were back in the truck with the right pipe and on our way to Louise's.

"Did you hear me in there?" I asked. "Just pretend it didn't happen."

"I can't pretend it didn't happen. Her husband knows."

"How?"

"I told him," Bobby said. "Or maybe he already knew. I don't know, Charles. But that's how."

I was laughing. "You're making this up, aren't you? Why would you tell him?"

"I didn't know he was her fucking husband. We were at that little bar, and we were talking, you know, just shooting the shit. He's asking me why I'm here, and I'm telling him, and he's asking me what I do for work, and I tell him, and I ask him and he says he's a retired cop but does some free-lance security shit. Anyway, we have some more drinks and he starts talking about how in the summer all these young women come down to the beach, and he whistles and goes, 'Damn nice sight.' And then I say I like the older ones, and he goes, 'Oh, yeah?' and I say, 'Yeah. Listen.' And I lean in close and say, 'Saw this lady the other night, right down the way,' and I'm describing her to him and he's getting all quiet and not looking at me. Finally he asks, 'What's her name?' and I tell him, and then the next thing I know he's got me round the neck and he's squeezing and the bartender's yelling at him to stop, and when he does stop, he goes, 'I didn't like you when you first opened your mouth. Come down this way again and I'll kill you.'"

"Get out of here," I said. "Why are you lying?"

"I ain't lying about this. That's the truth."

"So you're not going to tell me what really happened?" I said.

"That's what happened!"

"All right," I said, and I let it go.

"There's other places," he said. "There's always other places."

We were quiet for a bit. And as I had called him on his bullshit, Bobby called me on mine.

"So do you really want to go with me?" he said.

I didn't know what he meant at first, and so I said, "Go where?"

"Anywhere, away from this place."

I told him maybe, that I wasn't sure. That for as many reasons as I had to stay, there were an equal number of reasons to leave.

"I know you're busy with your mother," he said. "Christ, I am too, and she ain't even my mother. But what about when she dies? Sorry to say it, but it'll happen. There ain't going to be much else for you here. Especially if I'm gone."

I told him there was my daughter, and I told him that I had a feeling she wasn't doing good.

"How do you know?" he said.

I told him about seeing Mary, when I'd gone to ask her about burial rights a few months ago and found the courage to ask after Elizabeth and how she'd said she could be doing better but that she'd be OK.

"She could have meant something else," he said.

"If it wasn't bad," I said, "then why would Mary tell me? Why would she say anything at all that made it seem like Elizabeth wasn't doing well?"

"You think she wants you to worry just to worry?"

I did, but I couldn't see why.

"I don't know, Charles."

We were off the highway and driving Route 3, that long stretch of cracked, uneven road, back to Louise's.

While we'd gone to get the pipe, Louise had done what Bobby told her not to do: run the faucet. Water was all over the slanted floor, flowing into the thin space where the floor met the wall. Where it went, I don't know. It wasn't a lot of water, but enough of a mess to need six towels to clean it. It was an accident, her turning it on. Louise simply just forgot. But she didn't look at it that way. She sat in bed, crying.

"It's just a little water," I said. "It's all cleaned."

She looked at me. In a whisper she said, "Are you alone? Is he in the other room?"

Bobby was in the kitchen, on his back with half his body under the sink. I sat on the bed near Louise.

"Are you?" she said.

"Yes."

"How are you going to tell him?" she asked.

"Tell who what?"

She pointed at the wall, behind which lay Bobby. "Him."

"How am I going to tell him what?"

"That you're dead."

Even though she made no sense, the seriousness she said this with chilled me.

"I'm not dead," I said to her.

She yell-whispered, pointing at me. "You are! How are you going to tell him? Or am I going to have to tell him?"

"I'll tell him," I said. "I'll tell him."

She lay back in the bed and shut her eyes. I went to Bobby in the kitchen and watched him take apart the bottom of the sink. A flashlight was in the crook of his neck, and his hands were oily and wet. He made a scrunched-up face, squinting.

"If she asks if I told you," I said to him, "say I did."

"All right," he said, not even questioning it.

I went outside for a smoke. Louise's neighbor, shovel man, was out there smoking too, looking at his small, muddy lawn.

He hollered to me: "How's your mom?"

"Fine," I said.

"I hate to ask," he said, "but you got three bucks?"

I didn't have three bucks on me. Just change. I'd never noticed before, but he had a really thin and narrow head, and his cheekbones were sharp, like he never ate.

I gave him the change, and I told him that that was all I had.

"It helps," he said, sucking on his cigarette. "I need to catch the bus and get down to my appointment. I was late for the last one, and they were all upset about it there, and they were trying to kick me out."

I didn't know what he was talking about. "Sorry," I said.

"It's fine, it's fine," he said, counting the change in his palm. "Thanks for this."

He went inside, and I walked back inside and climbed the stairs to Louise's. Bobby was working on the sink. I asked him how it was going, but he must not have heard me.

"I told her you told me," he said. He tightened something. "This is done. Turn the water on."

I turned the sink on.

"Dammit, I'm good," Bobby said.

While Bobby cleaned up, I went in Louise's room. She was in bed with the blankets pulled over her head. She couldn't have been sleeping, I thought, and so I shook her gently.

"We're leaving," I said.

She looked at me. And it was her eyes that spoke: they skimmed over my face and the room as if everything was unfamiliar.

"Do you need anything?" I said.

She waved me away and rolled over. I could still see her looking about the room.

It was a flutter. That's the only way I can explain her state of mind. One minute she was over there, and then the next she was over here. But sometimes I didn't know where she was, where her thinking was at. And when I didn't know, I had to ask.

"Louise," I said. "Do you know where you are?"

She looked at me again. "Where I am?" she repeated.

"Yes," I said. "Do you know where you are?"

Never before had I heard such certainty in a voice. "I'm in my bones," she said, and she rolled back onto her side.

I stayed with her that night. Bobby and I had come in his truck, and he told me he could come and get me the next morning or late afternoon—not near midday, though, he had somewhere to be—and I said the morning was fine. Back upstairs, I shut her front door and locked it and went down the hall to Louise's bedroom.

She slept in the deep way she always had during those months of darkness when I was young. She stayed on her side, the blanket pulled up to her forehead. She made no noise, except occasionally when the comforter would crinkle. I kept the TV on as the only source of light, and I kept it turned down low. I could barely hear the voices, news anchors. Talking, updating.

The room was darker when I woke, and footsteps fell in the hallway. Not careful steps, but somebody hurrying.

Before I could say "Bobby?"—because I thought it was him, that he'd forgotten something and had come back to get whatever it was he'd left behind—a single hand came into the bedroom and reached for the light switch. The room lit bright and I squinted and stood up.

It was that man from next door. And when he saw me he turned the light off, yelled, "Sorry, sorry, I'm sorry," and hurried back down the hallway and out the front door, and maybe he meant to shut the front door but I'll never know because I was right behind him, after him, chasing, outside in the dark, watching him spring down the driveway and run down the street, and I lost him somewhere three roads down, near a gas station.

When I got back to Louise's, she was sitting up in bed.

"I shouldn't have been sleeping," she said. "Now he's gone."

I was out of breath. "Are you OK?" I said. "Did you see him?"

"Why would you do that?" she said.

"Do what?"

"He was coming for me," she said. "I told him I'd give him some."

"What are you talking about? Give him what?"

But she wouldn't say. I wasn't sure what was going on at the time, but the more I thought about it, the more I began to think she was giving him money. Why, I didn't know.

I called the police that night. Two officers came over, and I told them what happened. And I made the mistake of saying "I think" when saying it was the neighbor.

"You think?" they said, each of them. "You need to be certain."

"I'm certain," I told them, but the doubt was already there.

They said they would find him and talk to him, would take it from there. One of the officers said he was on this road a lot, and that he'd watch the house when he was on duty. It made me feel better, sure, but what if that man got away, was able to convince them it wasn't him?

The police found him, and he said he didn't know what they were talking about. They could not get him to confess—"I wasn't up there," he said, "so he didn't see anything."

If the officers were convinced, so be it. But I wasn't. After that night, I tried four times to find Louise's neighbor. He was never home, or if he was, he wouldn't answer the door. The last time—that fourth time—I didn't knock but stood on his steps and listened for any noise. But there was none except for the pigeons that whirred as soft as their feathers, up near the attic window.

9

On the day Louise brought up Fredrick's death, she wasn't agitated or upset. I went into her room, where she was watching TV in her recliner. "Hello, hi," she said, which was what she said when she wasn't sure who the person was. When she knew it was me, she would say, "It's not Sunday," except for when it was Sunday; then she would say, "What do you want for lunch?"

I asked if I could get her anything, and she pondered it. "No, nothing, thank you."

From the edge of the bed, I watched TV with her. It was the same show that always seemed to be on, that Dr. Something who solves crimes by cutting the body open and looking at the innards.

No wonder she thought about death so much. It was all she watched.

As the show played, I didn't listen. I was thinking about that man next door. I asked her again about him, asked if she gave him money. "Money?" she said. "What money? I don't have any money, if that's what you want."

She was quiet for a while. And then she said, "When do I need to be ready?"

I asked her what she meant.

"For dinner."

"Are you hungry?" I said.

"Is it dinnertime?"

It was a little past noon.

"So not for a few hours," she said. "I see. Have you called them for reservations?"

"Who?" I said.

"The Chocolate Moose," she said, a restaurant long gone now.

"You want to go out to eat?"

"If I do," she said. Except for the time I took her out to lunch and to meet Bobby, I never brought her anywhere.

It wasn't close to dinnertime, but I knew how she got in the evening hours. If I was going to take her out, I thought, better now than later.

"Our reservation is in an hour," I said, playing into her story. "You have to get ready soon."

She thought that was funny, and she pointed to the clothes she wore. "This is as good as it gets," she said. "I just want to do something before I leave."

For a bit, she tidied up the apartment. She washed dishes and set them to dry; she swept the kitchen and hallway floors, and bathroom. She vacuumed the living room, and she picked up bits of torn paper and junk receipts from the table and threw them away. With a small wastebasket in her hands, she checked each room twice for garbage.

"I didn't take too long, did I?" she said.

"You're fine," I said. "There's plenty of time."

"Not really," she said, and before she could leave me to think about that, I followed her.

She put on her shoes and asked if she needed a jacket. I told her no, that it was warm out, perhaps too warm out for October. As we went outside and I brought her to the passenger door of my truck, I watched for movement from the neighbor's house. Nothing.

"This is nice," Louise said as I backed out of the drive-way. "It's nice to get out."

I felt it too, what she felt.

"You know," she said, "my son never brings me out. Can you believe it? I just moved here last week—last week—and he doesn't even know it. I wonder how long it will take him to find out."

Too long.

"And he drinks an awful lot," she said. "At least he works. At least he has that."

I wish I knew who it was she thought she was talking to. Part of me thought to ask, "Do you know my name?" but that, I thought, would work her brain in a way it should not work.

"He hasn't been right for a while," Louise said. "Not for a while. Not since his father died. Maybe you can talk to him."

We were at a red light. A dump truck was in front of us, and I could smell the garbage.

"I can try," I said.

I felt Louise staring at me. "What will you say?"

"What should I say?"

"Maybe you're not the right person then," she said. "You need to know what to say."

We got off the highway and drove toward the dam and the main street that ran along it. The dam was not running, and at the bottom, jagged, dry rocks rose from the shallow bed like crooked, crowded teeth.

"My son lives near here," Louise said. "Just down that way. Let's go see him."

I turned the way she pointed.

"He might be at work," she said.

We drove on.

"Take this right, right here."

It wasn't my road, but I turned anyway.

"It's the next one," she said.

It was not. And I realized I was not alone here. We shared a mutual distance.

She took me down seven dirt roads, and on that seventh road she said never mind. If only she'd gone one road more, we would have made it. But instead we were going back, back the way we'd come.

"I don't feel well," Louise said. "I want to go home."

"You don't want to eat?"

She said nothing.

I drove past the bridge to the reservation.

"I want to go home," she said. "Take me home."

"I am," I said.

"Where are you bringing me?"

And then I slipped, called her Mom, telling her I was bringing her home.

"You're not my son," she said. "Pull over, stop, let me out!"

She opened the truck door as we were driving, and if she hadn't been wearing her seat belt, she would have completed the jump onto the passing pavement.

I stopped the truck and she struggled to get out. She did not know how to work the seat belt that I'd strapped on for her before we left. She yanked on it and bit it and kicked and screamed. The glove compartment popped open, and with her body weight she pressed down on it and it cracked and fell between her feet. She screamed, and then she quit. Her chest heaved. She didn't look at me. I touched her arm, and she started back up.

"Don't touch me," she said, and she swung her hand at me, at my face. "Who are you? You son of a fucking bitch, who are you?"

The whites of her eyes were red.

Cars passed by and did not stop.

I could not answer her question; I did not know.

*

I parked in her driveway and got out of the truck. I did not unbuckle her; I left her there. I did not know what to do but wait. So that's what I did. I waited and smoked and waited and smoked. I listened to those pigeons next door whir near the attic window, and I watched cars whiz by, kicking up dirt that floated and settled like a dirty, thin mesh net. I waited until she fell asleep, and I let her stay that way for almost an hour.

The truck ding-ding-dinged as I unbuckled her.

"You're home," I said.

She was calmer, but still on edge.

"I can do it," she said, getting out of the car.

I walked her to her apartment and brought her to her room. She sat down in her recliner.

"Has he told you?" she said.

"Who?" I said.

"My son. Has he told you why he didn't go with him that day?"

"Go with who?" I said, even though I knew who.

"His father," she said. "My husband. Why didn't he go hunting with his father that day? Has he said?"

"He has not," I told her.

"Can you ask him for me?" she said. "I'd really like to know."

"I will," I said. "I'll ask him."

She said nothing more. I was afraid to leave her, yet I was afraid to stay too. I made her some dinner. A plate of corn and brown rice and a slice of haddock, and I covered it with Saran Wrap and placed it in the fridge. When I went back to her, she had crawled into bed. I don't know if she was sleeping or not. A better son would have checked, or a better son would have stayed.

I do wonder who she thought she was talking to. Bobby? That's the only person I can think of. But then again, part of me thinks she didn't know who she was talking to. I don't know. I won't linger too long on this, because what does it matter who she was talking to?

I want to tell the full story, the full history of the family Elizabeth belongs to yet does not know exists, and to do that I have to explain Fredrick's death.

10

Am I at fault for Fredrick's death? is a question I've asked over and over again. I could have saved him. But does that make it my fault? I was convinced Louise thought so, and part of me felt that way too. Would I feel at fault when my mother died?

The reason I didn't go hunting with Fredrick is simple: my daughter was being born, and I was waiting, watching from my place across the river, for her to be brought home.

January 1991, either the fifteenth, sixteenth, or seventeenth. In the same way I do not know Elizabeth's exact date of birth—her exact arrival to this world—I do not know the exact date of Fredrick's death, his exact departure from this world. I do not know what I believe in when it comes to the afterlife, or the before life, but I've had this strange vision—when I was drunk, sadly—of the both of them passing by each other, one on the way in, one on the way out, their bodiless heads turned, bodiless eyes locked, knowing. A hello and a goodbye.

*

Fredrick asked if I wanted to hunt with him. I was outside my house, the one we'd built, in the cold, bundled up in a jacket, my body warm from drinking. A new snow had fallen the night before, about four or five inches. As I sat outside, I smoked, watching both the frozen river and Elizabeth's parents' house, waiting. Fredrick got out of his truck, and when he knocked on my door, I had to say, "Over here," and he made his surprised noise, "Ho, there you are," and he grabbed a cold metal foldout chair leaning against the side of the house and it opened with a loud creak and he pressed the chair's legs down into the snow next to me and sat in it, crookedly.

I knew why he'd come: the only way Louise would let him hunt was if I, or somebody else, was with him. It wasn't that Fredrick didn't want me to go—he'd be happy to have me along with him—but he knew I didn't like hunting. Fredrick wasn't old—in his late fifties—but Louise was worrying more and more about his health, about his ability to be out there in the cold and trudge through the snow, his ability to grapple with the immense weight of a dead deer or moose.

Fredrick was in fine condition. He was in better shape than me. But Louise wanted him safe. When she was in one of those dark places, she used to worry about anything and everything. A loose nail, a strange passing car, a heavy rain, a heavy snow, or no rain, no snow.

He sat with me, and I asked him if he had anybody else to go with him.

"Everybody's busy," he said. "I want to get out there now with the fresh snow."

"And she won't let you go alone?" I said.

"She probably would," he said, "but I don't want to worry her when I can avoid it."

I was quiet and so was he.

"I don't want to twist your arm into coming," he said. "It's fine if you don't want to go."

My eyes were set on Mary's house.

Fredrick laughed. "What if I tell her you're going with me? That would make her feel better."

"But what if something happens?"

"Nothing's going to happen, gwus," he said. "I'm going out tomorrow for the day, that's it. And I probably won't even get anything."

"You say that all the time, yet you always get something."

"It's best to expect nothing," he said. "That way you don't get your hopes up."

Across the river out back of Elizabeth's parents' house, snow loosened and rolled down to the river ice and spread like powder over glass.

Fredrick stood up and refolded the chair with a creak. "She'll call and ask you," he said.

"And I'll tell her."

*

I have this memory, and I don't know if it's true, where I felt he had something more to tell me, something more to say. It's a look on his face, but instead of saying what he wants, he says something else, that he'll see me when he gets back. And then he left. I think he wanted to say something more, and even all these years later I still feel that way.

Louise called that night and asked if I was going.

"Yes," I told her, and she asked if I wanted to sleep over there with them, so that way Fredrick wouldn't have to come and get me in the early morning. But before I could say anything I heard Fredrick's voice in the background, like it was far, far away, already departing our station. "I don't mind getting him," he said. "We have to go out that way anyway."

That voice, so distant. It was the last time I heard it.

He was only to spend the day out there at camp. He was supposed to stop by on his way back to "drop me off." And when he did not show up that night, I should have gone out there to find him. But I remained home and drank and watched the empty house across the river stay empty, going inside every so often to warm up and to get more to drink. I had taken the days off from work, and so I barely slept. One, two hours a night. I drank the rest of the time, and in the late hours I moved in and out of anger and sadness and worry as if they were rooms in a house I was pacing about.

Into the next day, into the next afternoon and evening, Fredrick did not return. It wasn't unusual. He oftentimes would stay longer than he had intended, longer than he had said he would.

And then in the morning on that third day—the seventeenth of January—tires rolled and cracked the snow in my driveway. I rose and turned to the coming noise. Of course it was not Fredrick. It was a taxi.

"Oh, thank goodness," Louise said. "I must have just missed him."

I stood from the chair but fell over into the snow, dizzy, and before I could try to get up Louise was in my face, looking at me, and so too was the taxi driver, a man whose gray hair stuck out from under his winter hat. They both lifted me up and propped me in the metal foldout chair. I don't remember what I said to her. It could have been any number of things, like, "I didn't go with him," or "I don't know where he is," or "He said nothing would happen." Whatever I said put Louise in a place I had never seen. She grabbed me by the jacket and was yelling, shaking me and shaking me. The taxi driver tried to pull her from me, and he could have if he'd wanted to, but I think all he wanted was anything but this. He stood back and watched as Louise shook me and screamed until she fell back onto the snow and sat blank-faced, her cheeks red, snow stuck to her eyebrows and hair.

She stood. "Get up," she said. "Start your truck."

"I can't drive," I said. I could barely look straight.

And so she drove the truck. On the ride she said nothing to me, and I said nothing to her. The drive would have been in silence if the radio hadn't been turned on to the lowest volume, but as it was there were voices with us, unintelligible mumblings with soft static. My window was not up all the way, and it made a slight whistle. We drove for over an hour with these noises.

Fredrick's truck was parked where it should have been: in a small clearing he had cut to make room for vehicles. The camp was a half-mile walk, and both Louise and I walked in the boot prints Fredrick had made. The shoes I wore were hiking shoes. Snow packed down around my ankles and every so often I would stop and stick a finger in my shoe and scoop out the watery snow, and each time I did so I had to hurry to catch up to Louise, who stopped for nothing.

The closer we got, the more I envisioned the scene: Smoke rises from the chimney. By the small shed an animal carcass rests, gutted and stiff. Louise and I both stand by the door, breathing. "Thank goodness," she says, and she opens the door to the camp and there he is—Fredrick. Sitting at the table, oiling his rifle. He looks up, and even if he is confused by our arrival, he says, "Ho, come in, come in," and like smoke he rises. He stands and walks to us. "Bang your boots good," he says, and he asks if we are hungry, and we say no but he starts frying something up anyway—salted pork or whatever meat he carved from the bones of the animal's sacrifice outside. And we unknowingly eat our way toward another, different future.

But no smoke rose from the chimney. No animals rested against the small shed. No voice greeted us when we opened the door into the camp. Everything was still. There was no smell except for the cold.

My head pounded. "Maybe he's still out," I said.

Louise brushed past me, and when I asked where she was going, she gave no answer, but I followed behind her. She found his boot prints, and they marched north into the woods. His boot prints pointed only away from camp; none pointed back.

We walked in his prints. Louise in front, me in back. I don't know how long we were out there, how long we walked, following where he had gone, but it was long enough to sober me up, and I got sick, sick, sick. I threw up time and time again as we walked and turned this way and that through sparse trees until all that came out of me was a groan. It was endless, where he seemed to go. It was like he was walking to walk; or he had been following something.

Daylight was disappearing. It was not dark, but I knew that if we did not turn around, there was a chance we'd lose ourselves and the prints and not make it back. Louise was way in front of me, and I had lost sight of her. I quickened my pace, and I caught up to her, but only because she had stopped walking.

Fredrick had shot something that did not die. Blood soaked the snow in patches, and every hundred feet we found the blood and his footsteps alongside it, and sometimes we found the large, bloody balls of shit—moose shit—and the outline in the snow of a monstrous body tired and wounded but that had risen to live.

I would have followed her all night, but she turned around and started back to the camp. Night beat us there, but we weren't too far behind it. I can't recall if any stars were out.

I still don't understand how she was able to summon the strength to pull herself together. Inside, she lit a small kerosene lantern and got the fire going. And then she went straight to the small cot pressed against the wall. She lay down and covered herself with a thin gray blanket. She faced away from the room. She had been so adamant about finding him, but when we got back to that cabin she fell into a deep sleep. One moment she was aflame; the next she was out.

I did not sleep that night. I don't know if Louise heard me tell her that I'd be back, but I spoke that into her ear. Before I left, I made sure the fire burned strong, and I made sure the door was shut tight.

I got back to the truck through the footprints we all had made. I still felt sick, and I was sweating. I drove all the way back to Overtown with my window rolled down, and I rolled it up only when I crossed over the bridge to the reservation. The wind whooshed hard over the ice. When

I made it to the tribal police department—not the old one, the one as small as my house—I realized I had forgotten my jacket at camp and was wearing only a T-shirt.

Fat Rob worked dispatch that night. His fourth heart attack finally killed him seven or eight years later. He sat behind a coarse wooden desk with a small lamp turned on that lit the hideous dispatch console, acquired when the tribe had been restored its sovereignty and began operating its own law enforcement. I don't know much about radios or dispatch consoles, but this one was old and outdated, which I realized when Fat Rob gave it little kicks every time the machine didn't cooperate.

Soon he was able to contact the officer on duty, Darren, who, before returning to the station, stopped off at the game warden's house on Rolling Thunder and woke up Shay. Darren arrived first, and I told him how Fredrick had gone missing, and then when Shay made it, I told him the story too. I drove between their two vehicles, pinched between silent spiraling red and blue lights, and we drove together out to the camp and parked in the clearing and Shay offered me a jacket and I told him I had one back at camp, but he made me take it anyway and he offered me a cigarette, which I took too, and then we all crunched the snow in single file through the path, both Darren and Shay lighting the way with flashlights while I hurried behind with the red tip of my cigarette and breath frosted, smelling the smell of smoke coming from camp.

At the camp I walked up the steps to the door, and before I could open it, it opened and Louise was in my face holding up a lantern, and she squinted her eyes like she had just woken up and the night was too bright for her. And then she said, "Did you find him?" and she looked past me at Darren and Shay with their flashlights pointed to the snow that looked like the fur of a white rabbit.

We were all inside. Darren and Shay asked questions, and Louise answered. When you got here, was the camp completely shut up? No fire? Nothing? Which way did he walk? How far? Were the tracks fresh? Did you find anything of his out there? Did you see any smoke or smell any? A moose? There was blood? So he was chasing something?

"We'll go," Darren said.

I showed them to the footprints, and I walked with them to the place where Louise had found the first blood of the moose, and then I could not walk anymore. I was shaking, and I felt dizzy. I was hot, overheated, and I crouched down in the snow and pinched the bridge of my nose.

"Are you all right?" Shay asked.

"I'm sick," I said.

"Go wait back at the camp," he said, and I tried to walk but I found it extremely difficult, like I was not in control of my legs.

Shay spoke to Darren. "I'll take him back," he said. "I'll catch up." And like an echo, I heard, "Radio me."

*

Halfway back, Shay had to help me walk. His flashlight shone every which way as I leaned on him, and he struggled to light the snowy path. We got back, and I didn't even know it. I could barely keep my eyes open, and I tripped on the first step indoors. The door opened, and for the second time that night Louise looked upon those on the camp steps hoping that one was Fredrick. She was no longer in the doorway when I went inside, and when I turned to shut the door, Shay had hurried away and gone back into the woods.

For the longest time I sat in the kitchen table's small wooden wraparound bench. Time passed by. I may have slept or dozed—I'm not sure. But I do know I wanted desperately—or needed—a drink. A beer or two. Liquor. Mouthwash. Sterno. Anything.

The next day arrived and Fredrick still had not been found. The sun was rising, but the inside of the camp was still dark. Louise was awake and she finally spoke to me.

"You look like shit," she said. My eyes were shut in the dark behind my eyelids, so there is only sound in my memory. Louise's knees popped as she knelt down and rummaged through the cabinets, the doors slamming shut. A can or two banged on the sideboard. A drawer opened and fingers sifted through clanking metal, the drawer shut, and then there was the short one-two-three-four-five-six grind of a can opener. The click-click-click-fwoo of the stove and the searing of something in a cast-iron skillet.

A crinkle of thin plastic, and then the smell of toast burning—"Dammit"—on the woodstove.

"Go get me water," she said.

The house was full of light now. Bright, white light. The sun behind me through the windows washed the back of my neck in warmth like heated water. I didn't want to move from it, but I did.

Part of a stream was not far from camp. Fredrick's father's camp used to rest right along it. There was nothing there then, not even the guide business. The walk there and back was only twenty minutes. I brought a blue bucket with a white handle, and when I got there I kicked a hole through the ice, below which the river still worked and flowed away. I got water and returned.

Louise did not eat any of the corned beef hash she had cooked. She ate only half a piece of toast and drank just a little bit of water. I ate a small pile of the hash no larger than a fist and a piece of toast plus the other half Louise did not eat.

Louise left the kitchen and the sideboard a mess, and I didn't clean it either. We were sitting in the quiet of the camp—listening to the crackle and pop of the woodstove—when she spoke to me, not asking for anything, her voice calm, as if the torment were over. But it wasn't over.

"I don't blame you," she said.

I didn't believe her, and that was not what I wanted to hear. For a while I didn't say anything. For her to say that,

that she didn't blame me, meant she had reached a conclusion, an end, even though we did not know for certain if that was where we were: the end.

"Did you hear me?" she said.

"It was his idea to lie to you," I said.

All these years later I saw how each of us told the truth, yet we couldn't believe each other. And that we didn't believe each other made each of us reconsider our own truth, our resentment, until it turned us against each other and in our minds we settled upon what was not true.

I blame you.

It was my idea to lie to you.

This was the friction in our lives. This was the moment we separated and had to try to love each other. Sometimes I would visit her in our old home, Fredrick's home that had become ours, but the weight of his absence was too much. She was better at keeping in touch than I was: always calling me every week or so, checking in and seeing how I was getting on. But I never answered her calls, never knew she moved from the house I'd helped her move into until years had gone by. And now, even as I was trying to bridge those years of silence, she was slipping away, both forgetting and remembering, remembering and forgetting into nothingness.

*

It was past noon when Darren and Shay returned. Only Darren stayed. Shay went out to the road to radio for help. They had found Fredrick stiff as iron and partly buried under the snow.

After Fredrick's body was removed from the woods, I tried to stop drinking. I don't know how long I made it, but I began to hallucinate. I started to see Fredrick in my house. I saw him outside. And when I did not see him, I felt him, his presence.

In a dream I saw him, which sounds comforting, but it was not: the dream was of his death. The gun had been fired: out in the distance the moose was hit and it ran and Fredrick chased after it for a long while and when he lost sight, he followed the blood and shit and he saw the wide brown fur of it out there lying down, and as he lifted the rifle again, the moose rose like a baby learning to walk and staggered through sparse trees, leaving behind a trail of odorous frost breath. Fredrick cursed and followed until again the moose rested, but Fredrick could not get a clear shot, and when the moose saw him again, it rose a time more and there in the woods the both of them were after life itself, which was somewhere in the distance, and neither reached it. The moose was breathing heavy, and Fredrick was a foot away. He was praying, speaking in a language that was not mine, and in the revered moment between the hunter and the hunted, the ascendancy of life itself spread its bright black wings over the horizon and over them both and the moose rose and charged Fredrick, who could not fire soon enough, and the moose rammed into him and collapsed on him, and the bone fragments from Fredrick's rib cage punctured his internal organs and he was dying, dying, dying, and the moose was dying, dying, dying. The dream ended before I could see who moved on first.

Now, I had to decide: Should I tell my mother the simple truth: that I did not go because I was waiting for my daughter to be brought home? Or should I reaffirm the other truth, the one she knew but wouldn't believe: that it wasn't my idea to lie? I didn't think either one of those would do any good. In a perfect world, Fredrick wouldn't have gone hunting—he would have been at the hospital with me, with Louise, with Mary's parents, Philip and Eunice, as Mary brought our child into this world for us all.

11

At our last doctor's visit, the doctor had mentioned the possibility of putting her in a home. But I didn't think it was necessary. Louise recognized me most of the time, though I knew that some days she didn't know who I was and that she was just pretending. But she still had not lost the ability to take care of herself. And then the doctor recommended a doll, but I didn't have one and so I gave Louise that stuffed elephant. The one I wanted to give to Elizabeth all those years ago. Her doctor had mentioned how some people with her illness responded well to having to take care of something. Did they really think it was real? I could see a small doll dressed as a baby in pajamas or in a jean outfit being convincing enough, but a stuffed elephant? But the elephant seemed to work for her. When she loved it, she set it on her lap as she watched TV, and every so often when I was there I would see her bouncing her leg so the elephant went up and down. But that was only sometimes.

That fall, she was sleeping a lot. She wasn't eating. She rarely talked, not saying goodbye when I left, and she said my name only so often when I visited. It saddened me, because she was never like this when she couldn't remember—that is, when she saw me but did not know who I was, when she lost touch with reality and took care of that stuffed elephant as if it were her child. When she went back to that dark place was when she knew who she was.

When I wasn't worrying about my mother, I worried about Elizabeth. Since the day I'd seen Mary to ask about burial rights and she said our daughter could be better, I'd started to arrive at all sorts of crazy conclusions. How could I not when her blood was Louise's blood? How could I not when the night after Louise's doctor appointment, after I gave her that elephant, two tribal police cruisers showed up in Elizabeth's parents' driveway, and all ideas pointed to the worst? I wouldn't find out anytime soon what had happened, but when I did, I learned my suspicions of blood and what it carries were not so crazy.

In mid-October I brought Louise back to her doctor, and I ended up getting a small checkup too. I had an accident while we were there, but nothing big. It was going on noon when I showed up to get her. Her appointment was at one. I still hadn't seen her neighbor, but I knew he'd been home. At the end of his dirt driveway he'd piled more garbage. Bicycles that were missing tires and chains; dressers with drawers off the tracks; sheet metal, one sheet black with paint; cardboard boxes, lots and lots of boxes, most damp from the rain we'd had; and a white couch with no cushions. There was other stuff, but I can't remember it all. I don't know why it was all there, and I don't even know where it came from. His house? Dumpsters?

When I went inside Louise's, she was asleep under the blankets in bed. I shook her arm, and it startled her.

"What time is it?" she said.

I told her.

"What time do we have to leave?"

I told her that too.

She was herself, or as much so as she could be. She knew my name and called me by it when she asked me to turn the coffee maker on. And she said my name again when she told me to turn it off and that she'd have a cup of tea instead.

I heated the water in her microwave until it was steaming and then dunked in a bag of this peppermint tea she likes, and when it was ready I set it on her nightstand and I had to wake her up again.

"I don't know if I can go today," she said. "I don't feel well."

"Then maybe that's reason enough to go," I told her.

She made a grunting noise.

"Sit up," I said, and I helped her with the pillows. "It'll help you wake up."

She reached for her tea, yawning.

"It's hot," I said. "Be careful."

I sat down in her recliner.

She picked up the mug and blew ripples across the top. Between blows she asked, "Is it raining?"

"No," I said.

"They said it's supposed to rain."

"Who?" I said.

She sipped her tea and made a pained face. "Jesus," she said.

"What?"

Louise sipped her tea again and then swore. "How long did you heat this for?"

"I said it was hot. Jesus said it's supposed to rain?"

She set down the tea. "Yeah," she said.

"You're talking about Jesus?"

Her tone was flat. "I'm messing with you. The weather people said it."

I laughed only because that's what I was supposed to do; and she did too. But I think both of us found it difficult to find things funny lately. It was hard to tell how much she really knew about her condition. I think she had an idea of what was going on but could not name it, like when you know the answer to something but you're pressured by time.

Louise yawned again and with her arms she slowly spun her body so her feet hung from the bed. Her face was scrunched up as she rubbed her ankle.

"Something hurt?" I said.

"Everything," she said, and she stood. She leaned on the back of the recliner for a moment and then took steps like her joints were rusted. As she passed by me, I could smell her. She did not smell terrible, but she smelled like she hadn't been showering.

It took her a while to get ready. She was in the bathroom for a long time. The sink sprayed and the fan hummed. Something fell and clanked on the linoleum. She left the sink on when she came out, and I expected her to be dressed in something other than her pajamas. She was not. She passed by me and her bed and went to her dresser and pulled out clothes from different drawers. Jeans, shirt, socks, all of it, and with a pile of neatly folded clothes in her hands she went back to the bathroom, but then came right out into the bedroom again and was looking for something.

"What are you trying to find?" I said.

"Um . . ." She looked on the top of her dresser and then in her nightstand drawers on both sides of her bed. "I don't know," she finally said. "Maybe it's in the bathroom."

The next time I saw her she was dressed and was in the kitchen.

I asked her if she was ready, and she said she felt she should bring something to eat.

"Are you hungry?" I said.

"Not really."

"We won't be gone long," I told her.

I helped her put on her shoes.

"Is it raining out?" she said.

I told her it was not.

Outside, she said it looked like it was going to rain and asked me to go get her jacket from inside. I did, and when I came out she was sitting in my truck and from behind the windshield she pointed at something and I turned around to look. It was the pile of garbage.

I got in the truck and started it.

"He sells that stuff," Louise said. "Goes around and digs in dumpsters to find it. Can you believe it?"

That was the first I'd heard of that.

"How do you know?" I said.

"He's tried to sell me stuff before."

"When?"

"I don't know," she said.

"Recently?" I said.

"Why do you care?" she said.

"I'm just curious. Was it recently?"

"A couple days ago," she said. "Can you turn the heat on? I'm cold."

I turned the knob to red and the fan to four.

"He came to your house?" I said.

"Who?"

"Your neighbor."

She mumbled two things. One I could not hear, and the second was "I don't know."

Rain droplets hit the windshield.

"Good thing I said to get my jacket," Louise said. "It's going to pour."

The rain stopped and then started again, but it was never more than a few drops here and there. Halfway to her doctor I turned the heat off, but she asked me to put it back on. I closed the vents on my side because I was sweating, like something in me was trying to get out, trying to surface.

Louise was quiet for the rest of the drive. There was an accident at a light a mile up, and we had to go a different way. Right as traffic was turning around and going back through a detour that had been set up, I caught a glimpse of a car and a truck, the front of the truck smooshed in and the back of the car crunched up. That's all I know; if anybody was injured, I did not see it. And Louise did not see it. For the rest of the drive she kept her head back and her eyes shut like it was something she had to try to do.

Louise said nothing when we got to the doctor. She struggled but succeeded in unbuckling herself. She got out of the truck and started for the doors that parted open. A cold breeze. Or maybe a wall AC. She took a seat while I went and told the man behind the sliding glass window that she was here for her appointment, and he handed me a clipboard with a form and a see-through pen with red ink.

"I don't know why I have to keep filling these out," Louise said, and since I didn't know I said nothing.

A few minutes passed.

133

"Here," she said, and I brought the clipboard and the form written in red ink back to the window. It was no longer a man on the other side but a young woman in giant spectacles who took the clipboard and started inputting Louise's answers into a database on a computer screen I could not see.

While I sat and waited with Louise, I saw the man come back to the window and sit down, and I was relieved to see him, to know he was real. I felt strange, like something was wrong or off; like seeing a glass of water too close to the edge of a table. I was anticipating something.

We waited close to thirty minutes. They said the doctor was backed up with appointments, which was hard to believe since we were the only ones in the waiting room and nobody had come out through the heavy wooden door leading to the back rooms. But then it seemed like all at once, patient after patient came out through that door, and a large line grew in front of the glass window and both the man and the young woman were busy scheduling next appointments and answering questions about when and where so-and-so's prescription would be. One man, an older man, got angry when the young woman told him he had no refills on file, and he told her that the doctor had just written him a script for them, that he'd just seen him, and the woman had to say that it wasn't in the system yet, and she had to get the doctor, Louise's doctor, to tell him that it would be ready later that day, and only then did the man leave and only then did the doctor come to the heavy wooden door, and he opened it with a clank and he said, "Louise?"

He said sorry for the long wait, and we followed the doctor through the door and down a white hallway with a few rooms until we got to one at the very end, and we each went in except for the doctor, who said, before shutting the door, "I'll be in shortly," and I don't know why but I felt as if it were me he was addressing, as if this appointment were mine, and I could not shake the feeling, again, that something was wrong with me.

A nurse came in and took Louise's vitals. When she finished, she knocked over a small jar holding long wooden sticks with swabs on the ends, and after she cleaned them up, she was gone. She was not very talkative, the nurse. She said nothing, not an "oops" or anything when she knocked over the jar, which was fine, because I had nothing to say and neither did Louise.

Red, yellow, and blue colored blocks were stacked in a thick wicker basket on the floor by my chair. I took a few out and stuck them together, and as Louise told me to leave that stuff alone, the door swung open and a doctor who had never seen Louise came in and I dropped the blocks to the floor and picked them up. I had no sense of embarrassment until the doctor said with a smile that closed up his eyes, "What are you building?" and he said it like I was a child, and so I said, "Nothing, just killing time," and when I'd put the blocks back in the basket I stood up for some reason—maybe to shake the doctor's hand—and then everything dimmed slowly to black and I expected to come out of it but I did not. The next thing I knew I was on the ground looking up at the doctor, who was looking into my eyes and talking and talking to me.

"Can you sit up?" he said.

I did.

"What's the matter with him?" a voice I did not recognize said.

"I'm fine," I spoke, and I stood up and walked to the chair I had been sitting in before. I sat.

The doctor knelt in front of me, the ends of his white coat draping the floor around him, and he questioned me.

Are you still dizzy? Have you eaten today? Do you have a history of this? We can take some blood work if you'd like. No, don't try to stand. Catch your breath. Breathe, breathe, breathe. In through your nose, out through your mouth. Good.

Some minutes passed.

"How do you feel?" he asked.

"I'm fine," I said, and I told him I thought I'd just stood up too quickly.

"Yeah," that same voice said. "I'm still here."

"Do you want to do some blood work?" the doctor said again.

"No," I said. "I'm fine."

"Do you ever feel anxious?" he said. "Do you get panicky?"

"Good Lord," the voice said, "he's fine."

"No," I said, which was partly true. Never before had that happened. From drinking and lack of food, sure, but not when I'd been sober and full. I could pinpoint the doubt I felt only because the doctor had brought up being anxious or panicky, and since we'd gotten to the doctor that day, I'd had a strange feeling like there was something in me that was slowly vibrating and numbing me. And every time there was a noise—the slam of a door, the squeak of a shoe on the floor, a cough, the sound of that sliding glass window behind which was a man and then a young woman and then both—my body was sensitive to it, and that sensitivity frightened me in a hard-to-describe way, like I'd known somehow I was going to be frightened by it even though it had yet to happen, and so that knowing what was to come only increased the fright or the fear. The only comparison I can really make is to playing hide-and-seek. It was like that—I knew somebody was hiding, and I knew to expect they'd pop out from somewhere, and so that knowing made it worse when they did, when the future came.

After I told the doctor no—that I never felt anxious or panicky—I knew he was going to say OK.

"OK," he said, but I had not known that while he turned his attention to my mother, the doctor would continue to pay close attention to me, glancing at me to make sure I was all right.

Her appointment should not have been very long. And maybe it wasn't, but it seemed that way. Louise was having trouble staying focused and answering the doctor's questions. She was forgetting. He asked her about the medication he'd prescribed for her, and she said, "What medication?" and he had to look at me and I had to say, "Yes, she's finished them," and then the doctor scribbled something on a sheet of paper and Louise looked at me and then at the doctor and she laughed hard and said, "I remember, yes, yes, I've finished them," but I don't know if she really remembered or if she just knew that was what she should say. And this went on and on until the end, which was after the nurse had come back and taken some blood from Louise and brought it to get checked and the doctor had come back with the news that things were looking good, and when he prescribed another set of medications and set out to say how they should be taken and when they should be taken, Louise looked at me and then at the doctor and again she laughed. "You're talking to me," she said. "I thought you were talking to him." And I told the doctor I'd run through it again with her and make sure she took the pills correctly, but then he went through the directions again because he had her attention.

My body had that feeling again, like we were done, or like we were going to be done. I stood up to leave with Louise but then I remembered I had things to tell the doctor. I wasn't sure if I should say them in front of Louise.

I asked him if we could talk, and he stayed seated in his little round swivel chair with his white coat hanging down, and he said, "Sure."

I don't know what he saw in my face. I know I tried to say something, but it did not come out, and he saw my eyes flick toward Louise. Whatever clues my face showed, he picked up on them. He turned to Louise, who stood with her purse over her shoulder as she studied the poster on the wall of the anatomy of a man, and he said to her, "You can bring this prescription up to the front if you'd like," and he handed her a sheet of paper he'd printed out and then signed. She took it and was glad to be out of that room.

I asked him if he was aware of her depression or her moods.

"All I know is what you tell me or what she says," he said. "Her medical history isn't very long."

I explained that that was because if she had gone to the doctor, it had been on the reservation, and that they would have her medical history, or more of it. She wasn't one to go. Only when Fredrick made her.

"She's suffered all her life from severe depression," I said. "My father—not my real father, my stepfather, the man my mother married when I was young—my father used to take care of her when she got in her moods."

The door opened and Louise came back in. "Is it this way?" she said, and the doctor went to the door and pointed down the hall, but then he told me to wait and he took her down the hall and back to the lobby.

He was not gone long. He came back and sat down. The door stayed open.

"What were her moods like?"

I told him that for days or even weeks she would lie in bed, that she barely ate and whatever talking she did was usually one- or two-word sentences, or else she spoke by not saying a word, that it was her silences that spoke for her.

"It would last for a few days or weeks?" he asked.

"Sometimes more, sometimes less."

He wrote down nothing of what I said.

"She still gets like this," I said. "But only when she remembers."

"What do you mean?"

"When she remembers things," I said. "When she knows it's me she's talking to, when she knows what year it is and where she is and where she's supposed to be and when she remembers fully who she is. When she's like that, when she's herself, is when she's most likely to slip into whatever dark place it is she goes to. She's been quite aware today of everything, and when I found her this morning, she did not want to get up and go to her appointment."

"Is this often?"

"I don't know how to quantify it," I said.

"Depression is normal," he said, "but would you say she's depressed more than she's happy?"

I told him yes.

"Do you think she will harm herself?"

I told him no. "As far as I know, she's just always waited it out."

"Waited what out?"

I will be honest—I was getting a bit annoyed with him.

"The depression," I said.

He stared at me, thinking. Or maybe he wasn't staring but was just thinking with his eyes facing me.

"What bothers me," I said, "is that when she doesn't remember anything, she is never depressed. I can't say for certain that that's true, but all the times she's been unable to remember me or the year or where she is or what she has to do, she hasn't been depressed, or hasn't acted depressed. She's never in bed but is awake and talkative. Of course, I'm not with her all the time, but the times I am, this is what I see."

Again, he stared at me or in my direction, thinking. He stayed like that for so long that when his lips moved, I expected more than the "OK" he let out.

"OK," he said.

"OK what?" I asked.

"Her appointment is when her ten days of medication are up, so when she comes in, I'll talk to her about this. There are some options that might help both her depression and her memory, such as medication or even electroconvulsive therapy."

I said that last thing back to him.

"ECTs," he said.

"You mean the things that fried Jack Nicholson's brain in that movie with the big Indian guy?"

Fredrick used to call him FBI for Fucking Big Indian because that's what he was. Fredrick also hated that movie, maybe because of the Indian.

"The treatment is nothing like that," he said. "It's been improved over the years and is still very effective in the short term."

"Louise isn't too old?" I said.

"No, but that's something I have to consider. We can talk more next time you're both here. And to see if this is something Louise would like to pursue as an option."

He stood up, and I stood up even though I felt I had more to say, and I think he saw that because he looked to be waiting for me to say something more, something on my mind, but all I said was, "Ten days, got it," and he let me pass first through the door and then he followed, and when we had not yet gone our separate ways but were already some feet apart, he asked me if I was feeling bitter. "I haven't been bitter in years," I told him, and I would not realize until after I'd left and was driving Louise home that he'd asked if I was feeling better.

Louise was waiting for me in the parking lot, looking up at the sky, which was no longer gray but a cloudless bright blue, and the sun at its zenith rayed down a sharp warmth, which would fade in the coming months as the sun distanced itself from us, when everything would whiten and gray and the life of the earth in these parts, except the pines, would wither and die, waiting to be brought back for the millionth or plus time.

12

Bobby seemed to care a lot for Louise. He stopped calling me to check on her and called her directly, and he was always curt with me when I asked how long they spoke for, as if he were embarrassed by the time spent on the phone with her. And this connection made me wonder why he didn't care that much about his own parents, who he—reluctantly—went to visit one weekend for a few days during the fall when none of his three brothers or one sister could make it. Around the time of his visit, his father's lungs were filled with fluid, and he was hospitalized. I was a bit relieved when Bobby left—I'd told him about the neighbor and what he'd done, and it got him riled in a way I had never seen.

The night before he left, we were sitting at the bar. He must have known that his father was ill, but all he talked about that night was the Celtics and how he thought they'd do this season, and when he had nothing more to say about them, when he'd run out of talk, he switched back to North Carolina and how he wished that woman's husband wasn't a cop.

"What are the fucking odds?" he said. When he had no more to say about it, but I could tell it was still on his mind,

I started talking to him about Louise's neighbor—"He's a wacko," Bobby said—and I told him about the garbage or junk at the end of his driveway—"I hear there's good money in dumpster diving"—and I said he liked to shovel and shovel and shovel the snow and even the mud when there was no snow—"Like I said, a wacko"—and he only got serious when I told him about the night he'd broken into Louise's house.

"What do you mean?" he said.

It was a mistake to tell Bobby.

"He broke in?" he said. "You were there?"

I told him the story, how I thought it was the neighbor but how I had a sliver of doubt because I'd been half-asleep.

"Don't doubt this," he said. "It was him. Who else would it have been?"

Maybe somebody else, I wanted to say, but he was right.

Finally, he said: "I'm going to see him. I'm going to knock on his door."

I told him not to, that it was over, even though I had plans to say something to the neighbor when I saw him. But Bobby wouldn't drop it. He was appalled I planned to do nothing.

"He broke into your mother's house," he said. "And you want to drop it? Let it go?"

He finished his beer and the bartender brought him another, and Bobby asked him for a quarter, and the guy didn't understand what for. I didn't either. And so he said he couldn't give him a quarter. "Check the register for one, I'll give it right back," and the guy said he couldn't open the register unless there was a transaction, so Bobby said never fucking mind and he asked me for a quarter. He pulled out a twenty-dollar scratch-off ticket.

"I don't like him," Bobby said, quarter scraping away the ticket dust.

I think he meant the bartender, but he could have meant Louise's neighbor.

"I'm going to talk to him," he said. "That's fucked up."

He scrutinized the ticket, which was all scratched off.

"Don't do anything stupid," I told him, and that was the end of it for the night. The next day he was gone, and I hoped that when he got back, he would have forgotten about it.

With Bobby gone to his parents, my mother sometimes here and sometimes not, and my helplessness when it came to my daughter, I thought of Gizos. He'd come to visit me once, and he'd planned to bring his son, who ended up not coming.

I can't say for certain which year he visited—I think it was in 1998. I guess I could check the library's newspaper archive, because it was also the year Lenno got out of jail. All I know was it was the first time I'd seen Gizos since he'd left the reservation. It was spring or early summer, the season when, some years, I worked the least. The ground was too soft and wet, so when I did work it was in the garage fixing equipment, and I could take time off with no loss of progress in the woods. When he did show up, I was able to see a lot of him.

Because it had been twenty years since that visit, how he was back then was still how I knew him. He had married a Lakota man—Dave, who hated to be called David—who he'd met in California at an Indian center in the city. Gizos was out there working for a company as a technical writer. I'd always thought that his reason for moving so far away had to do with his father. Maybe it did have a small part, but the truth was that he still maintained a relationship with Lenno.

What his father thought of his son's marriage to a man and their adoption of a boy is beyond me. I like to think he fixed himself, or pretended to be fixed, but I doubt it. Part of me believes he continued to hurt Gizos in certain ways. Not violently, since Gizos was no longer a boy, but mentally. Verbally. I guess that's still violence.

A few years before Fredrick died in '91, Lenno had been sentenced to prison for involuntary manslaughter. He was driving 110 miles per hour drunk on I-95 northbound when he rammed into the back of a car and the driver, a white guy, spun down into the median and smashed headfirst into the trees and was dead on impact. He had a wife and son. It was all over the papers and in everybody's mouths and ears on the reservation, but only until the surviving wife's cousins—these two men from up north—came down and tried to light Lenno's house on fire. Except it wasn't his house but Bethany Francis's place right next to the elder apartments, and then everybody talked only about that. And so they forgot about Lenno, or they stopped talking about him, and a new chief was elected. Fredrick said Lenno would have lost that year even if he hadn't killed somebody. Lenno ended up serving only nine or ten of the fifteen years he was given, and that's why Gizos had come up: his father had been released.

Gizos and his husband were not poor. Where they lived, they weren't rich, but up this way they had money. Lenno knew that about his son, and maybe that's why he held him as close as his sick spirit would let him. While he was in prison, he ended up selling his house to the tribe so he could pay the restitution the court had ordered. When he was released, he had nowhere to go.

For some weeks before he could visit, Gizos put his father up in a motel. Gizos told me this when we spoke on the phone, and he told me again when he finally came up. Because I'd told him, Gizos knew that my mother had sold Fredrick's house, and he told his father, who wanted to buy it. But the person who had bought the house from my mother planned to turn it into a museum, thinking that Thoreau's stay merited such a thing, which is what he told Lenno, who told Gizos, who then told me, and of course that guy's plan never worked out and the tribe bought it. So Lenno, Gizos said, was looking off reservation. I really don't think Lenno had money. I mean, where would he have gotten money from? His son was paying his motel bills. Even though he said his father was the one paying, this is what I think: Gizos was the one who was buying the property and was going to give it to his father.

Lenno ended up finding a place about an hour south, and that's where he moved to after he—or Gizos—closed on the house. It had been so many years since then, and I still wondered sometimes what had happened to Lenno, if he was still living in that place or if he was dead.

The last time Gizos and I had spoken before he made the trip up here, he said he was bringing his son, and I was relieved he didn't bring him. I don't want to say I was jealous. But something in me felt off every time I thought of Gizos's boy. Maybe it was jealousy—his child knew him, where mine did not know me. But he didn't bring the boy. If he had, I wonder how Lenno would have thought of him, how he would have treated him. I like to think he would have loved him.

Gizos stayed for a little over a week, and for the first few days he slept at the motel with his father. And then one day when he stopped by I noticed he had all his luggage in the back of his rental car, this ugly orange hatchback Subaru with mud caked all up over the chassis and doors. He was the type of driver that always backed into a place, so I saw all his stuff through the window when he parked.

The front of my house was a giant mud puddle, and I had set down square pieces of chipboard and set foldout chairs on top of those, and that was where I was sitting when he arrived. He came over from his car, and I can still remember that sharp sigh—a real one—that he let out as he sat. And then he asked if he could stay with me for the rest of the time he was here.

When I said yes, he offered to pay me.

I told him no.

We went hiking one day up to Katahdin and we went to the coast and he bought some craft beer from Bar Harbor Brewing, which was a type he liked, but he didn't drink when he was with me, maybe because I was in AA. We went to the movies one day and watched *The Truman Show*, and when we left, we kept saying to each other, "You'd tell me, right, if I were in a TV show but didn't know it?" and every so often one of us would pretend to talk into some invisible radio and mumble that the other was on to us.

Gizos told me he wanted to find his mother, but that he didn't know where she would be. We were sitting in the chairs on the wet chipboard covering the soggy and muddy ground.

"Did you ask your father if he knows?" I said.

"He won't tell me," Gizos said.

Maybe this was why he'd had all his luggage with him that day. Maybe they'd gotten into a fight.

"Your birth certificate?" I said. "Her name must be on that."

"It is," he said. "Willow Wintle." He puffed air from his mouth. "Isn't that a nice name? Willow Wintle. Willow Wintle."

He kept saying the name but grew quiet.

"Have you thought to look for your father?" he asked. "I mean your biological father?"

"No," I said. And that was the truth. I still don't know where he is or if he's alive.

"Why not?" he asked.

"I always felt I had a father," I said.

I was kind of like Elizabeth. And based on what I knew, how I felt about my own father, I expected nothing to come from this story I wanted to give her. But I didn't know if anybody else had lived within such a strange set of circumstances as I had, as she had, as we had.

"Always?" he said.

"Sure," I said. "I grew up with Fredrick, and since my earliest memories he's been there."

"But you must think about your birth father? Or have wondered about him?"

"I have, yes," I said. "But I've never wanted to find him."

I could see why Gizos thought I might be like him: we were both without a blood parent. But there was a difference between us: I had somebody to fill that space, while he did not.

"I sometimes worry that our son—Dave's and mine—will wonder about his birth parents too much, and that wonder will pull him toward them, to find them, kind of like how I want to find my mother. Did I tell you I know his birth parents? I don't *know them* know them, but I know enough. They're not together. I know more about his mother than I do about his father. They were both bad off. Very bad off. Well, I think the mother more so than the father. The boy was addicted to drugs when he was born. His mother is Coeur d'Alene and his father's Tukudeka or Shoshone—I forget which, but I think it's Tukudeka—but he's not on the census.

"Dave and I had a long talk before we adopted the boy. I get that it's best to put Native children with Native families, I do, but we worried about his culture, what he, this Coeur d'Alene and Tukudeka boy, was losing by growing up with a Lakota and Penobscot. What would his culture be? Would he take Dave's? Mine? Some mix of both?" Gizos laughed. "This is such an Indian thing to worry about."

It was, and still is. There are too many unnecessary things to think about when it comes to existing as a skeejin.

"But the boy had nowhere to go," Gizos said. "I mean nowhere. His mother didn't want him, his father didn't want him. The boy's grandmother on his mother's side was dead, and the grandfather was too sickly. I worry he'll wonder about them and only find out that his place with them was never real or could not work out, that his culture may have been, since the beginning, inaccessible to him. But here's the thing: he's Coeur d'Alene and Tukudeka. He can't be Lakota or Penobscot. He can only be what he is, and he'll always be there. I just hope he grows up to know that, to understand it. That's his blood.

"He is cute though," Gizos added. "Damn cute. Funny what wins in the end."

For one of the only times in my life, I felt like an outsider around Gizos. This was something I had no claim to talk about—as in I had no Native blood—yet I knew and still know what it was like to both not belong and belong, what it was like to feel invisible inside the great, great dream of being. We're all alike, even when we're not.

When Gizos went back to California, I stopped going to AA for about two weeks, and of all the people to get on my back about it and to worry, it was Bobby. I started to have these strange existential thoughts, like I wasn't really real. It's hard to explain exactly, because I knew I was real, but I didn't feel it. It was like my spirit did not match my body, as if my body were where it should be but my invisible innards were not. I could not for the life of me reconcile my existence.

And I did fear these strange feelings would take Elizabeth should she learn of her blood, learn that she had a secret part in her and that, in this world, that part might erase another. But she needed to know that her blood was her blood. Nothing could take that away, and nothing could even come close to capturing it, especially not percentages on pieces of paper. Because we're more than that. Or at least she was—she'd got it in her, that connection to a past time and people, no matter what anybody said.

It's not always funny what wins in the end.

13

While he was visiting his parents, Bobby called twice from a number I didn't recognize, and since I didn't recognize it, I didn't answer. But when the phone stopped ringing and then not fifteen seconds later again started its brrring, I picked up. He sounded sober, which I found interesting because it was past ten in the evening and he was usually drunk by then.

He didn't have much to say, really, and he didn't know when he'd be back. He didn't even fill me in—he spoke as if I were up to speed with where he'd gone and why he'd gone there, and I thought about pretending I had no idea what he was talking about. But he sounded down, so I thought better of it.

The only specific thing I can really remember that he said was, "He's going soon, so I'll be here till he's left," and whether or not his siblings would be joining him he did not say.

Sometimes Louise got overwhelmed by the elephant, her baby, and she got snippy and sharp with me. The first time this happened was a few days after I gave it to her. She was sitting in her recliner with the elephant in her arms. I was sitting on the bed, and I thought we both were watching TV, but she was not. She was trying to put the elephant to sleep, or so I suppose, because she said, "He won't get any rest, and you're not helping."

At first it took most everything in me not to laugh, and if her face had not been so serious, I would have.

"You never help me," she said. "Never."

I asked her what she wanted help with, and she said I should know.

"It's not rocket science," she said. "It's a baby. And I need help."

"Do you want me to take him?" I said.

"No," she said, and she put her head back and shut her eyes.

I laughed about this that night, and even Bobby thought it was funny when I told him on the phone. He said she never acted that way when he was around, and he said that maybe I was shit with kids and she was just pointing that out. The next time I saw the elephant in her arms, I laughed to myself about the seriousness with which she took caring for that stuffed animal and again her jab at me for not helping.

She wasn't always like this, wasn't always scrutinizing me. It was rare, that behavior, and when it happened, it never lasted very long. Around the fifth or sixth time it did happen, though, it became unfunny. Bobby was still gone, and so I had been with Louise for quite some time. Louise was in her recliner, and she had set the elephant in the bed, right behind me, had it tucked between two pillows. The TV was on—that same show that always seemed to be playing, the one about the mortician. I don't know how long I'd been there, but I was getting uncomfortable on the bed, so without thinking I took one of the pillows holding the elephant in place and I used it to prop myself up on my elbow.

Louise said, "You're unbelievable."

I put the pillow right back, but it was too late.

"Unbelievable," she said again, and she rose and went to the bed and took the elephant.

How do you correct such a mistake as this?

"You're lucky you didn't wake him," she said.

I could only play along. "Sorry," I said, holding back that laugh.

She was shaking her head, looking down at the elephant or at something past it, some idea in her lap, and then said what sounded like, "No wonder I'll leave you."

At first it made no sense, just gibberish. But that night at home I couldn't stop thinking about it, couldn't stop trying to make sense of it. It came to me the next day as I was out in the woods on a small job, working the skidder. Did she mean my father? My real father, the one she had left? Had she seen him sitting on the bed, taking his son's pillow? Had she thought that child, that elephant, was me as an infant? That seemed to fit, seemed to make sense, and if that was the truth of this situation, it was such a strange feeling to be both so loved and so hated at the same time.

I didn't know what type of hatred my mother felt for my blood father. While nobody can fix what's been done—nobody can erase the memory—I thought I could at least try to be better, in her eyes, than my father, even if it was just for a stuffed elephant, even if it was for a daughter who didn't know her blood father.

Bobby came back and wanted to meet me at the bar, and I left him hanging. I intended to go, to meet him, but when I stepped outside, I saw Roger coming back home, and with him, in the bed of his truck, was a bed, a mattress. Maybe full-size. It was wrapped in plastic, because I'm sure Roger smelled what I smelled: rain.

He carried the mattress by himself across the yard and up the stairs to the house, where Mary held the screen door open for him, and when she tried to help him carry it, he set the mattress down on the steps so it was slanted, and she tried to pull it but it was too heavy. He carried it all the way in by himself, and he went back to the truck and grabbed the bed frame, long metal boards that had been disassembled and taped together into a bunch. As he carried them up the steps, Mary was not at the door, and he struggled to get inside but he managed.

He then left in his truck, and he was back again before too long. This time he unloaded boxes. Many boxes, twenty or more. And baskets. One was a nice utility basket, filled with blankets, and another, worn, had pots and pans sticking out. Mary helped with this load, carrying a box indoors and going to get another. Roger carried two boxes at a time. None fell from his grip, even though he moved with haste, the way an animal might when it has fallen behind in building a nest, a home.

Again, the truck emptied. Again, gone and back in little time. This time, he had brought back a large object, and only when he stood up in the bed of the truck and removed the blanket that covered it did I see that it was a dresser with what I think were many stickers stuck to one side (it can be hard to see from so far away). Roger needed help carrying the dresser. I don't know who helped him load it in the back to begin with. Maybe he'd done it himself, had exerted the last of his energy. He needed Mary's hands, her strength. But before they carried it indoors, she brought him water in a cup, which he drank in one tilt.

My phone rang and I ignored it. Roger and Mary unloaded the dresser, and Roger walked backward up the steps and through the door propped open with a cinder block. When it was inside, Mary came back out and with her foot she pushed the cinder block off the steps and shut the door. Neither of them came back out for close to thirty minutes, and in the meantime I stayed outside, sitting, and I went indoors only once to get a jacket.

During that silence, I thought I heard yelling from inside their house. But the shouts could have been from somewhere else, carried downriver by the wind. When they came out, Mary stayed on the steps and Roger got in his truck. If they said anything to each other, they did so quietly. That was my curse, my distance.

Gone and back, and it was the last trip. In the back of the truck were two nightstands, each a different type of wood. One a two-drawer mahogany, the other taller and built of light wood the color of sand. Besides those two items was an assortment of things like a tall lamp and a mirror and a wardrobe box filled with what, I don't know.

And then there was Elizabeth, up front. I noticed she was there only when she got out of the truck and Mary shut the door for her and walked behind her up the steps.

And then she was gone, and I thought I wouldn't see her again that night. Roger carried each item in. Mary did not help. When he finished unloading the nightstands, he walked to his truck but turned around and spoke with somebody—Mary or Elizabeth—about something. Whatever it was, he said he'd get it.

After he'd gone, Elizabeth came outside. She had on a sweatshirt with her hood up as she sat on the steps, cigarette between her fingers. When did she start smoking? Could she hear me from there? I wondered if I was that far away.

When she was done, she was gone again, and in her long absence, with no distractions, I felt it, the wondering, the speculation, the why, until I settled on my worst fears. How can I possibly describe what I felt? How is the spirit's rapid descent accurately captured? What I felt was not unlike the rumble of the ground to an ant crossing a freeway.

Roger came back, and with him a man I could not recognize. The sun was going down and night was coming.

Out back of the house they made a fire, a small one that crackled and sprayed flamed ash. They fed it logs, kept it burning, until all was dark except that side of the river. Their bodies were just bodies, their features disfigured by shadow and occasionally by the fire smoke as it swirled this way and that, a screen of gases and water vapor. The smell was calming.

For what I had thought—the why of it all—I felt this was ceremonial. Fredrick had done something similar for Louise countless times, and I kept thinking this even when Elizabeth and Mary joined Roger and the man out back around the fire.

My side of the river was pure dark. No lights were on in my house, and I sat where I had all afternoon, in the same chair. But I was there, felt present at that fire, the one I so stupidly thought was ceremonial. It turned out it wasn't. It was just a fire, the life around it, and they all cooked with the flame. Two of them held long sticks and handed around a bag, their shadowed heads rising as Elizabeth blew out the flaming tip of the stick before eating.

This is ceremony too, I suppose.

The fire did not go out for hours. Elizabeth left first, then Mary, and then Roger and that man but not until late in the night. It was two in the morning when he and Roger drove off together, and when they came back, they were in separate vehicles. One was Elizabeth's car. They left once more, but only Roger returned. Only after all this did the fire die. But still: it glowed red until the sun rose—the fire burned all night in the cold of fall.

So that is what I saw: Elizabeth coming home. And I didn't think it was a good thing.

14

Once Elizabeth arrived back home, I rarely went anywhere. I went to check on Louise once—wanting to make sure she was locking her door—but that was it. I stayed outside, every day, watching, acting like I had things to do in case anyone spotted me from across the river. And after a while, the strangest thing began to happen. Late at night, somebody kept ringing me. If I didn't pick up, whoever it was didn't leave a message. If I answered, they hung up. It went on for eight days total.

At first, I thought it was Bobby, calling drunk about something and then hanging up when I answered. He could get weird, fifteen, twenty beers in. But I asked him, and when he said it wasn't him, he seemed sincere about it.

So somebody else was calling me, and I started to think it was Mary. The calls came after midnight, around one in the morning. For a few nights I took my house phone outdoors with me and waited in the cold, cold fall for the call. As I waited, I watched across the river for any life, light, any movement from within Elizabeth's parents' house. But I saw none. And of course the call came. I sat on the steps, holding the ringing phone. Across the river the house was quiet, stilled, no light or movement from within. When I answered, the caller hung up. If it was Mary, I thought, she was calling quietly, discreetly, from somewhere in the dark of that house.

I thought it was her, trying to build up the courage to tell me what was wrong with Elizabeth, especially since Elizabeth wasn't going to work; she was home all day except sometimes when she left with Mary.

I went out and bought a new phone at Best Buy that could display the digits of incoming calls. I was excited to see what number would come up, and when the call came— same time, one in the morning—I was ready, pen in hand, to write down the number that lit up on the small rectangular screen on the phone. But no number showed.

I had no goddam clue I had to add that caller ID to my phone from the phone company. So that's what I did the next day. Right when they opened at eight. It turned out the calls weren't coming from Mary. The call that came in that night was from a motel in Sterling, Colorado. When I called the number back, nobody answered. I thought to try it again, but I held off until late morning, and when I did call back, somebody answered, a woman, and she said she hadn't used the phone, that she had just checked into the room. I asked her where she was, and she said none of my business, and so I said, No, no, what state are you in, where is this call coming from, and she said Super 8 in Sterling, Colorado.

The next night the call came again, this time from a number I couldn't trace, so I had to call the operator and pay an extra fee for the information. The operator had a nice voice, like he was meant to do what he was doing, and he said the call came from South Yankton, Nebraska, and he said the phone wasn't registered with any business, or it was a pay phone.

The next night, the call came once more. This time from Iowa City. They were getting closer and closer and closer to me. What next? I thought. Illinois? Indiana? Massachusetts? Portland? Overtown? Maybe all of this was coincidental, I thought, but there was something too neat about it. I won't lie: I was a bit worried. It was like somebody was stalking me, coming for me.

My obsessive worrying about why Elizabeth was home and the mysterious callers made me forget about Bobby for a while, and I wish it hadn't, because maybe I could have prevented him from beating up Louise's neighbor and getting arrested. But instead, I spent my days outside, tending to a yard that needed no tending, tinkering with my truck that needed no tinkering, tidying the riverbank where garbage had floated downriver and gotten stuck, and the whole time I made it look like I was doing these things, but I was really watching for my daughter across the river. And at night it was much of the same, except I'd sit out on the porch with that phone in my hand and my sights set on something I thought was coming. It got to the point where I wasn't eating anything, and it reminded me of the days I used to drink, which sort of snapped me out of whatever I was in and got me to leave for a while.

Bobby didn't tell me right away about what he'd done. We were at Louise's, watching her after her first ECT treatment, and he was telling me about his father's passing. We were in the kitchen, and he didn't seem sad. In fact, I was the one who brought up the funeral.

"Was it a nice service?" I asked him.

"I don't know," he said. "It was a service. My sister organized it. She organized it before he even died. It was like she saw his death, had everything planned, right down to the meals at the funeral parlor."

"Were your brothers there too?" I asked.

"No," he said, and that was as far as he let me in on the matter.

Bobby got a glass of water, drank some of it, and started to tell the story.

It had happened after Bobby left the bar that night— the night I was supposed to meet him, the night Elizabeth moved back home.

"I got him to admit it," Bobby said, and he finished the water.

I didn't know what he was talking about at first, so I asked, "Who?"

"What do you mean, who? The neighbor. You should have seen the look on his face."

I was stunned. Bobby leaned on the sideboard and I stood in the center of the kitchen, listening to him.

"I came up here after the bar the night you didn't show up," he said, "and parked along the road and waited, just shut my truck off and was in the dark. I really didn't think I'd see anybody. Christ, it was going on midnight when he came out. That little fucker. I didn't know where he was heading, but he shut the screen door all soft and walked down the steps and started digging around in that pile of shit he's got. That sheet metal was loud too. I heard it through my closed windows. I'm surprised it didn't wake up the whole street.

"Right, so he's digging and digging and tossing shit, making all this noise"—Bobby was waving his arms—"and so I get out of my truck and let the door shut quiet and start walking toward him. 'You,' I say to him. I'm right at the beginning of his mud driveway. He turns around and goes—this is what he says—'Me?' Me! That's what he says. 'Yeah, you,' I say back. Who the fuck else would I be talking to?"

"You said that to him?" I asked.

"No, I'm telling you that. Listen. 'What do you want?' he says, and I say, 'What do you got there?' And he says, 'I already sold what I want to sell. The rest is mine.' The rest is his? I couldn't see that well, but I imagine everything there—all of it—was crap. I step closer to him and just start talking like meeting, at this hour, is normal. I ask him where he goes to find stuff, and he has loads to say about that: on Tuesdays he's up at Burlington Coat Factory, that's the day they dump merchandise, and then on Wednesdays he's over at Old Navy—the one by the on-ramp to 95 south, not the one near the mall—out in the back, but he goes there at night because workers can see the dumpster during the day and they phone the police, and then Thursdays and Fridays he goes around all the other stores because he doesn't know the day they dump out stuff. Can you imagine doing that? Something's got to be wrong with you."

"Did he ask what you were doing?" I said.

"Yeah, he asked, after he ran out of shit to say about the art of dumpster diving."

Bobby leaned forward and looked out the kitchen window at the neighbor's house. He leaned back again on the sideboard.

"And I tell him I'm there to see him," Bobby said, "which he again says he isn't selling anything else. I tell him he misunderstands me. I'm there to see him about something that happened. 'What happened?' he asks, and I say, 'You know what happened,' and I point up at Louise's window. He knows right then what I'm talking about, and he bolts for his house. But I grab him by the shirt and yank him back. 'What were you doing up there?' I ask him, still pointing, and he says, 'I don't know what you're talking about, I wasn't anywhere.' Bullshit, I say to him. There's something about seeing a frightened face at night that's scary, the way his porch light reached and lit his face so the bags under his eyes looked sunken and dark."

Bobby laughed. "Poor kid," he said.

"So what happened?" I said. "You beat him up?"

"I didn't beat him up," he said. "I just slapped him around is all. I didn't even punch him. I open-handed him a few times, and then he started screaming real loud and kicking me and digging his fingernails into my face, so I held him in a way he couldn't dig at me, had to put him on the ground and put my knees over his arms. I was about to punch him until he says, 'I'm sorry!' Just like that: 'I'm sorry!'"

"You know there's something obviously wrong with him, right?" I said. "He's not all there."

He waved off what I had said. "He is now," Bobby said. "I'm sorry—who does that, breaks into an old lady's house?"

I asked if he'd found out why the neighbor had done it.

"He didn't say," Bobby said. "I asked him why, but by that point in time he was spitting at me and trying to squirm away. I started to get up—I felt I'd scared him enough—and as I did, I heard an engine, tires on the road, coming down our way. That skinny-headed fuck flagged them down before I could get in my truck. And as luck would have it, it was the police—'We watch this place closely,' one of them said—and when they had me in cuffs, two more showed up and even an ambulance to check out the neighbor, whose name is either Brett or Rhett, and Brett or Rhett started to act real hurt and was taken up to Saint Joe's while I was taken to the station. All they had there was one little tiny cell, and they didn't even put me in it. They let me sit in a chair in one of the back offices. Christ, I could have escaped if I wanted to."

Bobby continued to tell me how they'd treated him well. The two officers who had shown up and arrested Bobby were the two I'd spoken with when the neighbor had broken in, so they knew the case. They also knew about the neighbor, Brett or Rhett—he had all sorts of strange charges in his past; he'd once stormed a store butt-naked, or so Bobby said—and so they didn't see Bobby as a vicious criminal but more of an idiot who could not behave under intense circumstances. So maybe that was why they didn't put him in a cell or cuff him when they brought him to the station. Or maybe it was because he was white.

Bobby had no remorse for attacking the neighbor, but he was upset about being caught. He was facing criminal charges and would have to go to court, and until his hearing in December he was unable to leave the state, which got him angry, and while he was cursing, getting another glass of water, I asked who had bailed him out.

"Someone you don't know," he said, but I knew Bobby had no one besides me, and so Louise was the only person I could think of.

15

I was at Louise's, sitting on the bed, when she started talking to me about Bobby's father. I wasn't supposed to leave her alone after a treatment (you have to sign a paper saying you won't), but I didn't want to be at her place, because I couldn't stop worrying about Elizabeth. All Elizabeth did was go in and out of her house, taking smoke breaks, always wearing her hoodie and a pair of basketball shorts. She'd never been like that before—it was a strange sight. She was dressing differently. I was so used to seeing her leave in a blue dress or jeans with a red blouse that seeing her in the same outfit every day had me worried. It reminded me of my mother, the days she would stay in the same clothes. I wanted to be home, wanted to be able to watch and see if Elizabeth or Mary or Roger would come home and give something away by saying something loud enough to hear, but Louise's ECT treatments took up a lot of time. At first it was one every so often, a gradual upward climb, and then she was up to three a week: Monday, Wednesday, Friday.

Bobby had brought her to one once because I'd had to work, and I thought he'd take her again if need be, but he had found the experience to be a bit worrisome, especially the part when the nurses or whatever they were brought her out and she walked slowly, sloppily, to the wheelchair, and her eyes were glazed and jellied as she handled the stuffed elephant.

There was something peaceful in her face when her treatments were over. When she sat in that wheelchair after a treatment, her face was the most restful I had seen it, like the electricity had put up a wall blocking the terribleness that can be human feeling. I wonder what, exactly, she felt.

While I was visiting with her that day, she was having difficulty remembering, was sitting in her recliner with the stuffed elephant, and then she said, "That poor boy, that poor boy."

When I asked who, she couldn't give a name.

"You know," she said, but I didn't know. And I don't think she did either. I don't think she even knew who I was that day.

"Remember?" she said. "That boy. The one whose father just died."

"Bobby?" I said.

"No, no, that's not it."

Who else would she be talking about? It's only now I have this strange thought that she could have been speaking for all boys everywhere.

"I saw him," she said. She held the elephant in the dip of her arm and scratched its head. "He was very upset about it."

"About what?"

"His father," she said. "Poor, poor thing. I couldn't console him. Not one bit."

"When was this?"

"I don't know. Does it matter? The boy was upset. Was crying so hard he could barely breathe. I said to him, 'You must have loved him so much. He was lucky to have you as a son.' And at that he cried even harder. I cooked him a meal. I asked him what he wanted, and he tried to say he didn't need anything, but I said, 'No, no, you need to eat.' I made him eggs and a can of corned beef hash I've had since, jesum, I don't even remember when, and I made him some grilled bread. Did I mention my toaster's broken? I had to make it in a frying pan with some butter. He stopped crying by the time he went back home."

I never really knew what the two of them did or talked about when they were alone. Honestly, I never thought much about it until it was clear Louise knew things I didn't, and I imagine Bobby too knew things I didn't. I used to think they just watched TV like us, her and me. I never thought differently of Bobby after that. Maybe I did, but in a good way. He became more human, more knowable.

I asked Louise if, as he ate, he stopped talking about the death of his father.

"Oh, no, Lord no. That's all he talked about that day." She paused. "Do I smoke?"

"Do you smoke?" I said.

"I want a cigarette."

Louise had never smoked.

"Maybe that boy left one of his."

She got up from the chair and carried the elephant in her arms. She puttered around the bedroom, looking on top of her dresser and in drawers. When she found none, she sat back down.

"Does he give you cigarettes?" I said.

"Who?"

"Bobby—I mean that boy."

"Just forget I said anything."

If the elephant were a child, its leg would be broken; Louise was sitting on it in a way that it had bent backward.

That doctor was on the TV, and the narrator was talking about the standard Y incision.

"I do hope he's feeling better," Louise said.

And from what she said then, Bobby's father—or the boy's father—worked all day, every day, his entire life to support his family. He worked at a lumberyard that no longer existed, doing work similar to mine, and he was up every morning at three and didn't get home until six in the evening. He worked most Saturdays, and on Sundays he spent most of his time tending to everything else, from fixing the house to repairing their car, an old four-door Buick that I guess he still had, or did until he died. When nothing else needed to be done—or what could be done was put aside—Bobby's father, Andrew was his name, worked on projects in most seasons besides winter. He built his children a tree house, and he built his wife a garden shed—"about the size of a small cabin," Louise said. And one summer, when he had no projects, after he'd helped his wife landscape the yard, he borrowed an excavator and dug a hole out back of the house and made a pond where frogs croaked in the tall, tall grasses, and where two ducks returned each summer and had their babies; and when time was kind and opened up to him an empty space in an afternoon in which his biggest wants and dreams could flourish, he tinkered with the truck he'd hoped to drive one day but knew he never would: a red tarnished Chevrolet from the late '40s.

What a life, I think now, one I would have given anything to have.

"The boy was upset most about that," Louise said. "That his father never got to finish the truck. I think he said he had to sell it. Not the boy, his father."

"Why?"

"He didn't say."

"And you didn't ask?"

"Why would I pry?" Louise said. "He was upset enough as it was."

I don't know why I said this next bit to her, but I did: "Did it occur to you that maybe he wanted you to ask about it?"

"What do you know?" she spat. "You're just a boy."

*

Before I went home that night I left a single cigarette on her dresser, and as I was leaving through the front door, I looked back down the hall and watched her shadow rise to the dresser and then fall back down and disappear.

Mary used to sleepwalk. Before I bought the phone with the caller ID, I thought maybe she was calling me in her sleep.

She didn't sleepwalk all the time, just some of the time. The way she slept, it was like she was always fighting something: she twitched and closed her eyes tightly. She never complained about getting poor sleep, but to me it looked very unrestful. Occasionally, I woke to find her sitting up in bed, talking. Nothing coherent. It was always mumbles or one or two clear words here and there. Once, I woke to her pulling my hair, and she leaned in close to my face and said, "Stay out of my way."

In the late spring—almost summer—of 1990, I found Mary in the kitchen in the middle of the night, messing with the wall clock. (This was when she began to stay with me the most, when she had three dresser drawers full of clothes and makeup in my bathroom.) I really didn't like that clock; the numbers were roman numerals and always confused me. She had taken the clock off the small nail and was twisting the dial in the back. I don't know what she was trying to do, what her brain was telling her, but she kept twisting and twisting the knob in the back until both the big and little hands were where she wanted them—some specific time in the past.

In the morning, we were drinking coffee at the table, which was what we always did before work. She asked why the clock was off the wall and why it was set to the wrong time. I usually told her what she did in the night, but for some reason I lied and said that in the night I had woken and the ticking of the clock had disturbed me, so I'd gone and taken it off the wall and removed the battery, which I'd since put back in, but I had yet to reset the time.

She righted the time and put the clock on the wall.

This was the day she would tell me she was pregnant.

When I got back from work that day—the day after Mary took down the clock—I found her on the porch steps, in shorts and a long-sleeve black shirt. Her hair was pulled back, as it always was when she was home, or when she was comfortable. Usually I found her like this: on those steps, holding a lit cigarette. But on that day, she held nothing.

She told me to sit down and she scooted over and between us set my overlarge lunch pail streaked with motor oil, and she said without looking, "I'm pregnant, Charles," and to that I said, "No shit," not knowing—and still not knowing—if that was appropriate, but my intent was and still is that of joyful surprise.

"Yes shit," Mary said. "Yes shit."

I said we could build on my place, if she wanted, that I could put in a new bedroom, and I even recall saying I'd get things done, things I'd intended to do but had not, like fix the leaky sink and get at the mold that was spreading on the wall beside the refrigerator. But Mary looked at me with red and watery eyes, her cheeks the light pink color you'd get if you rubbed a pink flower across a piece of white paper. And she said, "The baby can't be yours."

I asked her what she meant. How could I not? But Mary wouldn't tell me. She stopped talking. I got angry. Why wouldn't I? I was yelling and yelling and yelling, but then I began to beg her. "Would you please talk?" I said. "Say something, anything."

She said it had to be this way.

"Why?" I said. "What do you mean?"

But then she rose and went inside and was back out no more than five minutes later, and in her hands she had black garbage bags filled with her clothes. I stayed on the steps as she brought the bags to her car. She came back to me, and I didn't know that that was the last time I'd see the Mary I had loved, the one I had grown up with and thought I'd spend the rest of my life with.

She did not say goodbye to me that day, and she did not give me a hug or anything of the sort. All she said was, "This is for the baby, you have to understand that."

I never knew what her plan was. I pieced it together from over here as I watched my world unfold in someone else's hands. And when I knew, I knew, too, the why. Then I understood immediately: she wanted Elizabeth to be "Native." There was a time I did think that Roger really was her father, that Mary had something going on with him, but then it did not make sense why over the years she would come back when she did, to see me, and even that one day when she brought her, my child.

No matter what she did, no matter how big the lie was, Mary loves Elizabeth. It was for her she did this. It was for those who would come after her. It was for a chance at something greater. It goes deeper than blood.

I was a mess after, and all these years later I still was. After she left that day, having told me she was pregnant, I had so much hope she would come back, that we would be a family, that I'd build that extension, our child's bedroom, that I'd fix the sink and the mold. And over the years I'd watch Elizabeth grow before my eyes and I'd teach her what I could—maybe not a lot, since I'm not the greatest of men, the greatest of fathers—and then down the road she would have a brother, or a sister, just some small body that the child would look at and see and admire as the soul's responsibility to love, and the two of them would grow up together and fight and laugh and fight and cry for the other until they were both old enough and began to go separate ways but were forever held together by the invisible rope of having experienced each other, and they both would watch us, their mother and father, get closer to the Silence until we entered it, and the rest would go on, and on, and on.

16

The building where Louise got her ECTs administered reminded me of a spider. I was telling Gizos that as we walked inside with Louise. I'd been surprised when he showed up, but also not surprised. He'd been on my mind. He was back for reasons that seem all too familiar to this story, for reasons concerning death: his father's liver was going.

As we walked, I told Gizos that if you had an aerial view of the layout of the building, if you could look down from way above as if you were a cloud, it would be exactly like a spider. The very core, the body of the building, was the main entrance: a security guard was the first person you saw when you entered. He was a tiny, tiny man with pale skin and a shirt and pants too big for him, was always making sure we carried nothing sharp that a patient could get hold of. Past him was a lady behind a desk, who knew us now, and let us—Louise and me—go by without name tags (they made Gizos wear one, though). Louise usually sat in a wheelchair, which I pushed, even though she could walk. Eight hallways branched out from the spider's body, and they each ended in a dead end. I had walked them all, waiting for Louise, so I knew that at least all but one ended with double doors that read "Exit," the signs lit with plastic red flames. The one hall I wasn't sure about was inaccessible unless you were visiting somebody who was under watch or somebody who was severely depressed. When you made it to that door you had to ring a buzzer, and the overhead camera would turn with a vrrrr and if you were permitted to pass, the door would bing and the locks would release. It was a place my mother would have gone, could have gone, and, I thought, still could go.

It's hard to believe that Elizabeth knows this place.

I should have known. I shouldn't have been surprised. The moment I wheeled Louise down that spider's leg and into the ECT waiting room, the moment I saw Mary sitting there on the little green bench, a magazine spread open and hiding half her face like a scarf, the moment Louise, not quite herself but partway so, said to her, to Mary, "Were you here last time? I remember you," and the moment Mary and I looked, horrified, into each other's eyes like we had been here before, not quite in this place but in this feeling of dread and warning and rupture, that was when I realized whose appointment was before Louise's, who I would see wheeled out through that door.

*

Elizabeth did not come out for some time. It was in this waiting that I began to understand how long these treatments could last. Louise, once, was back there for an hour and a half.

At some point after the first few moments when Louise and I were settling down in the chairs, waiting, I remembered that he, Gizos, was with us, off using the bathroom. It's so hard to remember and make two monumental moments coexist, but it's true: on the day I learned the truth about her, Gizos was with me. And now, looking back on that time in the waiting room, I wish he had not been there, hadn't been with us, hadn't shown up after all these years, unchanged except that his skin was growing a bit paler and coarse. I wish he hadn't had car trouble that morning, hadn't said he would come, that he could do nothing else without a car, that he'd love to see Louise. If he hadn't been there, Mary and I could have ignored each other, but when he walked through that door and he saw her, Mary, he could not help himself. He had to talk to her. He called her doos and got so close that Mary had no other option but to give in and set her magazine down and rise up from the cushioned bench she sat on.

"I heard about your dad," Mary said. Two people from the same place, the same people. They did not embrace, but Gizos had his hand on her shoulder. While Mary went to the bathroom, Gizos said he felt a sort of discordance between him and her, and I told him it was probably because I was there.

"Why's that?" he asked.

"I'll tell you later."

My wait for Elizabeth to come out, even though it must have been a little less than an hour, was the longest wait of my life, and that's saying something when I consider the wait for her to come home from the hospital, and then the wait to find Fredrick, to learn what had happened to him. The blood she did not know about that ran through her body was tainted, flawed. This was why it was so important she know all of this, who I was and who her grandmother was. This was why her body's secret history was important to know.

I did not want to look at her when she came out through the door, wheeled in the wheelchair.

"So young," Louise said. "That poor girl. So young."

I shushed her, which made her speak more. "I'm just saying that it's a shame. That's all I'm saying. That's all."

Gizos began to talk to her, to distract her.

Elizabeth was gone so fast from that room. And she spoke only once, and it was when she was down the hall and almost out of earshot. Mary whooshed her away.

Louise almost did not have her appointment that day. Something in her became irate and uncooperative. As the nurse came to get her, Louise asked Gizos if he was ready. She did not remember him, and she kept referring to him as Gus, like she was afraid to mispronounce his name, and she was convinced he needed to go back there with her.

"I don't trust that man," she said. I think she was referring to the doctor. "Gus needs to be with me. He needs to."

Maybe I would have handled this situation better if, you know, what happened hadn't happened. I'm not proud of it, but I screamed at Louise, crouched right down to her level and yelled inches from her face: "You're going back there and that's that! Got it?"

"Sir"—that's what the nurse said, Sir—"don't you yell at her like that."

"Fine," Louise said. "It'll be your fault then. Like everything else is."

Nothing happened except for regret.

I heard her. I heard Elizabeth as Mary wheeled her out the door.

"Who were they?" she asked.

"Nobody," Mary said.

Is there a word that means something is both true and false? I've looked, and I've yet to find one. I can come up with statements that are the example. "I am your father" is one that comes to mind.

*

Back at Louise's, I told Gizos. I told him the secret Mary and I shared, that that girl, that young, wonderful girl Mary had had with her, was our daughter. And for the first time ever, I said out loud what I wanted to do, what I planned to do: tell her the truth.

"What?" was all he said, but I didn't say anything because Louise cut us off and asked Gus to make her tea, which I made but told him to bring to her when it was ready. We waited in the kitchen while the microwave warmed water for tea; I was sitting on the windowsill, blowing smoke into that sharp fall cold. Gizos stood in the center of the room.

Gizos knew about our past, Mary and me, but I didn't think he wanted to believe what I said, that Elizabeth was my daughter and that I wanted her to know the truth. And there's no real point here in going back through it all. He just didn't want to believe it, and when he asked why she would do that—why Mary would lie—I told him why, and he said that was ridiculous, and I said that was the truth, and he said something else was going on here, and I told him there was nothing going on there, that if there were something else I would have figured it out over these past twenty-some-odd years, and he said I could have missed something, that she—Mary—wasn't like that, and I said to him, So it was me, then? No, that's not what I'm saying, he said, and I said, It sure sounds like it, and he said, Well maybe, and I said, Well maybe what? and he said, Nothing, nothing at all.

"Forget it," he said, but he didn't stop there. "You can't tell her."

"It's none of your business," I said.

"Sure," he said. "Just my thoughts."

"Just your thoughts."

Louise yelled from the bedroom, asking about her tea.

Before he brought Louise the tea, which he spilled a little of on the floor, he said it one more time. "Don't."

I wanted to say, "You don't want me to tell her the truth? You don't want me to give her the part of her she doesn't know belongs to her? You would have me deny her her full story?" but instead I pointed to the floor and said, "Clean that up after."

17

I kept taking Louise to her appointments. I did think about asking Bobby to help. But even if I had wanted to, I don't think he would have let me ask the question. After I told him what had happened, he was too busy saying "Jesus Christ" over and over again as I drove him to the bar. "Jesus. She was there?"

I was driving Bobby to the bar, and he had no other words. Nothing sympathetic, I mean, but that's him. What he jumped on and stayed focused on was that I said I was going to tell her the truth.

"Charles," he said. "You can't tell her the truth. Look at her. You've seen her."

She reminded me of my mother, except younger and not my mother but my own child.

Bobby continued, "It'll put her over the edge. She's gone all her life knowing one thing to be true. Why would you fuck that up?"

He had some other words to say, but what stuck with me the most after we talked was this: "What do you expect to get out of this?"

Elizabeth was Mary and Roger's daughter. Nothing could change that. And so I expected nothing to come from telling her except that she would know there was more to her story than she had thought. I didn't hope she'd love me. I didn't hope to be brought together. All I wanted was that she know the history that was hers, that this history wasn't lost or wasted because of the illusion we'd tried to live in so neatly, that there was a life she could have lived and been a part of, and that she know she was as much a part of me as she was not. That's the truth, the absolute truth.

When I dropped Bobby off at the bar, he thought I was going with him. "You coming?" he said, and I told him I had to be back home to see if Gizos had got on all right with the car troubles. Bobby really wanted to meet Gizos because he lived in California ("I've always thought about moving there, that might be a nice spot, Charles"). Before I left him at the bar and before he shut the truck door, I told him that I would stop back by later and take him home—but when I did, he would not be there; the waiter would tell me that he had left in a cab.

Gizos was not at my place when I went home. Why would he have waited for me? His father was dying. On my kitchen table he'd left a phone number that went direct to the hospital room where his father was laid up. I called him, and he answered in a very low and quiet voice.

He couldn't talk long, he said, because the doctor—his father's doctor—was going to be on shift soon and would stop by the room to talk. His father was sleeping, and Gizos said he was unsure if the doctor would wake him, Lenno, but that he hoped he would just let him sleep.

"He probably will," I said about the doctor, yet I had no clue. I just thought I had to say that.

Before we hung up, Gizos asked if I was going to visit. I didn't want to, but he'd come to me to visit, and he had come to see Louise, even though that coming had more to do with his car crapping out and less to do with the fact that he hadn't seen her in many years, but I do think—no, I know it—that he would have seen her or made time to see her regardless.

On the drive out to the hospital the next evening, I found a sense of calm. That Elizabeth was getting help made me feel better, slightly. And so while I drove, I thought about her briefly between my thinking of Gizos. He hadn't come clean about it, but I had a feeling all those mysterious calls were from him. He had mentioned driving cross-country to get here, that he could have flown but that he wanted to see the land between here and there. It made sense that the calls had come from everywhere—he'd been moving in a straight shot cross-country, but with stops each night between places.

It was only when I got to the hospital that I questioned if I was supposed to bring this dying man something. What do you get a man you hate? What do you get a man who has done so much wrong?

I settled on nothing.

Lenno's stomach was swollen so much that he looked pregnant. He was unconscious while I was there, and he had a tube shoved down his throat and white tape all around his mouth. In that room with Lenno, I felt compelled to act in some peaceful manner, and so I stood beside his bed with my hands on the bed rails, and in my head I said a prayer for him, said some words about a death with no suffering, but he looked like he had been suffering for some time. Maybe what I meant was that I hoped he stopped suffering. I could see the veins lining his skin, not just on his swollen belly but all along his arms and bruised hands, and I could not—and I still cannot—help but feel sorry for him, even though I disliked him the most out of anybody I had met in my life.

Seeing somebody so helpless and close to the Silence puts things in perspective.

Gizos and I did not stay in that room for very long. We went down to the cafeteria. I expected a flavorless meal, but the chicken thighs and mashed potatoes tasted fine. I ate while Gizos didn't. It might have appeared he was drinking coffee, but he'd been holding that same Styrofoam cup when I showed up, and then, at that table, he only stirred it with a red stirrer.

He told me he hadn't meant to tell me what I should do. About Elizabeth. He was talking about that, looking into his cold coffee and stirring it.

"It's all right," I said, which was what I'd said when we talked on the phone the night before. When he apologized.

"It's not any of my business," he said, "but does Roger know?"

"I don't know," I told him. I really didn't know what Roger knew, what he didn't know, but I thought it would be stupid of me to say he did not, that he was unaware, and so I wanted to say to Gizos, "I think he knows," but then I knew Gizos would ask me why I thought that, and I didn't want to get into it.

I asked Gizos how long his father had.

"I'm leaving in two weeks," he said, "and so I expect sometime between now and then."

I asked him if his father had been conscious at all while he'd been here visiting, and he said he had been a little bit at first, but that he'd grown quiet even when he seemed to be awake and aware.

I asked Gizos why he cared so much about his father. "Like you said, it's not any of my business, but I just want to know."

He shrugged and said, "I just do."

We're not so different, Gizos and I, when it comes to why we love who we love.

We left the table thinking we'd come back, but we wouldn't. We went out front of the hospital, across the street near the bus that would head into Overtown to pick folk up, and when I lit a cigarette this guy walked by with a big hiking backpack that wasn't too full and he asked for a smoke, and he took the one I gave him and lit it and kept on going down the road without a thanks or nothing.

"Where do you think he's going?" I asked Gizos. I felt like we were kids again.

"How should I know?"

"But where do you think?"

He paused so long I didn't think he'd answer. Then he said, "He's got a date. A good one by the looks of it."

"Then why the backpack?"

"West's a long way away. And it's going to go so well she'll ask him to stay."

"And will he?"

"Oh, no," he said. "He'll chicken out, and he'll go back home to his wife."

"He's married?"

"Of course. A few years back."

"And what happened?"

"They both got tired," Gizos said.

"From what?" I asked, and the feeling of being a child once more disappeared. We were grown right then.

He paused, thinking. And then he said, "They don't know."

The outside gray darkened the sky, and we walked down the cracked sidewalk around the corner to the parking lot and found my truck, whose window I had left open.

"I want to ask you something," he said.

"What is it?" I said.

"Do you remember when we stopped talking?"

I told him yes.

"Why?" he asked.

"I felt it was just easier that way," I said.

"Easier than what way?"

"Than going on as we were."

"And how was it that we were going on?" he asked.

"Whatever it is you want," I told him, "I don't have it."

"But you do," he said, and I had nothing to say.

It took some moments for me to realize what he wanted. Love never dies, and he wanted me to love him in a way I could not. But even if I could, I thought, what about his husband? What about their son? It would be impossible—I had already destroyed so much. Any more would have destroyed me. I loved him—I did—but not how he wanted. And he loved me so much he wasn't able to accept it.

Before he left me there by my truck, walking away through the lines of parked vehicles and then around the corner and out of sight, back to his father, he said, "I'm sorry," and he wrapped his arms around me.

"For what?" I asked, but he did not say.

The sides of our faces pressed together in equal weight, and we held on for one, two, three, four, five, six, and then he let go. Maybe we looked at each other before he turned away. Maybe we didn't.

*

I met up with Bobby at the bar. Under the hanging lights he asked me where that guy was. I think he was embarrassed to try to pronounce Gizos, because he messed it up once and then started referring to him as "that guy." I told him he left.

"Left?" Bobby said. "What do you mean, he left? I told you I wanted to talk to him about California."

For a long while we sat in silence.

"Why are you so quiet tonight?" he said.

"Just tired," I told him.

"You don't have to sit here with me," he said. "I can get home fine. I might stick around and see what these dance parties are like."

"It's Tuesday," the bartender said. I want to say he was standing there cleaning a glass, but the truth is that he was leaning back on the counter, almost right between us, like we were his friends. "They only have them on Thursday and Friday."

"Since when?" Bobby asked.

"It's always been that way," I said.

"Maybe so," he said, "but I'll get home fine. Go. And when you talk to that guy, would you ask him what he thinks about California?"

"Sure thing," I said.

18

When I picked Louise up early for her next ECT treatment, she asked where her baby was: "I need to bring him," she said, and so I said I'd get him while she got in the car.

"Thank you," she said. "I do really need a break."

Usually, on the days she brought the elephant, she would tuck it by her waist, right next to the seat belt. But today she looked panicked, and when I put the truck in reverse she said, "No. Not without a car seat."

"He'll be fine," I said.

"You *would* think that. You're not taking us anywhere until the conditions of this vehicle are safe enough to do so."

I tried to suggest that maybe he could stay home. "He looks like he's sleeping, anyway."

She laughed at that. "That is neglect, and I'm a better mother than that."

I had no idea where to get a car seat. She wouldn't even allow me to drive the truck anywhere, so I could not go and get one at the store.

"I'll be right back," I said to Louise, and she told me to start the truck and put the heat on.

I went straight to the neighbor's door. The screen door had no springs, no mechanics, and so when I opened it, it flung back and banged the side of the house and slowly crept back to me. I knocked once, and then once more. Nobody answered, but I thought I heard noises. Again, I knocked, but nobody came.

The pile of garbage or junk that he kept on the ground was soaked, especially the couch and pillows, and all the boxes sagged. I had only just begun to dig when the neighbor's door ripped open and he said, "What the fuck are you doing?"

Was this all I had to do to get him outside?

Louise spoke from the truck. "Rhett, honey, hi."

Rhett waved to her and then came down the stairs to me, right by the pile of garbage. He said the words slow, each syllable a jab in the chest.

"What—the—fuck—are—you—doing?"

I had no reasonable explanation for what I was doing. It was his stuff, and I had no right to go through it, even though it was just garbage.

So I just said it. "Please tell me you have a car seat? I'll give you anything you want for it."

"Why would I keep a car seat in this pile where it rains?"

I thought of the couch, but said nothing.

"How much money do you have?" he said.

I didn't know, so I took out my wallet and checked. I had no cash on me.

"Look," I said to him, and I explained why I needed it. "It sounds ridiculous, I know, but I promise I'll pay you when I come back."

He turned away and went back up the stairs and inside the house. I thought he was not coming back, that his leaving was the end of the conversation. But as he got indoors, he yelled to someone.

"Do we still have Corinne's car seat?"

A woman's voice spoke, but I could not hear what she said.

"Huh?" Rhett said.

Again, I could not hear what she said.

"The car seat! Do we still have it?"

"Why?" I heard her say that.

"Someone needs it," he said. "Do we or don't we?"

I think she said "No."

"You don't know what you're talking about," Rhett said. "We do too."

He disappeared from the doorway, and both the screen door and interior door were wide open. He was not gone long, and when he came out and down the steps, he held in one hand a car seat.

"Sorry about the crumbs," he said. As he handed me the car seat he said, "How old's the baby?"

I don't think he understood at all what I had explained to him, so I tried again, but he just looked at me and shook his head. He turned away.

"Thanks for this," I said. I don't know why I said what I said next, but I did. "You won't need this soon, will you?"

He laughed. "The state took our kid. Just leave it on the steps when you're done with it."

I looked at the crumbs in the car seat—there was even most of a deformed cracker lodged between the armrest and seat cushion—and I wondered where, in this world, the mouth was that had chewed this food.

For all the trouble Louise had put me through in wanting a car seat, she didn't even buckle the elephant in. She set it in the car seat and then set the car seat on the ground between her feet, and she had the heat cranking through the bottom vents.

I never would have guessed Elizabeth went by the name Ellie.

I imagine the last thing she wanted was to be bothered as she waited for her appointment; the last thing she imagined was that an old, senile woman would wheel herself over to her and say, "Hello, what is your name?"

"Ellie," Elizabeth said.

She was kind.

"And yours?" Louise said.

Mary, too, was kind.

"Mary," she said. "I'm her mother."

"Mary was also Jesus's mother," Louise said.

"That's true," Mary said.

"Is your husband's name Joseph?" Louise asked.

"It's Roger," Mary said. "He'd be here, but he's working."

"That's your father?" Louise asked.

"No, that's my husband," Mary said. "He's Ellie's father."

"And he's working?" Louise asked.

"Yes," Mary said.

"Men do need to work." Over her shoulder, she glared at me.

I went to the window to get the clipboard with paperwork from the woman behind the glass, and as I sat and filled it out for Louise, she grew quiet. Mary asked after her stuffed elephant, and I wondered if she recognized it. Then Louise asked if she, Elizabeth, wanted to hold it.

"Sure," she said. "What's her name?"

"It's a him," Louise said.

"What's his name?" she asked, but Louise didn't answer.

Elizabeth held him for only a moment, no longer, before Louise wanted him back.

"He's tired," Louise said. "I'm sorry."

"That's all right," Mary said.

"He needs to be put down for a nap," Louise said. "Don't you, darling?"

Louise wheeled herself over to me.

"Where is his car seat?" she asked me.

"In the truck," I told her.

"Why didn't you bring it in?"

"I'll go get it," I said.

I returned the clipboard and paperwork to the woman behind the window, and I walked back down the narrow hallway to the entrance, and I went outside to the truck but remembered my keys were in the locker—they didn't allow some items in the building, yet I never understood keys—so I had to go back and get them, and then go to the truck. Having gotten the car seat and put my keys back into the locker, I made it back to the waiting room to find Elizabeth not there.

I set the car seat at Louise's feet, and she put the stuffed elephant in it.

I asked Louise if she wanted a magazine, but she didn't answer me. I got her one anyway, a *National Geographic*, an issue about the cosmos, and I didn't think she was going to look at it. She had it on her lap with her hands folded over it. But then she started to look at it, began to flip through the pages, pausing only to look at the photos, and the bigger the picture, the more time she spent inspecting.

There was noise—there's always noise—but even so the room was quiet. The loudest sound came from Louise as she turned, rather roughly, the pages of the magazine. Mary still sat where she had, right across from us on that bench with green cushions, and she looked to be reading a magazine, but her eyes did not move. They looked down at the magazine and stayed straight. I looked back to Louise, who wasn't reading and instead was looking at a photo. Without taking her eyes from the page, Louise asked, "Have we been to space?"

Mary answered her. "We have," she said. "A few times, I think."

"For what?" Louise asked. "To find out we can't get away?"

"What do you mean?" Mary said.

"Never mind," Louise said. "Pass me another."

I got up and grabbed a different issue, which I gave to her. This one had a photo of a young woman in a safari shirt standing in a forest and holding a camera. The caption said "Becoming Jane," or something like that.

Again, Louise just stared at the cover for some time before she began to flip through the pages. But then she went back to the cover and held the image in front of her face.

"Do I look like her?" she asked.

"A little bit," I said. "Do you think you do?"

She didn't answer me. At least not in a way that responded to my question. She set the magazine down and looked right at me.

"Does my mother know I'm here?" Louise said. "Where is she? Can I see her?"

I was glad Elizabeth was missing this.

"Do you want to go for a ride?" I asked Louise. "In the wheelchair?" I did not want to answer her question.

"I want to see my mother," she said. "Where is she?"

"She's not here," I said.

"Is she home?"

I went to the window and told the woman I was taking Louise for a stroll, that I'd still be in the building, that if I wasn't back by her appointment, to come looking.

"Of course," she said.

I turned Louise around and pushed her toward the door. "I can't steal this," she said about the magazine, so I took it and tossed it onto the table.

"Do you want your baby?" I said about the elephant.

"I have a baby?" Louise said.

"He was talking to me," Mary said, trying, for some reason, just a human one, to ease Louise's spirit.

And Louise said to me, "She should want her baby."

We were away from the room and going down the hall when Louise asked where we were going. I said for a short walk.

"Is my mother walking too?"

"Maybe," was all I said.

"She's here," Louise said. "She is."

Fredrick used to call them Goog'ooks—spirits. It's like you're not alone, like something is just over your shoulder, peering.

That's what I felt. And maybe that's what Louise felt too. But it was only my body's remembering something I did not—this woman, Louise's mother, from a time that I had no memory of. And I wonder, looking back at Louise wanting her mother, how strange it is to want something you did not like, or something that seemed a bad part of your life. But maybe, like most things, it wasn't all bad.

On our way back through the hallway to the waiting room, we passed Mary pushing Elizabeth out in the wheelchair. I did not look at her. I kept my eyes down at the floor, and I looked only to make sure we would pass by them with no accident.

As we passed by, Louise said, "I remember you."

19

That night, after Louise's most recent ECT treatment, I was dreaming of Fredrick—we were driving to some unknown place in the middle of a snowstorm—when Mary woke me.

"Get up" is how she said it.

I really don't know if her unannounced visit frightened me. Maybe I thought I was still dreaming, which might explain my saying, "Is that you?" when I walked out into the kitchen, which was too warm. I'd left the heat cranked. The light above the sink was on, and she was by my cupboard, crouched down.

"Do you not keep your coffee here anymore?" she said.

"I do, but I'm out. The last of it's in the maker. Turn it on."

We sat in silence while the coffee brewed.

I somehow knew she would come.

I wanted to smoke—needed to smoke—even though I didn't do that in the house anymore, but I felt something momentous was about to occur, and so I asked her if she minded if I smoked a cigarette, like it was her house.

"Yes," she said. "I do. I don't want to go home smelling like one."

The coffee finished brewing, and Mary went to get some. There was only a cup's worth.

"Drink it," I told her. She got a cup from the red drying rack and poured the coffee. She put two sugars in, no cream.

"Dairy rips me up inside," she said, sitting. Thin steam rose from the cup, and she blew it away in a swirl. She seemed to take a sip, but I didn't see her swallow. Maybe it was still too hot and so she only touched her lip to the coffee, checking. She set the cup down.

"How'd you get here?" I asked her. "Did you park down the dirt road?"

This time she did drink the coffee, but I could tell it burned her tongue.

"No," she said. "I paddled over. It was quicker."

I stood up to look out the window.

"Roger didn't hear you leave?" I asked.

"Maybe," she said. "But he knows I'm here."

"He knows?"

Mary laughed. "He's always known."

I wanted to ask Mary why, if Roger knew, she hid the canoe, but then I realized why: for Elizabeth.

I sat back down.

The obvious question to ask was why she was here, especially if Roger knew. And I would have asked it if she hadn't started talking.

"She's sick, Charles," was how Mary began. "She's been sick her whole life. When she moved out, when she'd been teaching third grade for a few years and had bought her house—which she's thinking of selling—before all that, I thought she had been cured, that what she'd suffered from had gone. But it hadn't gone. I guess I was just hopeful. Since she was a little girl, she's been ill. Not physically, I don't mean, but in her spirit." She paused a moment. "No, that's not true—she was sick physically for a few years when she was eight or nine. She suffered seizures, but the medication helped with that."

Mary started laughing, and I asked her why that was funny.

"It's not, it's not," she said, but she kept laughing. Maybe she needed to laugh.

"Listen," she said. "Before we knew she had epilepsy, we—Roger and I, I mean—Roger and I used to think she was just a bad kid, one of those children who would grow up to be criminals, like that boy who set the community garden on fire—did you hear he did it because he was bored? Anyway, Ellie's epilepsy's gone, if you're wondering. I once had Marissa over—do you remember Marissa? It doesn't matter—Marissa was over once on a Saturday, and this is when she was studying to be a manicurist, which she never finished, and she was doing my nails at the kitchen table. She was gluing on acrylics. Ellie had been watching TV in the living room, and she came into the kitchen and stood right between Marissa and me. She had this blank look on her face, and she looked me in the eyes. I asked if she was all right, if she was going to be sick. That's what she looked like. Her face was pale and her cheeks were sunken. 'What's the matter?' Marissa said to her, but Ellie kept on staring at me. I scooted in my seat so I was right in her face, and as I went to speak to her, Ellie slapped me. And I don't mean gently. She smacked me hard, right across the cheek.

"I grabbed her by the arm and brought her straight to her room. I think it was the only time I yelled at her—I mean really yelled—and she started to cry. Of course I thought she did it on purpose. Who wouldn't think that? Marissa—she's always been nosy, she gets it from her mother, but then again so is everybody on the reservation—Marissa stuck her head in the room. 'Is everything all right?' she said, and I took her back out to the kitchen, where we sat back down at the table and I asked her to finish my nails. One of the fake nails she'd glued on me had come off.

"'What was that all about?' Marissa asked me, and I really didn't know, which is what I said. 'Does she do that often?' she asked. I told her no."

Mary went to the microwave and heated her coffee. As it heated, she kept talking.

"Later, when I went to her room, I asked her if she was sorry. 'For what?' Ellie said. 'For hitting me,' I told her. 'I didn't hit,' she said. 'I didn't!' We went back and forth until she started to cry again."

She stopped the microwave before it beeped at zero. She came and sat back down.

"She never hit me again, and it took a few more weeks to find out something was wrong. She was not remembering things she did, and then finally she had a seizure at school during lunch. After a sleep test, the doctors were able to explain what was wrong with her, which included her not remembering moments, things she'd done."

Mary laughed again. "That slap though. I'll never be able to take it seriously, since I know she couldn't help it. It was a hell of a smack. My face was bright red for at least an hour. I was, and still am, glad she got better over the next few years. She was eventually able to come off the seizure medication, and she's not had a seizure since then. Well, she has, because of her treatments now, as you more than well know, but those are controlled. How long has Louise been sick?"

"A year or more," I told her.

"No," Mary said. "I mean with her depression. I take it that's why she's getting treatments."

I explained what I could to her, that she'd been sick all my life—"Sounds like Ellie," Mary said, not knowing the weight of those words—and that she was confined to bed for weeks while Fredrick tended to her.

"She rolled her ankle," I said, "and on one of our visits to the doctor I mentioned her depression to him. He recommended the treatments, for her memory and for her mental health."

"And are they working?" Mary asked.

I shrugged. "It's not like her memory can be improved. I think this treatment was more for her depression. Maybe they're working. But her memory has been the same. Sometimes she remembers me, sometimes she does not."

And for the first time, I felt frightened about losing Louise. Gizos was gone forever, and besides Bobby, she was the only other person I had in my life who knew I existed, however rare it was for her to recognize me, to know I was her son. Although I couldn't recall the last time she'd looked upon me with the knowledge of who I was. I hoped she knew it was an accident. That it wasn't my fault.

I cleared my throat. "Other than her memory issues," I said, "and the bouts of her not feeling well mentally, she is doing all right. She's still strong in her body."

"I want you to know I was sorry to hear about your mother," Mary said. "That day you came by to ask about the burial. I've always liked Louise, and I've thought about her from time to time. She was always kind."

It was my turn to laugh. "She was, and still is. I don't know who it is she thinks I am, but she has a big issue with me."

"So I saw," Mary said. I don't think she meant what she said next to be malicious, because she does not know the story about Fredrick, but it did set me to wonder darkly. "You think she knows who you are but still treats you like that?"

Fredrick was a dream now, but he was still very much alive between my mother and me. Had I missed my opportunity to tell Louise the truth once again? To report back to her about what her son had said, why he hadn't gone with his father that day?

I want to say I told Mary I had thought about that, that maybe Louise knew who I was but still treated me badly. But all I said was, "Maybe."

"I remember the first time I brought Ellie to the doctor's," Mary said, "when she wasn't feeling well. This was in high school. She was up all night and sleeping all day. That's a bit dramatic. It wasn't always like that, but for the most part she couldn't sleep at night. Only during the day. The doctor asked if there was anybody else in our family that suffered from depression. I felt like saying, 'We're Indians, of course it runs in our family,' but I didn't say that. I told him yes, which made Ellie look at me. She asked who, and I told her Roger's mother, which was not true, but she was not alive to say otherwise. After, Ellie asked her father about it, and he told her that that was the truth. I don't know why she had difficulty believing that, but she did."

"So what did the doctor do for her?" I said.

"Gave her medication. She tried a few over the course of a year and some months, and then she settled on one that she kept taking through the end of college. But they stopped working, and she stopped taking them. She's since gone back on them while also going through the treatment, which is helping. She'd gone back to that pattern of stay-ing up all night and sleeping most days, but now she's starting to sleep through the night again. She'd sit outside and smoke—I don't know where she picked that up—and play on her phone or just sit. I watched her once from the kitchen. She stayed outside for hours."

"I've seen her out there before," I said.

"I figured you had," Mary said. "She thought once she heard a Goog'ook outdoors, late at night, heard this jingle"—she waved her hand and wiggled her fingers—"echo across the water. She told us the next day, sometime in the afternoon. She thought Roger should smudge."

I thought of the phone calls and said as much to Mary.

"I thought it was you she heard. Roger smudged though, to make her feel better."

We were quiet a moment, and then I said, "So they're working," but Mary took that as a question.

"Yes," she said. "As I said, she sleeps through the night, and she's up early. She's even started talking about going back to work."

"I thought you said she lost her job?"

"I didn't say that," Mary said. "She took this year off, and they didn't hire somebody new but instead got a long-term substitute, or something like that."

"Is she going to go back next year?" I said.

"She hasn't said just yet."

We were quiet. My chair creaked. Again that rush of wondering why she was here, and Mary seemed to hear my inner thoughts: she answered the question I never posed.

"Gizos told me," Mary said. "He called me last night. That's why I'm here."

"Told you what?" I asked, but I knew.

Mary got up and heated her coffee for six seconds. There was barely any in her cup, and so when it was done warming, she drank it all.

"Do you have any tea?" she said.

"Check in the cupboard."

Mary crouched and dug around in the cupboard for the tea I knew was not there. Her knees popped as she shifted cans and bags of flour and sugar and containers of salt and pepper all around, looking for tea. When she found none, she poured a glass of water.

"Your water's gritty," Mary said.

"What is it you want?" I asked.

"You need to keep the story to yourself."

But it was already let loose.

"Who else knows about this?" she asked. "Who else have you told?"

"Gizos knows, and he only found out recently, and somebody you don't know knows. He's non-Native and doesn't care about anything except drinking and leaving here. Just them. And now you."

"And Roger."

"Then why isn't he here? Why is it only you?"

She said nothing.

"I'm going to tell the story," I said.

"You can't," Mary said.

"Why? Tell me why. Tell me one good reason."

"What good does it do for her to know?" she asked.

"She has a right to know."

"And so the past twenty-seven years of her life won't be true?" Mary said.

"Of course they will," I said. "And that's what I want to say. I want to make it clear that knowing her history will only make her more real, more true. She has a right to know."

"Charles," she said, "it's sometimes best not to know. Take Roger. He knew from the very start what I was doing as well as why. Sure, he was an exceptional father to Ellie, but there were days I was afraid he would back out of this. I was afraid he would leave us."

"But he didn't," I said.

"Let me finish—" she said.

"And that's why he's her father," I said. "That's why he will always be her father. That's why she will always see him as so. All I will be to her is a man who told her a story and who is her biological father. All I will be is a history she had no part in but nonetheless belongs to. What damage can that do?"

"Let me finish," she said. "How different would it have been if Roger hadn't known, if he had thought she was his?"

"What kind of question is that?" I said. "We can't know. All we can know is that would have been the cruelest trick to have been played, even more so than what you did to me. I wondered whether or not he knew about where she came from. I felt sorry for him, when I thought that way. What am I saying—this is not about Roger. This is about Elizabeth."

"Ellie," Mary corrected.

"This is about her," I said. "All about her. Maybe that's why she's sick—maybe she needs to know her full story. Have you thought about that? Maybe her body and mind know something is missing."

"I don't know what you're talking about," Mary said. "But please, consider what I'm saying, what Gizos has said. You can't let this story get out. She can't know. It has the potential to ruin everything I've worked toward giving her as well as everything you've sacrificed for her to be where she is and who she is."

"I never agreed to sacrifice anything," I said. "And percentages on paper don't mean shit."

"In a way they don't, but those percentages, those numbers, also do. And you need to understand that. By giving her this story, you're creating a situation where she's learning more about herself, yes, but she's also questioning who she is—or at least I would, if I were her. And her learning all this on top of managing her well-being? It could break her, Charles. This could break her. Your daughter. Let her keep living knowing what she knows."

Maybe I was blinded by my experience, by my own suffering, by my deepest desire—that she know I exist, that she know we were part of a story or a history that very much mattered, not in some grand scheme of things but in a simple way concerning our spirit.

"I can't do it," I said.

Mary threw the water from her cup in my face, and then she left through the front door. She did not close it, and the cold rushed in across the floor and brushed my ankles. I went to the door but did not close it. It was dark out, but in the glimmers of light shining from behind me and lighting the steps and the air around me, snow was falling, gently in large flakes. Mary yanked the canoe from around the house and guided it into the water. She got in, and with the paddle she pushed herself away from the riverbank. I closed the door before I saw her make it to the other side, but as I sat back down at the table I thought I should watch her leave, and so I went back to the door and looked through the glass window. The river is not so wide, and so she made it back home. I could not see her, so I turned off my lights and went back to watch. No lights shone from across the way, but I could make out the movement. In the dark, I watched her as she shimmied the canoe up the small incline and over the dying grass, and she flipped the canoe over against the house.

I locked my door and could not go back to sleep.

20

A few days after Mary visited me, Louise got sick and was unable to go to her ECT treatment. She had a high fever, and I brought her to the doctor. I don't know how long we waited, but it was a while. And the whole time I kept thinking about Mary and what she had said. I still stood by what I'd said to her, still planned to do what I'd said I would do. It had to be done. It was our daughter's, all of it.

The doctor did not sit for too long with Louise, and it probably would have been faster if she had talked some. I don't know what was the matter with her that day. She said no words at all, though she was conscious and able to hear and move about. And so for all the questions the doctor asked, I answered them.

He thought it was just a cold, and he gave her some cough medicine. She wasn't coughing terribly, I said, but he said just in case it should get worse.

I asked him if it was OK if she missed her appointments, which he didn't answer right away and instead asked if they were working.

"I don't know," I told him. "Maybe. But is it all right?"

"It's fine, yes. Call them and tell them what happened. Say you'd like to reschedule."

I stayed with Louise until late afternoon, watching TV on low and listening every so often to her breathing as she slept. Before I left to go pick Bobby up from the bar—he'd called and asked for a ride—I checked her fever, which was gone. I told her I was going home and that I'd be back in the morning. As I was on my way out, her phone rang and it was Bobby again, asking where I was.

"I'm coming," I said.

I had every intention of telling him what had happened with Mary, but I never got the chance. When I picked him up he was loaded, had sixteen beers in him, or so the bartender told me when Bobby wobbled off to piss, which was also the only time he was quiet. He talked and talked and talked about how angry he was at the neighbor, at the court date, how it was "fucking up" his plans.

"I'll kill him," he told me. "That's why you, Charles, you, you, you have to talk to him. Tell him to drop the charges. I'll kill him."

I didn't disbelieve him, so I suppose that's why I decided to try and find him first—Rhett, that is—when I went back to Louise's. Maybe he would drop the charges.

It was only a little past six when I brought Bobby home. He was falling asleep at the bar, and the bartender helped me carry him out and put him in my truck, at which point he was miraculously awake, like the five or ten minutes he had dozed off had somehow been enough to strengthen him.

"How's our girl, anyway?" he said as I drove him home.

"She's good," I said, and I was about to tell him about Mary.

"Does she remember us?"

He meant my mother.

"Maybe," I said.

"I've got to go see her," he said. "It's been a bit. Pull over."

I stopped on the side of the road and he got out and puked. He wiped his mouth.

"Better out there than in here," he said. He shut the door. "I've been thinking," he said. "You should get your land appraised so when we move you can sell your lot and that shitty little house of yours."

"You thought that?"

"Fuck you," he said, laughing. "But really. It'll give us some more money."

"I'll think about it."

"You do that," he said.

Bobby coughed and spat out the window.

"I'm gonna call Louise when I get home," Bobby said. "Do you think she's up?"

"Don't bother her," I said, and I meant it. "She's sleeping. She's got a cold."

"You said she was good. What do you mean, a cold? She go to the doctor's?"

"Yes, he said it was a cold."

"She got a fever?"

"She did."

"And you left her? Jeez Louise," he said, and then he laughed until he was coughing. "I said that to her once. The jeez Louise. Couldn't get her to laugh all day, but she thought that was pretty funny. You got a cigarette?"

He asked that as he was taking one from my pack sticking out of the console.

"I should call her," he said, blowing smoke out the open window.

"Don't call her," I said again. "She's sleeping."

He was quiet, and after a time of silence he said, looking out the window, "You shouldn't have left her."

He could have meant anybody right then.

When I got home, I could hear singing and drumming—an honor song—and I looked around for the source of the noise, but it was nowhere to be found. It was a ways away. And then I saw something else, across the river by their house. The tribal police were just leaving it. It was just one cruiser, and all I could see was them driving away, and behind them followed an ambulance. No lights were on. It was one of those quick flashes of a moment, the tail end of something, and so both cruiser and ambulance could have been coming from down the street and just so happened to pass as I was looking about for the drumming and singing.

The singing and the drumming grew louder when the wind quit blowing. If she was home, she probably heard it. I sat outside and listened for a while, wondering, and then it came to me. Lenno. It's not that I wanted to be right about that; I felt I had to be right about it. I hopped in my truck and drove over to the reservation, and I watched them from the parking lot of the football field, right next to the school. I don't know for how many days they'd had the sacred fire burning, but it was still going, and not even fifty feet away was the drum, seven men—one of them must have been Gizos, but I could not tell—around it, and around them a dozen or so people, all singing.

I did not stay very long, but long enough to feel part of it. Because I suppose I was. And how strange that after all these years I still remember the words to that song, and I drove off singing them:

kchee-da-mee-d'haa-da-moo-neh dun elee
    ul'naa-buy-ol'dee-yagw
nijee ul'naa-bettook maa-weeh-laa-neh
kchee-da-mee-d'haa-da-moo-neh dun
wedaa-beksol-dee-yagw
nijee ul'naa-bettook we-jooh-kem-dol-dee-neh
we-jooh-kem-dol-dee-neh dun gizeeh-ol-lugw
elee boon'lugw eeyo wskit-ka-migk
wey-yo-hey-hi-ya-ya-wey-oh-hey-ho-hey-hi-
    ya-awey-yo-hey-hi-ya-ya-wey-yo-hey

21

I went to Louise's the next day, on a Saturday. Her door was locked, and I unlocked it with the key. I found her in the living room, a garbage bag opened and partly filled by her feet. She was going through all the junk mail she'd had piled up for who knows how long, tossing pieces. But what caught my attention was a cream-colored cord hanging out of the black bag.

"Hi, yes, come in," she said, as if I had knocked on her front door. She did not take her eyes from the mail as she tossed envelopes in the garbage. Two or three pieces lay flat on the floor around it.

Louise coughed once, and then once more.

I grabbed hold of the cream-colored cord and pulled it.

"Leave it," Louise said. "I won't have it anymore."

"What?" I kept pulling until from below the many envelopes her phone emerged.

"All night," Louise said, "that machine would not stop making noise. I had to rip it out of the wall."

"You can't throw away your phone," I said.

"I don't use it," she said.

"What about when I call?"

She tossed an envelope into the garbage.

I hooked the phone back up in the kitchen, and I hung it on the wall where it had been, that part of the wall whiter than the rest of the kitchen. I expected it to ring, but it did not.

In the living room, I put my hand to Louise's forehead, and it was warm.

"Help me," she said.

"You need some Tylenol?"

"With the mail," she said.

Most of the day was spent going through her junk mail in the living room—taking a break only so I could cook her an early lunch of canned green beans, microwavable mashed potatoes, and this ham from a can I fried in her skillet. I wrapped half of it up for her dinner and gave her the other half, which she picked at as she watched TV. I made sure she took the Tylenol I set beside her plate. For the entire time we worked together, gutting envelope after envelope, she said nothing, and every time I asked her a question about herself, she responded with short answers, mostly, "I don't know, sir."

The quiet bothered me intensely, like the sun beating down on my neck. And I couldn't take it anymore, feeling so alone, so I asked: "Do you have any children?"

I felt like a stranger.

For a moment she thought on it. "If I do . . ." she said. A brief wait, a second, and then she asked: "Do I?"

Before I could answer she cut me off with a wave and looked back at her envelopes, many of which were upside down, so I don't think she was reading what they were.

"I don't know," she said.

She was dozing when I left her that day, and I thought it might be time for her to go into a home. Not that she couldn't take care of herself—she could do that. But I was concerned that she was forgetting too much.

I called Bobby when I got home.

"What the fuck did I tell you?" I said.

"Goddammit I thought I dreamt it," he said.

"She threw her phone out because of you."

I was nowhere near him obviously, but I imagined him rubbing his eyes.

"I'm sorry, Charles."

"She's too sick for this shit," I said.

"Then maybe she shouldn't be on her own," he said. "She can live with me. I'll watch her."

"And get drunk and bother her all night? What happens when you move away? What then?"

He knew what he'd said was ridiculous, and that it would never happen, but even so he still argued with me because that's what he does.

"The neighbor isn't dropping the charges anytime soon," he said. "So it looks like I'm here for quite a while."

I had seen him, Rhett, when I was leaving Louise's apartment. I was trying to pay him for the car seat, but he seemed to have forgotten and wanted only one thing. "Stay away from me," he said. "You're friends with that lunatic, aren't you? He's getting sued for all he's worth."

"I ain't worth much," Bobby said when I told him how the neighbor had put it.

The next week, Louise did not look well. She was pale, and her skin was very warm. And she was coughing more. But she would not stay home and in bed. She kept saying she was fine, and so I listened to her and said we'd still go to her appointment. "I have to be there," she said, and when I asked her where, she did not answer me. I thought, however, it was better to take her. The doctor there might see her sickness and help convince her that she was unwell.

I really expected to see Elizabeth there. We sat in the waiting room, and I kept wondering: Had her appointment been changed? She did not show up in the hour we were waiting for Louise's treatment. Louise rested in her wheelchair, and at her side slept her elephant in a car seat I'd bought for her. She kept taking it out and rubbing its face, and she'd take its trunk and massage it between her bony fingers.

The door to the treatment room opened, and the nurse said Louise's name.

"Here," Louise said. "I'm here." She tried to rise from her wheelchair, but she collapsed back into it.

"I'll wheel you over," I said, "and the nurse will take you the rest of the way."

She tried to rise again, but again she failed.

The nurse came over.

"I'll push you," she said.

"I'm hot," Louise said. "I need to breathe."

"Stay seated," the nurse said.

She felt Louise's head, put her hand against her cheek.

"Is she sick?" the nurse asked me.

I told her about her cold.

"Let's bring you back so the doctor can see you." And then to me she said, "You can come with us."

Louise's fever had returned, and it was the highest it had been—102.9. I told the doctor what I could—that she had been sick, that she'd seen her normal doctor, that he had prescribed her cough medicine that she had not yet taken because her fever had gone away and the cough wasn't as bad as it had been. As I spoke, the doctor listened to Louise's lungs, checked her mouth and throat. Both of us listened to her cough, which spoke more to him than to me.

"Take her home," he said. "Call and reschedule when she's better. And monitor her closely. If she gets any worse at all, take her to the emergency room."

He looked at his watch, and he never glanced back at us.

When I wheeled her out of the treatment room and down the hall to the waiting room, I expected to see Elizabeth sitting out there with Mary. Where are you? I thought. Where she normally sat, on the green cushioned bench, were two women, and a young girl, about five or six, red all around her mouth, was sitting on the floor beside the elephant in the car seat, looking at it. I'm sure she had touched it.

"Get," Louise spat at her, and the girl scooted back, quickly, to the women she was with.

I carried the car seat and the elephant as I pushed Louise back to the truck.

When the first snowstorm of the season hit, and all the pine branches bent under the weight of snow, I fantasized about—prepared for—Louise's death. It's always a cold that gets the elderly, or so we hear, but still it catches us off guard. We act surprised by something that is not quite surprising—it's expected. It's more unexpected for them to survive the cold, to get better, to live on.

But Louise recovered. I checked her temperature with the thermometer. It had gone down 0.4 degrees, and then the next time it was down more, and then again, more, until it was normal. She still coughed a little bit here and there, and she still was picky with her food, but at least she started to eat.

Before the storm hit, Bobby stayed with Louise while I went up north for a job. I came back Tuesday night to find him sleeping in the recliner, Louise sleeping in the bed. The TV was on very loud, and the first thing I did was turn it down.

I shook Bobby awake. "You can go if you want," I said to him.

"Storm's coming," Bobby said.

"Wake up," I said.

"I am awake. Shit. A storm's coming."

It was not until the eleven o'clock news that I saw what he meant. A nor'easter would hit Thursday evening and would go out to sea at some point, the soonest, according to their models, late Friday evening or early Saturday morning.

Before the storm, I left Louise to go back to my place and make sure the windows were shut and locked and to get my shovel and a flashlight and a small kerosene stove that used to be Fredrick's. Before I went back to her, I went to the store for batteries and kerosene and canned food and three packs of cigarettes and cold cuts and bread, which was almost sold out, and I bought a cribbage set that came with a deck of red cards in case Louise wanted to play.

When I got to Louise's, she said the phone wouldn't stop ringing, and it rang right before she could finish the sentence. It was Bobby saying he wanted to come and stay with us, but he never showed up. I told him I didn't want him there if he was going to drink.

"I won't," he said. "I swear to God I won't have a drink while I'm there." I pressed him about it. "I won't," he said.

"Christ sakes. I won't." And so I said fine, come on over. But he never showed, and he didn't answer when I called his house, so I figured he couldn't stay sober for a day or more. I thought it was good of him. Why have two sick people when one is enough? He had said he was cutting back on his drinking—how much, I didn't know—because he wanted to be ready for his court date, which would be here soon. He was convinced he was going to get his case dismissed, especially with my testimony, which would be what, I didn't know.

The news was right about the storm starting Thursday evening. The flakes fell few and far between around six. I was outside Louise's place, smoking, watching past my smoke-and-cold breath as the white drifted like fuzz to the ground. For dinner that night, I made Louise canned soup. It was mainly broth, which she had some of but not all, and I made two sandwiches with cold turkey. I drank water, and then I made tea for Louise and me but she took only one sip of hers to swallow a Tylenol, and then her tea got cold and stayed cold all night on her nightstand.

All Louise did was sleep, which was something I still could not do. I think I did get some sleep around four in the morning for about an hour, but for the rest of the night I was awake. At two, I went outside for a smoke and I went to my truck and got my shovel, and I smoked three cigarettes while I cleared from the driveway and front steps what snow had already fallen, about four inches. Shoveling got me thinking about Fredrick. He hated to shovel after all the snow had fallen. He liked to break it up. He'd go out and shovel in thirds. As a boy, I was always with him for some part of it. And since then, I'd done the work the same way he did it: in parts. He'd always said it was easier on the body that way, and I agreed.

All day Friday it snowed, snowed, snowed, and I'd go out in it and shovel, but could not keep up with the snowfall. By late afternoon, I'd shoveled and cleared away the snow. For a time, I leaned on the shovel and watched some children in oversize coats build a fort, a tiny dugout in which they crawled until their mother told them to get out, and then they turned their attention to a green sled, which they used to slide over and over again down into a ditch. By the time I looked back at my work, the ground was covered again.

When inside, I started to worry about Louise. She was in a deep sleep, her fever burning, and she kept shivering. Once I thought she'd stopped breathing, but she was just barely breathing. If she did have to go to the hospital, then it was best I keep the driveway as clear as possible, even though the roads were barely plowed. They were drivable, but dangerous. I worked to keep the driveway clear, going out every forty-five minutes.

When the wind came, the lights would flicker once, maybe twice, and the house would shift and creak. I could never tell if it was my blinking that caused the lights to flicker or if it was actually the lights. But they did blink once, I know that. I was inside, getting ready to head back out, when they dulled and came back on, and I was surprised to find them still lit when I finished shoveling the snow and went back indoors.

Before Louise got better, I sat near her in the recliner, waiting to go back out and shovel more, and I thought very much about her getting worse. I was sitting there, my eyes on the TV but not taking it in, and I imagined myself rising from the chair, standing over her as she slept. I nudged her shoulder, trying to wake her. But she did not wake. I said her name: "Louise, Louise, Mom, wake up," but she did not. She was sweating, the saltwater drops sliding down her temples. Her pillow was soaked, her hair damp. In that vision, I checked her temperature, and it was too high, too high, so high that I saw myself run down the hall and put on my boots and not tie them, and I went two steps at a time to the outside, where I started my truck and cleaned off the snow just enough to see, and back upstairs I tracked snow on the floors as I raced to her bed. I threw the blankets off her and sat her up, but she could not hold herself steady, so I set her back down and went, hurriedly, to get her jacket. Again I sat her up and wrapped the jacket around her, over her light pink pajamas, and I stood her up and guided her down the hall until I realized she was light—so light, like dust, or like how I imagine the weight of a star to be, just the dot of it in the dark sky, in the middle of your palm—and I picked her up and carried her out the door and to the truck, and I almost dropped her in the snow but I didn't because the fierceness with which we love gave me enough strength.

This is where a winter storm brings you.

Like Fredrick's shoveling, like my shoveling, this vision was broken up into parts. I did not think at all about it while I was shoveling. I was thinking only about getting back to her, and when I did, I would pick back up where I had left off, except I did not envision too long a drive, only a quick bumpy and snowy road that I skidded over once and we were there, in the emergency room, waiting to be seen. There, the noise of snow falling was all I heard, that muffled quiet. We were there, I envisioned, for days, and I'm wondering only now if I thought about the storm, if I wondered about its ending while I stayed in the apartment with Louise, while the children played with their green sled. In that moment—in that fantasy—I don't know, but I do know in this imagination she did not make it. She was gone.

And I let the sadness take me, and it gripped me so tightly around the throat I could not breathe. The vision and its effect were over with a blow of my nose in a tissue, the weight of possibility, the weight of expectation, released, no longer pushing down on the top of my head. I felt like I had gotten over something, some sadness, had come to some exaltation. At the same time, I felt like something was yet to come, something big, something so big that if I hadn't made room for it I would not have made it, that the grief and sadness and fear yet to arrive would have been too much to carry.

When her temperature finally went down, she was not all better, of course. There was no miracle during this storm, or maybe there was, but she was well enough to sit up with her eyes open and stare at the TV. I made her breakfast: a fried egg and toast, the yolk broken, runny—"Can I have some water, please?"—and she pecked at the yellow, sticky pool with the corner of her toast, which she ate completely. She left the white of the egg. After, she went back to sleep, and I woke her only to take her temperature again, which was normal.

When she woke next, it was Saturday afternoon. I had slept most of the morning, and my lower back hurt, either from sleeping in the recliner or from shoveling. Maybe from both. But when I woke, she was not in bed but coming back into the room.

"I thought I was going to pee myself," she said, sitting. "I see it snowed."

"It did," I said. "How do you feel?"

"Tired," she said. "I had terrible dreams." She rubbed the space between her eyes.

I did not want to know what she'd dreamed.

Louise yawned, looked at me, and said my name. "Charles." She said it again. "I heard you crying."

I told her I wasn't crying, but she only looked at me and then looked to the floor, the space between us. She went to speak but did not. Do I tell her? I thought. Do I bring it up or let it go? I let it go. If that was one of the final times she spent knowing herself, knowing me, did I want to ruin it by pushing her into some dark depth about some truth that did not even matter? What difference did it make in the end? He had died. And she already knew why her son had not gone with him. She just wouldn't believe it.

Louise lay back in bed and asked for some tea, which I brought her, and I asked if she would be OK for a few hours. I wanted to go home and check on the place, see a neighbor the road over from me to ask to use his plow.

"You don't need my permission to leave," she said.

I was out the door and in the hallway when she asked what tomorrow was.

"Sunday," I said, and I asked why.

She was quiet.

Again, I asked why.

"I don't know," she said. "I feel like I have something to do."

The sun was out, and the miles and miles of snow shone bright white. The roads were not that great, and they were narrow from the banks of dirty snow. I took the highway, and everybody except for a select few in large trucks drove forty-five.

I drove straight to my neighbor's. He was not home, but his driveway was plowed and at the end, pressed into a pile of snow, was his plow. I didn't think he'd mind if I took it, which is what I did. I hooked it up to my truck, the metal of it cold on my hands, and I went back down the driveway and hung a left and drove down some ways. I slowed, tried to lower the plow, but it would not, so I had to get out and see what was the matter. I'd missed a plug.

It did not take me too long to plow. When I finished, I returned the plow.

The power was out, and my place was chilled. It was times like those I wished I had a woodstove. I did not plan to stay, but I ended up falling asleep on my couch for some hours under a blanket. It was not a restful sleep. The sun shone so hard on the white snow outside that the brightness woke me every so often, and when I was sleeping good, was in a real deep sleep where dreams would come, my stove beeped and my fridge banged and hummed. The power returned, and so did I to the world.

Louise was sleeping again when I returned to her place. She stayed sleeping while I took a shower and while I boiled pasta and twist-popped open some ready-made sauce that

I poured on it. I made her a plate too, which I set aside on the kitchen sideboard. She woke sometime after I'd eaten, and I checked her temperature again. It was still normal.

I stayed with her again that night. She rarely spoke. In fact, I remember her speaking to me only two times the entire time I was there. The first was when she asked me if we were getting another nor'easter, and when I told her no, she waved me away and said she'd heard we were going to get one, that I didn't know what I was talking about, so I agreed, "We're bound to get another one," to which she said nothing and didn't look at me.

The second thing she said was also a question. She asked for her baby, which was right beside her in her bed. After that, she did not speak, but she did laugh quite a bit at the television. We were watching the Justice Channel, and the show featured reenactments of 911 calls. The one she laughed at the most was about a woman who was in her own apartment when a man broke in. The woman hid in the closet with her son and was on the phone with 911. She had a gun, but the dispatcher kept telling her to put it down, officers are on the way, put it down on the floor. As soon as she did, you could hear the man crash through the closet door and the woman screaming, and the 911 dispatcher saying, "Ma'am? Ma'am?" and more screaming and yelling, and all of the fight was made louder by Louise laughing hysterically at this story of violence, laughing so hard she had to wipe tears from her face.

*

I wasn't sure Louise knew who I was anymore, but I was quite certain I was nobody. And as I sat there I felt myself slipping away to damp depths of sadness as I had done the night before, and I was thinking and thinking and thinking about how, in just the past year, I had just started to know her, but then I began to unknow her, getting farther and farther away like watching a boat drift from the shore and head out not to some other land but to an open water that never, ever ends. And she did not even know this, that she was on the boat.

22

When Louise was better, I brought her to her next ECT treatment. Again, Elizabeth was not there. I thought about going to Mary's work to ask about her, to see if she was OK and ask why she was not at her treatments. Instead, I went to the lady behind the glass and asked after her.

"I can't discuss patients," she said to me.

I asked her again.

"Sir," she said.

And then I said it. "But I'm her father."

"Name?" She typed something and looked at her computer screen.

"Charles Lamosway."

"That's not the name we have here. You said you were her father?"

"Never mind," I said, and I sat down.

The longer I waited for Louise, the larger my worry grew, and the less rational my thinking became. It's hard to say exactly how I felt, but however it was pushed me to think that I had to go to Mary's work. My bones could not withstand the pressure of having to wait at Louise's apartment with her until it was obvious the treatment would not cause any problems, until I could leave her and go.

Back in the truck, Louise lifted up the seat cushion and set in the empty space the car seat with the stuffed elephant, and the farther away we got from the spider-legged treatment center, the more I forgot she was there. Every now and then she massaged the stuffed elephant's gray hair, and her movement in my periphery, the reminder that she was there, frightened me.

I should have brought her home first, and I should have waited there with her until I knew I could leave. But I didn't.

We drove over the bridge to the reservation, and as we passed by our old home, I watched Louise stare at the house covered in snow.

I remembered the offices had been moved, and so I went to the correct place this time. I parked in back of the tribal offices, in the spots against the small decline that leads to the river.

"Can you wait here?" I asked Louise. "I'll only be a second."

She looked out at the river, and I got out of the truck.

"Are you bringing me home?" she asked.

"Soon," I said. "Very soon. Wait here, and don't get out of the truck."

I reached in and turned off the engine, and I locked the doors.

Behind her desk, Mary was typing. Her eyes flitted to me and then back to the computer's screen.

I shut the door behind me.

"Leave that open," Mary said.

"No," I said.

She stopped typing and set her elbows on the desk.

"What do you want?" she asked.

"What happened to her?" I said.

"Please leave."

I said it again.

"She is fine," Mary said. "Now leave."

"Where is she?"

"I won't say any more than that. She's fine. Now go."

"I haven't seen her at the treatments and I haven't seen her outside the house, so I find it hard to believe that she's fine."

"She's fine. She's not home with us, but she's fine."

"So she moved back home?"

"She's fine," Mary said. "Now leave."

"I want to know."

Mary stood up and walked around her desk to the chief's door, which was closed. She knocked.

"You'll leave," she said. "Now."

"Fuck you," I said, and I left.

I drove to Elizabeth's house. The one she was thinking she might sell. I knew it was hers because all the houses on this road were plowed and tended. Hers wasn't. The driveway was buried in a snow that was cold and hard. No smoke climbed out of her chimney, and no lights were on. When I honked my truck's horn, nobody came to the door, to the window. I did not enter her home, but I walked around the house in the snow and looked through the windows, the ones with the blinds open. It was nearly empty; none of the furniture I'd seen brought back to her parents' house was in the home.

Mary hadn't been lying, but from what I could see, Elizabeth was nowhere.

"Whose house is that?" Louise asked me when I got back in the truck.

"A friend," I said.

"When did they build that house?"

I backed out of the driveway.

"I don't know," I said.

"It's too new for this street," she said.

We drove, hearing only the hum of the heater. It was a bright blue sky day, but the air was frigid. As I headed to the bridge, once again we drove by our old home.

"Where are you going?" she asked, her head turned back, her eyes on our old house.

"I'm bringing you to your house," I said.

"It's all your fault." She said it so flatly, so matter-of-factly.

I knew what she meant, so I didn't say anything; and she also knew what she meant, exactly what she meant, and by my silence she knew I had understood her.

Maybe she was right; maybe I'd gotten it all wrong. Maybe it was all my fault.

Bobby's court hearing was later that week. I picked him up from his house in the morning. He was dressed nicer than I'd ever seen. A blue checkered button-up and brown slacks and brown sneakers. He told me not to smoke as we were driving, but then he said, "Leave the windows open. It'll be fine." I keep a roll of blue paper towels in the back seat for when I check my oil or poke around under the hood of the truck, and Bobby took the roll and ripped a few pieces for the sweat pouring down his face. I didn't think it was nerves—I could smell the old alcohol on him, squeezing through his skin and emerging to the air of the world.

We got to the courthouse early. It was in downtown Overtown. Most of the roads were one-way, and the concrete sparkled with the cold of the morning. I parked in back of the courthouse, this old stone building with copper or brass signs with dates and words. They're moving this place somewhere else now, somewhere newer and closer to the jail.

We were early, but people were outside, some smoking in nice suits and some rubbing their hands in old loose clothes. Bobby said nothing while we waited. He wiped his face with another blue paper towel.

The truck was warm, and so when I got out, the cold bit hard, so hard that for the rest of the day I would be unable to shake that chill from my body. I walked beside Bobby toward the door, and by the door he turned and leaned against the wall and lit a cigarette. He rubbed his eyes with the hand that held his long 100. He smoked it so fast his ash grew long and orange like a traffic cone.

We waited and waited. For what, I didn't know. I was waiting for Bobby, sure, but what was he waiting for?

He looked at the sky and I said, "We should go inside."

"How's my hair?" Bobby asked.

I don't know why, but I laughed at him. Maybe it was the stubble on his cheek that he missed.

"What's so fucking funny?" he said.

"It's fine," I said. "Looks fine."

Under the stubble on his cheek, his jaw clenched and released, as quick as a pulse.

I never gave any testimony. The court didn't allow it. I sat and sat and sat and listened and listened and listened to all the cases. A woman who stole a chicken and vodka and Legos from Walmart. A man on bail who got caught with cocaine. A young woman who crashed her car into a store, not by accident. And Bobby, who slapped my mother's neighbor around. Only a few people that day were sentenced to time—the woman who stole the chicken and vodka got three months; she had prior theft convictions—and the rest were hit with fines or probation or both. Bobby got a fine of $300 and six months' probation with one month served.

"He didn't even want your testimony," Bobby said when I drove him home, but I wasn't there fully. My mind was on the courtroom, the murmurs of voices, some with power, some without. I sat in two places: in the truck, turning left with Bobby yapping in my ear, and in the courtroom, situating myself on the polished oak bench, thinking about how much the judge reminded me of a man I never knew: my father, the blood one. I saw no resemblance in him, nothing, and I still can't quite figure out why I thought this, why I think this. Maybe it was because he was over there, across the way in a high seat, hunched over, looking, looking, untouchable at that distance but untouchable regardless. Always untouchable, but there, hovering. And he knew this, that man up there. Like all fathers, he knew this.

I dropped Bobby off at his house, and he said, "You were a real fucking help today, you know that?" and I thought that was the end, but before he shut the door in my face, he told me he'd need a ride home from the bar later. It didn't end, but continued.

I left him and took Louise to her treatment. Elizabeth, again, was not there—of course she was not there. The waiting room was colder than it had been in the past.

"A technician is working on the heat," the woman behind the glass said as I handed her the forms Louise had filled out.

The TV was on in the waiting room. The Weather Channel. Louise had a hold of the stuffed elephant, and she watched the TV.

"Look," she said, pointing. "A storm's coming."

The report was about Montana, and I told her so.

"But it'll come for us," she said.

This was the last week of her treatments.

"What did she say?" Louise asked. She was looking at me. I think she meant the weather lady.

I told her I didn't know.

"You never listen," she said. "Never."

I took her home, stayed the required number of hours, and told her I'd see her tomorrow.

"Don't forget the list," she said. "I need things from the store. It's on the table."

There was no list, but I pretended to take it.

23

After almost two months, Elizabeth reappeared. It was the middle of winter, the new year, and her birthday had passed. I first saw her when I came home from Louise's—she was outside shoveling snow at her parents'. I watched her from inside my house. When she finished, she went to the shed and came out with a foldout chair, which she opened and set right in the middle of the hole she had dug. I didn't know what she was doing, but from where I stood, I could see her from her chest up as she sat. And she was facing this way, looking across the river at my house. For the next few days, off and on, she sat there, smoking, rarely taking her eyes away.

If the news hadn't made the storm out to be the worst one Maine would see in years, I wouldn't have come—I would have stayed at home and tried to see, through the falling snow, my daughter.

"I knew it would come," Louise said to me about this second nor'easter. The wind shook the house, and the air whipped through the window screen and whistled.

"Don't whistle back," Louise told me sharply, which was something Fredrick used to say. It had been some time since she'd made any mention of Fredrick, even by use of phrases. But that day she began to act removed from where the ECTs had put her, or where I had thought they had put her—in a better place—and instead seemed to be embodying some time now long past, a time we all hoped to forget.

I was staying with her through the storm. That was the plan, anyway.

"It started in Montana," Louise was saying. She was sitting up in bed, explaining to me how she had told someone it would make its way to us, this storm. She was confusing me with me, and this storm with the one we'd seen the month before on the Weather Channel in the ECT waiting room.

"He thought I was a liar," Louise said.

I said, "He sounds like a jerk."

The snow started at about three in the afternoon. I made Louise dinner, and she ate it—all of it, which led me to believe that she was well—and she finished it before the six o'clock news was over. In each of my hands I held a plate—mine, hers—and I walked them to the kitchen and rinsed them and washed them with soapy bubbles, and I put the pots and pans I'd used in the sink and soaked them with hot water. I was away from Louise for some fifteen minutes, spraying and wiping the counters and scrubbing the pots and pans I had soaked for not very long so it was still hard to scrub them clean. When I got them clean, I set them with the other dishes to dry on a red hand towel and cleaned the sink and the sideboard around it. Drops of water had dripped from the tips of my fingers, dotting the floor, so the floor was wet and I cleaned it, and on the floor below the trim of the baseboard I saw dirt and dirt and crud and more dirt, and so I swept. I was in mid-sweep, the pile of dirt and crumbs and a loose lentil and a grain of rice or two and a tangle of thin hair at my feet, when I heard what sounded to be Louise on the phone.

It was. Behind me the cream-colored cord ran around the corner to her bedroom. I stepped over the pile and ducked under the cord as I went to her.

"You don't advise it?" she was saying.

"Who are you talking to?" I asked.

With a wave of her hand, she told me to be quiet.

"OK, well thank you for your time," Louise said. "Good-bye."

She held the phone out to me. "Hang this up," she said.

I did, and then I asked again who she was talking to.

"None of your business," she said.

I finished in the kitchen, went outside for a smoke, and then found myself back in Louise's room and sitting in the recliner. Louise was no longer sitting up but was lying back with her arm over her forehead. For the longest time I thought she was sleeping, and it was only after I watched two and a half episodes of that doctor show that I heard her crying.

"What's the matter?" I said.

She said it three times, each louder than the last: "Shut up, shut up, shut up! My head."

"Do you want ibuprofen?"

Through her crying, she said, "I want you to shut up. Do not talk to me. This is your fault." Here, she sat up. "All of it is your fault! You, you, you . . ."

She plucked a tissue from her nightstand, lay back with it, and rolled over onto her side, facing away from me.

At around ten, I went outside to shovel, and across the way next door the neighbor sat out on his porch, smoking, drawing with his finger in the freshly fallen snow. I paid him no attention; I just simply shoveled away what snow had fallen so far, but at some point, a woman yelled, which startled me, and the neighbor, Rhett, flicked his cigarette and got up and went inside, the red ember fading out in the snow.

I made myself coffee when I went back indoors. I didn't want the coffee, just the warm mug in my cupped hands.

I did not watch the news, but at a quarter to eleven a preview showed for the next hour's news. Louise's room was dark except for the glow the television, and I sat in the recliner, mug in hand, watching right as the news anchor said, "The search continues for a missing Indian Island woman. More at eleven."

Louise was sleeping, snoring in little bursts, the tissue held tight in her hand. I shook her gently.

"Louise," I said. "What did you see on the news?"

She grunted and would not look at me.

"Louise," I said again, nudging her. "What did you see?"

She looked at me with her eyes barely open. "It's your fault," she said. "All your fault."

I tried to wait for the news to come on. I waited for ten minutes, and when it did come on, they did not talk about the missing woman but kept saying they would, soon.

I suppose it was panic that pushed me toward the door and into my boots and coat and outside to my truck, and as I turned the key and the engine flared on and the head-lights flashed and the snow fell in their light I realized I was leaving her.

I went to the neighbor's and knocked.

He pulled the door open and then pushed the screen door so it nudged me back. "What do you want?" he asked, and I told him, too quickly, what I needed. He looked at me. "Sure, I can do that," he said. "Lois is a nice lady. Just give me a second." He was gone down the hall to his girlfriend or wife or whoever the voice belonged to, I don't know. He came back and followed me outside. He stopped walking.

"What do you think of this?" he said, lifting something from the pile of garbage. The snow fell off the object like an animal was shaking it loose. But I was rushed, and I don't know what he was trying to show me.

"Later," I told him. "I really have to go."

He dropped whatever it was back into the snow.

"I'll be back soon," I said. "Or as soon as I know what's going on." I tried to give him some advice, some guidance on how to talk to Louise—who he kept calling Lois—and I could not, and still cannot, believe what he said.

"I know how Lois is," he said. "I used to take her for walks to the store." He pointed down the road. "She walks fast for an old lady, and I told her that. I like her, and so does my lady. Listen," he said, but I had no time, although I'm very curious now to know what he wanted to say. That's my life, though—not knowing, but wishing.

I thanked him too many times on my way to my truck. He passed through the headlights and falling snow to the stairs to Louise's, and he banged his boots on each step as he climbed. I was gone before I saw him enter the house. When you're in need, even the person you hate or distrust the most is someone you can rely on, especially when they, the hated, know they are needed for something important.

The first turn I took, the truck skidded, and so after that I drove more careful, but not careful enough. On straight roads I drove too fast, and every once in a while the snow fell too hard and I lost sight of the road. But I thought nothing of the condition of the road then, just the weight of my foot on the pedal and brake and what that news anchor had said. *The search continues, the search continues, the search continues, the search continues. More at eleven. More at eleven. More at eleven.*

I took I-95 instead of the back roads. Every few miles, signs flashed yellow to drive forty-five. I did not. I don't know how fast I drove, but it was probably closer to sixty, and I even passed two plows.

I stopped at a red light. There were no cars, just me in my truck and the snow falling slanted through the streetlights. I went to light a smoke, but I realized I had forgotten them. So I did nothing but focus on driving, on my two hands gripping the wheel. When the red turned green, my tires lost traction and the truck's back end swung left, right, left, then steadied when the wheels found something to grip.

Nobody would have known people were out searching for a missing person. The streets were empty, both in Overtown and on the reservation. After I crossed the bridge to the reservation, I parked in the church parking lot and rolled my window down. There was the sound of falling snow, the noise outside not unlike pressure in the ear, but without the discomfort. I thought I heard a plow approaching, the metal scraping the road, but no vehicle passed by.

I waited in the church parking lot for I don't know how long, and I didn't quite know what I was waiting for. A sign, something more to push me to Mary's house. The feeling to act had disappeared, reason had come back to me. My plan had been to go to Mary's, but now that I was so close, I was second-guessing. This is silly, that's what I thought. It was silly to think what I had thought, to hurry as I had and ask the neighbor to watch my mother while I chased after something I thought was falling apart. But that had been my life: a pursuit of only remains.

I drove home. Not to Louise's but to my house. The dirt road wasn't that covered—much of the snow had landed on the pines—and I could see turned-up dirt frozen hard, my old tire tracks. I drove through the soft falling white down to my house, and I could see a light on inside—the kitchen light above the stove. I turned it off when I went indoors and left the house in darkness. For a time, I stood on the porch with no light.

I watched. Across the river, all was quiet. The yellow of a kitchen light lit the window of her parents' house. The porch light was off, and so I could not see the driveway too well. Maybe both of the cars were there, I thought. What was I doing? What was my plan? I had wanted to go to her parents' house to make sure it was all in my head, that it wasn't her, but then, cowardly, or wisely, I had decided not to. It could have been anybody they were looking for. And so I had come to my house? For what? To see what? The same thing I always saw across the river: an untouchable past, present, future.

I kept watching across the river. Waiting. Ten, fifteen minutes. The cold was that real cold, the Maine cold. And then the lights came. Headlights. No cars had been parked in the driveway, as I had thought. Across the river and through the trees, the two lights swung and shone all the way from over there to here, and the vehicle parked in their driveway, pulled right up to the end, where the little hill down to the river began. The headlights shone, and in the light the snow dropped faster and faster and faster, my eyelashes wet with snow and so too my shoulders, and in the one or two seconds that the snow slowed I saw the footprints—not mine—leading from the end of my porch down to the river and across the frozen ice, where they disappeared up the bank on the other side.

The footprints, smaller than my own, were not fresh. Snow had filled them in partway. And so I walked in them—or I should say I walked over them, step by step, across the river. The person was moving from the car and up the porch steps. I hurried, and somewhere the ice split just enough for the sound to crack like a bone into the night.

Through the falling snow I looked, and the person stood still on the steps. I breathed heavy, hard, and maybe it was that noise that stopped the person too; they heard the sound of this human. But then the figure was gone, only for a moment, a glance, and then the porch light flicked on. I climbed up the bank, fell on my knees into the snow, and then rose.

"Where have you been?" It was Mary. She was on the porch, holding the screen door open with her leg, the wind whipping the snow indoors.

My chest was heaving. The snow, even in the footprints I had walked in, was deep across the river to this side.

"I've been trying to find you," she said. "I've been driving all over the place in this shit weather to find you. Come inside."

"Should I take my boots off?" I said to her.

She didn't answer me, so I left them on.

The lights were bright. Mary disappeared down the hall-way and into a back room, and while she was gone the warmth of the indoors revealed how heavy my clothes were, how soaked with melted snow, with water.

Puddles and streaks of dirty water and salt covered the kitchen floor from boot tracks. Mary came back down the hall, and she stood in the middle of the kitchen.

I asked her. "So it's her?" I said. "It's her?"

She didn't answer my question.

"Sit," she said.

"But is it her?"

"Just sit," she said. "Please just sit." And at this she began to cry. Not quiet crying but crying with tears and heaves so loud it rocked the flesh of the fleshless, my spirit.

"What is it?" I said. "Is it her?"

We were both on our knees amid the dirty water covering the linoleum and the tiny, tiny rocks that pressed into my kneecaps and later left bruises, and the closer I moved toward her, the more she shook, and when I was near to her, just inches, she began to swing at me with her closed fist, back and forth at my arms again and again and again, screaming the incomprehensible into my ear, which she pulled at once or twice, tried to rip it off my head. If she didn't stop, if she didn't slow, I would have let her take me piece by piece by piece, if that was what it took to know.

"We didn't know it would go like this," she said. She was shaking. Her face was wet, her nose running, and she wiped at it with her sleeve. "We didn't know. We told her. We had to."

"Told her what?"

Here she stood up and looked down at me. "What do you think?" she said. She went to the kitchen sink. She wet her hands and wiped her face. I stood up.

"Roger will be back soon," she said. She wiped her nose on her sleeve. "And maybe the game warden. You can go with him. They're upriver right now, looking along those banks. They've checked all the others."

"When did this happen?"

"Earlier," she said. "Before the snow started to fall, before we got home from work."

"That's when you told her?"

"We told her weeks ago, Charles, because what if you told her—what would she think of us?" Mary said. She didn't look at me. Over the sink, she held a glass of water, but she did not drink from the glass.

"And what happened?" I said.

"Exactly what I told you would happen."

It was around here that I wondered if I was dreaming. Mary said something. Was I dreaming?

She repeated only part of what she had said. "Are you?"

I was awake. "Am I what?" I said. It was like bugs had burrowed under my skin.

She dumped the water and let the glass roll from her palm into the sink.

"Am I what?" I asked again.

"Thirsty."

I told her no.

She sat at the table, but I did not.

"She was on watch," Mary said. "When you came to my work that day."

"What do you mean?"

"She was on watch," she said again, "up where she was getting her treatments. They have that ward. That's why you did not see her. That's where she was. Behind those locked doors in the west part of the facility. You know the ones. You've seen the doors. They'd take her in the morning for her treatments, before any appointments."

"How long was she there?" I asked.

"Long," Mary said.

"Why were they watching her?"

"You know," she said.

"I'll have some water."

Mary never told me how it happened, how she chose to try it. I never want to know. Or do I?

I got a cup and filled it. I sipped the water slow until a single drop remained at the bottom. I refilled it and went back to the kitchen table, where we sat in silence for a long, long time.

We both rose at the sound of a car approaching the front of the house, and we both sat back down when the plow passed by, kicking up snow and leaving behind brown, brown dirt. We did the same again when the plow passed by once, twice, three times more.

Again, nothing to say, but everything to think about until, for me, the thinking was too loud to keep in.

"You asked where I was?" I said.

"What do you mean?"

"When I came over," I said. "You asked where I had been. You said you were looking for me."

"I was," she said.

"And you came to my house?" I asked.

She said yes.

I was quiet. Then I told her she left my stove light on.

"You must have left it on," she said. "I didn't go inside. I drove down your dirt road, and when I didn't see your truck, I backed up and went to meet Roger near the river, the place near the dam. After the dam. I should call him and see where he is."

Mary stood.

"Wait a minute," I said.

"It's been almost two hours," Mary said. "I'm calling."

"Just wait a minute. Or don't. Call him. Fine." I went out the door and down the porch steps. Mary yelled after me, the noise muffled by the snow falling. I crawled down the snowy bank to the river and I found the way I had come. I stood up and I crossed back over the river, following my prints, under which the smaller ones were buried.

They belonged to her.

I followed the prints to my house and up the porch and inside, Mary still yelling to me from across the river all the while, a faint calling. Maybe the melted snow in the kitchen was from me, but I knew the wet linoleum down the small hallway and the wet carpet in my bedroom was from her. On my knees, I pushed my palms into it and felt the damp and dirt. She was here, had been here, in this house.

24

After that, it did not take very long for Roger and the game warden to show up, as well as two tribal police who had been out there searching with them. We were inside Mary's, all of us. Roger, Mary, Mel the game warden—the nephew of Shay, the man who helped search for Fredrick—and two officers whose names I did not know. One was white, I'm pretty sure, and the other tribal. We all stood over the table upon which lay a wet map of this side of the land, the page ending at some unknown boundary. Someone said something about following the tracks for as long as we could, and something about dogs, dogs, they might pick up the scent. For a time, standing there at the table, I was drunk on embarrassment: I could not help but feel like some drunken uncle who had caused so great a problem that others had to clean it up. What if, all those years ago, I had just never let Mary do what she did? What if I had said no, that I wouldn't allow it? What if I had said fuck blood quantum? But that was not how it went.

Roger stood there, sweating, the wet tips of his hair sticking out from under his blue hat. He said nothing to me while we stood in the kitchen. No—I did not expect him to say anything to me. The mess that Mary and I had made had put Roger in such a place. He reminded me of Fredrick.

I crossed the river alone. The ice cracked once, twice. The others drove on the roads. Afraid I would ruin any of her marks, I waited on my porch for them to show up. The police lights shone through the bare trees on the road, and they grew brighter and brighter as the cars came to my house and parked. There was only one cruiser. The other officer had gone to get a dog, as if they just had them in storage. The police lights were so bright I could not see behind the cruiser to Roger and Mary and the game warden as they parked.

I showed the footprints to Mel. The snow fell hard and fast, and he wiped his face as he walked, shining the flashlight at the white ground. Around the house, he knelt in the snow and dug his gloved finger into the fresh powder.

"They go this way," he said.

I've been here before, I thought. And there was something more to think about, right then, something I knew that would have been powerful if it had come to me, but her father spoke to me for the first time and stole my attention.

"We'll find her," he said.

*

We kept going and going and going out into the cold dark of the earth that we disturbed with all our hollering.

My hands were numb, and I walked with them in my pockets. Snow filled in the tops of my boots, and my ankles too were not warm. I was losing feeling in my body; it was as if I were separating into two things, each not unlike the other but not whole. And the snow fell harder and faster and harder—it was said that overnight the storm would be at its worst, an inch or more an hour—and it kept coming slanted and harder and faster until not even our flashlights could penetrate the wall of falling snow.

"This isn't safe," Mel said. But he did not mean for him. He was talking to Mary, to Roger, to me. Our group of six had stopped walking, had our backs to the snow falling so dense around us, the cold as deep as it had been this winter, and we had to holler to one another. The tracks, the prints, stopped there, and the dog had no sense of where to go, had got turned around and tried to go back the way we'd come. Mel said he'd radio another county for help, that they'd meet him out this way, and that they'd press on.

The four of us—the white officer brought the dog back—followed our tracks back to my house, where we had set out from. It did not seem to take us very long to return, and that was because my mind was preoccupied with what Mary and Roger were going to do—would they come in? Would they stay? Or would they go back to their home?—or because the falling snow was deafening in its own quiet way, a thing to be focused on intently, like a room furnished with only the spinning of a fan.

"Can we wait here?" Roger asked. In the porch light, his wet face sheened. And Mary's, too, was wet like that, and inside I would see she'd been crying. It was those tears that reminded me of Louise, and I wondered how she was.

I made coffee. We each held a mug, but nobody drank. I had hung our wet clothes, our jackets, hats, their gloves, above the floorboard heater all along the wall, and I had given a quick call to Louise, who had answered and given no indication that the neighbor was there. I suppose I should have expected that he'd leave. Before she hung up, she said I had woken her and not to call again.

Roger and I sat at the kitchen table across from each other while Mary stood by the front door, looking out into the storm. It was close to three in the morning, and our coffees grew cold. Nobody heated their mug in the microwave. I had never turned off the coffeepot, so I could smell the coffee burning, but I let it burn.

Every so often Mary would speak. It was always a mumble or simply words to herself, but each time Roger would say, "Huh?" She never said anything back. She was speaking just to speak, like that act was the only thing keeping her going, keeping her awake.

"I can't sit here anymore," Roger said.

"There's nothing we can do," Mary said. She did not take her eyes from the window.

"It's slowing down out," he said.

It was not slowing down. It was easy to trick ourselves into thinking that.

"They've been gone a long time," he said.

It was now around four in the morning.

"When it's light," Roger said, "I'm going out."

"You're not," Mary said.

"I am," he said.

She said nothing more.

Roger asked where the bathroom was. I told him, but then he said he'd go outdoors, and while he was gone, for the first time since we'd been there, Mary said something to me.

"Do you think they'll find her?" she asked.

"Of course," I said.

"Of course," she repeated.

While Roger was outside the power finally cut out. It would not return for three days.

"I have a lantern," I said, and I went to the closet in the hall. I crouched with a lighter, looking through a box. I found it, but it would not turn on. The batteries in it were dead. I knew I had no more, but I searched like I did, and as I searched the front door banged shut and Roger coughed and Mary told him I was looking for a lantern. I went through as many boxes as I could until the metal of the lighter was too hot and burned my fingers. In the dark I leaned against the wall. Then light—Roger had set his flashlight upright on the kitchen table. But I felt I needed batteries, felt I needed this lantern, so I kept on looking until what I found was the absence of something.

"Hand me your flashlight," I said to Roger. I needed to know with certainty. He brought it over.

I shined the light in the closet.

"You find the lantern?" Mary said.

"No," I said.

My gun was gone.

It was like a click, an alignment.

"Where are you going?" Mary said. "Those are my gloves."

I dropped the gloves to the floor.

"She took my gun," I said, and I did not wait for them to follow.

Dawn had not yet come. I could not see anything but the falling snow and the trees before I bumped into them. My hat kept slipping down over my eyes. Three, four times I tripped, trying to walk in the deep snow, and, stupidly, I had forgotten a flashlight. I didn't even know if I was going the right way or if I was going toward the tracks. I was near them, or so I thought, running horizontal to them.

Was that Mary yelling? Roger?

I yelled her name. I crossed a neighbor's driveway, right up near the beginning of it, and so I knew I was off track, and I cut back into the woods a bit, managing to find our old prints, almost filled with new snow. I followed them, going off in this new direction, and before I knew it I had gone too far right and found myself along the river-bank, and I stepped on thin ice, below which was hollow. I dropped down to my knee, my shin scraping against the thickening ice, an injury that would later require stitches, but that would be the least of my problems. It was a struggle to get back up, but when I did, I went more inland again until, once more, I came to the road.

I zigzagged in this way: to the road, to the river, to the road, until I knew how to stay centered. They called after me, and only now do I wonder why it was me they were looking for, not her—did they think I would lead them to her, take them to her? I kept on through the dark and rising trees and cold falling snow until the sky grew a little bit brighter, just a smear of light, straight ahead to the east, that lit the sky as if far away a fire blazed.

But it was only the sun.

Here, the shivers began. I ran for so long, the cold getting colder, that I forgot what I was chasing. Her? Fredrick? Louise? Myself? I began to talk to nobody. Out here in the cold lay only trees and snow and snow and more snow up to my knees, my thighs. It went deep, as do most things if you look hard enough. My running turned to walking, then limping. The sky grew a brighter and brighter gray with each step, but there was no sun to be seen—it was behind the dense clouds. I remember thinking my hat was down

over my eyes, but it was not: I could not lift my head. My
fingers had no feeling. Neither did my ankles, my feet. Time
passed the way it does when you don't pay it any attention:
fast.

More light.

My pant leg was frozen to the blood that seeped from
my shin wound, and it hurt when I tore it, when I peeled
the fabric from the skin. The wound must have bled again,
because it got warm. But then again, everything got warm:
my head, my neck, my torso and arms and fingers, my waist,
my thighs, my knees, my calves and my ankles and my toes.
My chest.

I shed my clothes, piece by piece, as I stumbled along,
until I felt I could no longer go on. I fell backward into
the fresh powder, and when I lifted my head, I saw the
hidden sun, and when I rested my head back, upside down
and looking not east but west, I saw a sun too, blazing, it
seemed, like it had crashed into the earth and was setting
the world on fire.

She wasn't out here. We had it all wrong. We were all
going in the wrong direction—or we had failed to notice
when she turned around.

I smelled the smoke.

I don't remember how long it took me to get there,
I don't remember how many clothes I was wearing, but I do
remember thinking, So what, I didn't rescue him then and
I wasn't going to rescue him now. But her. I could rescue

her. And she was this way, not toward the east but toward the west, the future.

Fredrick's house was on fire. Fire trucks and ambulances and police cruisers and their red and white and blue lights lit the air as I made my way back to my house and called for Mary and Roger. I ignored their questions about what was happening as I crossed the frozen river, the both of them behind me. The bright lights lit the snow that fell like ash.

"Why aren't you putting it out?" Mary asked the firemen.

"Our lines are frozen," a firefighter said. "We're waiting for Overtown to come—" He looked at me. "Are you OK?"

I wasn't. I barely had any clothes on, my leg was bleeding, and my head hurt like it had been cracked by a rock. Before I could even tell him no, two EMTs brought over a blanket and wrapped it around me as they guided me toward the ambulance. They were preparing to settle me in the back when Mary screamed so loud and hard I knew a part of the world was about to die. I turned and looked and one officer dragged Mary from where she stood, and then three took hold of Roger.

"Get in the ambulance, please," an EMT said to me.

I looked at Mary, who yelled with what she had left. "She's in the house, Charles! Right there! I see her! She's in the house!"

Part of it, the left side, crumbled, and smoke and flame billowed. I felt the heat, and I pushed the two EMTs from me, took the blanket and wrapped it around the face of a man who tried to grab me and yanked him to the ground. I passed the fire truck and lifted a steel axe from two hooks, and I ran for the house. The firefighter closest to the home went to grab me but I raised the axe, and he took several steps back as I limped for the house, the house that would be gone in the morning.

The main door was a wall of fire, and so I went into the small garage with the old ash-pounding machine, went right to the far wall. On the other side of that wall, I knew, was the living room. I put my hand to it and it was warm, so warm, and if I had been here under any other circumstance I could have easily just fallen asleep against that wall and fallen with the rest of the house. But I lifted the axe and swung and swung and swung, the way Fredrick and I would cut wood, and I eventually split the wall enough that I could fit through.

She was in sight: she was across the empty room, leaning against the other wall, two wooden boards across her lap as she awaited the approaching flames.

"Elizabeth!" I told her to hold on. What little clothes remained of my pants were on fire, literally, my skin burning. I patted the flames out as best I could with the wet blanket the EMTs had thrown over my shoulders, and when I took one step there was a small yet distinct pop and then a searing pain in my side. I looked up, and Elizabeth had my gun, Fredrick's gun, Joseph's gun—her gun. She kept it aimed at me.

I was on my knees, crawling in the fire toward her, hands burning. "Don't," I said. She pumped the .22, but before she could fire another shot at the only real target—my head—two things happened: the front of the house collapsed, and then jets of water sliced through the snow and cold and ash and fire and blinded us both like light that burned hotter than fire, than the sun, and before I could say one more word to her, a burnt two-by-four dropped from the ceiling and put me to sleep.

25

I woke two days later. The room was lit only by the hospital's hall light. I thought I was alone. Machines beeped when I pulled wires from my gauze-wrapped arms, and then a hand was on me.

"Jesus Christ," Bobby said. "Don't go nowhere."

"Where is she?" I asked, but he was gone.

I felt I had somewhere to be, except I did not have the strength to bring myself there. I wondered how Bobby had found me here. And I asked him later, in the morning, after I had slept again and dreamed of fire and water.

He sipped coffee from a white Styrofoam cup. "Your mother told me," he said.

And I wondered how she knew. And before Bobby explained, in those brief moments, it was as if she loved me more than anything, as if some miracle had occurred, some vision, maybe sent by Fredrick himself, had spoken to her, told her what had happened to me.

But no. Bobby had called Louise after the storm to see if I was there, and she said, "Who? Stop calling. Don't you know she's missing?"

"Then I saw it on the news," Bobby said. "That she'd been found and that someone else was brought to the hospital. I don't know why, but I just felt like I had to call around and ask for you. Sure as shit you were here. They didn't tell me a goddam thing. I had to tell them you were my brother, and only then would the fucking bitch tell me you were alive."

I suppose this was the miracle: the part where I woke up and Bobby was there.

I was in the hospital for nine days, and before I was discharged, I called Mary. I don't think she wanted to ask how I was feeling, but she did. And when I told her I'd be fine, she said, "That's good," and we were both silent until I asked her about Elizabeth. "Her thighs are burned bad," she said. "They did two skin grafts."

"Is she here?" I asked. I coughed, and the bullet wound made me wince.

"She was," she said. "But they moved her back to the building where she gets her ECTs. She refuses to see any of us. We can't get in to see her. She only has one name on her visitors list, and it's not Roger or me."

"Maybe it's me," I said.

She hung up.

26

I went up to the facility to see her. It was half past four on a Wednesday, and I parked in the same lot I parked in when I took Louise to her ECT appointments. I got out of the truck, my leg hurting and my neck a bit sore. My body was broken still from the search, from the fire. It was almost dark when I limped to the front doors; a last sight of blue cut across the horizon, right above those tall pines. The security guard—not the tiny, tiny man with pale skin; I don't know what happened to him, maybe he had moved on somewhere else—stood up from behind his desk. Before he could speak, I said, "Just car keys, I'll get a locker," and he sat back down and looked past me to the outdoors, as if that was what he wanted. Or maybe a smoke.

I told the woman behind the desk I was there to visit somebody. I said that. "Somebody," like Elizabeth was still a secret. And the woman said I'd missed visiting hours, that they were from two to four Monday through Friday and ten to six on Saturday. When I left, not a sliver of blue remained up above: just the black licorice of the night sky. And no stars shone, but they were there, and I'd see them on the highway as I drove home on that last stretch of 95, where the lights are few and far between, crumbs to an ant.

On the drive home I was relieved, and maybe it was that relief that had blinded me to the fact that I had not even checked to see if I was on the visitors list. So all that night I barely slept, thinking about how dumb I was for not having asked. Even when I did fall asleep, I could never stay asleep for more than five minutes, one reason being I kept thinking about Elizabeth and the other being the pain in my leg. This went on until four in the morning, when I decided to just get up and watch the sun rise, and it rose, but the day was a cloudy one, and all I saw was the change from dark to light gray, hazy, clouded in the way wax sometimes gets.

I had to wait until two, and that waiting reminded me of the day Mary planned to bring Elizabeth to see me. I stuck around home for some time, but by ten I had begun to feel restless, and so I drove up to Louise's. When I got to her, she was in the living room, the elephant in her lap as she sat at the table and played games in a book filled with crosswords and word search puzzles and sudoku.

Louise looked up from her book but said nothing.

I asked her if she wanted coffee or tea, and with the pencil she held she tapped the mug in front of her.

"Do you want it heated?" I asked.

"No," she said.

I asked how she was feeling.

"Are you a nurse?" she asked. I didn't know if it was an honest question or if it was a taunt.

I went to ask if she knew my name, but she cut me off.

"I shit myself this morning," she said, writing something in the margins of the sudoku she played. "That's how I'm feeling."

I asked stupidly, "Where?"

"Where do you think?" she said. "In my pants."

I told her I'd be right back, and I went to her room. A few months ago, she would have cleaned the mess. But now she had not. I stripped her bed of the soiled sheets and carefully brought them to the house's basement. A sink was down there, and under the water I washed out what I could before loading the sheets into the washer. Back upstairs, Louise continued to work away at her game.

"Did you change your clothes?" I asked her.

"I'm not an animal," she said.

I could smell it.

"I'm not saying you are," I said. "I'm just asking."

"You're the animal," she said. Now she looked at me. "A dog. Nothing but somebody's dog."

I could see it now, all of it. It ran down her leg and up her back and down the chair legs.

I called her Mom, and she said, "I'm not your mother."

"Louise," I said. "You have to wash and change. Come on."

"I already did," she said, setting the elephant upright on the table. It fell forward on its face.

"You did not," I said to her. She needed to see. I felt this was the only way: I ran my hand along her back and showed her.

That face. Like all things she knew to be true were turned upside down. Like all things right were now not right.

She said, "But I did. I know I did. I know I did. I did." Her hands were covered as she stood up and looked at it all. And here she said, looking me in the eyes, trying to touch my face with her shit hands, "Charles, you, Charles, I did. I did." She walked toward her room, and in there she pointed to a pile of soiled clothes in the corner I had not seen before.

So she had. "But it happened again," I said.

I led her to the bathroom, and I turned on the shower.

"Wash off," I said, "and I'll bring you clothes."

While she sat in one of those white shower chairs under the water, I cleaned the living room chair and its legs and the floor below it all. And then I brought her clothes down to the laundry room and set them to the side until the sheets were done. Back upstairs, I brought her fresh clothes and draped them over the towel rack and let her know they were there.

I was sitting in the living room when she came out. The clothes she had on—just pajama bottoms and a long-sleeve shirt—were wet, like she had not dried off before putting them on.

"I'm going to lie down," she said to me.

I checked the time, and then I followed her.

"Your sheets aren't clean yet," I said.

"My sheets?"

"I put them in the wash," I told her. "To clean them."

"But I cleaned them," she said. "Go get them."

"They'll be wet," I said. "Do you have other sheets?"

She didn't answer me. She got in the sheetless bed and pulled the blankets up to her neck.

"Are you cold?" I asked.

"Am I?"

"I'm asking. Are you?"

"No," she said.

"I can put the heat on if you are."

"I'm not," she said, and she rolled onto her side.

I put the heat up just a bit.

"I'll be back," I said to her. "I have to be somewhere. And when I'm back, I'll dry your sheets and cook you something to eat."

"You have to see another patient?" she asked.

"Another patient?"

"You're my doctor, right?"

"I'm not your doctor," I said.

She paused a moment, rolled over, and looked at me.

"The nurse," she said. "Wait. No, no, that's not right. You're not the nurse."

"You're right," I said. "Do you know who I am?"

She looked at me like you look at a puzzle. "I do," she said with what seemed to be a smile but could have easily been a frown, and she rolled back onto her side.

It was half past two when I parked in the lot of that spider building. I sat in my truck for I don't know how long. Ten, fifteen minutes. I smoked two cigarettes and dumped out the truck's ashtray in a small bag I kept in the back for garbage. And then I smoked another.

I could not bring myself to go inside. It wasn't because I didn't want to—I did—but I felt unprepared. Like I was coming with nothing, which wasn't far from the truth. But I needed to bring her something, didn't I? I started the truck and went down to that Rite Aid near downtown, and I bought two bars of Hershey's and a *People* magazine and spearmint gum. And after I checked out, I started to worry I smelled bad, like shit, and so I went back in and bought some body spray, which was too strong, but I used it anyway. I drove back with the windows down, trying to blow that smell away, and I grew cold with the air cutting across my knuckles. When I made it back, I had to park in a different spot because somebody had taken mine.

It was three fifteen.

"It's for somebody who I'm visiting," I said to the security guard as he looked in the bag. He told me to give it to the woman behind the desk, that she'd make sure the patient got it.

"I can bring it up," I said to him.

"You can't," he said. "They need to search it."

"But you just did," I said.

The woman behind the desk spoke. "Bring it over here."

"It's food and a magazine," the guard said.

I brought the bag over.

"We have to take the staples out," she said about the magazine. "Who is it for?"

"It's for somebody who I'm visiting."

"Does the somebody have a name?" the woman said. A Styrofoam tray of rice and curry the color of wet sand lay on the desk in front of her. Her white plastic fork was stained brown.

"Elizabeth. Elizabeth Francis."

She typed something on her computer. "Your name?"

I told her.

"Hold on one second," she said. She picked up the phone and made a call.

"If I'm not on the list, that's OK," I said.

"It's not that—"

She was not on the phone for too long. "There's no last name here," she said. "Can you check with her?"

A minute or two of silence. Then she put her hand over the receiver. "This will just take a second," she said to me.

Of course Elizabeth wouldn't know my last name. Or maybe she'd forgotten. Or maybe she didn't care to remember.

"So it's right," the woman said. "OK, thank you."

The woman wrote my name on a tag, which I pressed to my shirt. She said that once they—I don't know who—had gone through what I'd brought, they'd give it to Elizabeth. And then she told me where to go. Left down that hall and to the door with the buzzer. When the door buzzes and unlocks, go straight. On the left is the elevator. Take it to the third floor. Then there's another set of doors. Ring the buzzer. "They'll bring you to her," she said.

They did not bring me to her, because as I passed through those last doors, she was right there, waiting, the staff and patients and other visitors going about their business while a man with a yellow over-the-head radio earmuff walked up and down and up and down the hall, talking to nobody. She was right there and I didn't even know it, among them all, near the main desk, and I walked past her, right past her to the desk, and asked this tall man with glasses where I could find Elizabeth Francis.

"I'll go get her," the man said, but then he asked another to get her, and it was the other—a very old man with a gray beard—who said, "Sure." And when he rose, he said, "Oh, she's right there behind you," and all of them—the tall man with glasses, the old man, and a young woman who was standing beside them—they all laughed.

She was wearing blue hospital pants and a gray hoodie that said "Penobscot" across it.

"I got you some—"

"Come with me," she said, and I followed her. The hallway was long and warm.

We reached the end of that hall, and against the wall were two blue plastic chairs. She sat down in one, each of the corners rounded.

"This floor is for retarded people," she said. "See that guy down there?" She pointed down that long hallway to the man with the yellow radio earmuffs, who was running in circles. "He thinks he's a German spy. He keeps telling me they're keeping him here against his will, that they caught him trying to transmit sensitive government information. At least once a day he tells me he has a secret, a secret so big it could change the course of human history. Are you going to sit?"

I sat down.

"The floor below us is for people on watch. People who aren't like him are down there. There were no beds, so they put me on this floor. What I'm saying is that I'm not like them. Or maybe I am."

"You're not," I said.

"I'm joking—I know I'm not."

We were quiet for some time. Elizabeth lifted her legs up and tucked them under her.

"Did she tell you to come?" she said.

"Who?" I asked.

"My mother."

"No," I said. "She said you were here. I thought to come up."

Elizabeth put her hands in her sleeves. "My mother kept saying that it was the right thing to do. Telling me the truth. Why did she tell me?"

"Because she felt it was the right thing to do?" I asked.

"Why? Why was it the right thing to do? Why, all of a fucking sudden, did she tell me? Look, I'm not in this place because of what she said. I'm not. So don't sit there and look sorry. I'd be here no matter what. I just want to know why."

"Why she told you?" I said.

"Are you listening to me?"

I told her why. And she listened to me, in that chair with her hands in her sleeves. I told her that my plan was to tell her the truth, that I felt she should know it, that she deserved to know the history that was hers. We are made of stories, and if we don't know them—the ones that make us—how can we ever be fully realized? How can we ever be who we really are?

"So what are you saying?" she asked. "You think my life would have been different if my mother married you and you raised me?"

"I'm not saying that," I said.

"Well, what are you saying?"

"I'm saying there's more history that belongs to you than you know."

Elizabeth stood up and went into a room—a woman in there yelled at her to get out—and she came back and sat down. "You have ten minutes before visiting time is over," she said. "Can you tell me that history in ten minutes?"

"No," I said.

"You better try," she said. "There was a reason why I tried to shoot you. This is the only time you have with me."

I got what I could out. I was lucky in that they let me stay a bit longer. But there was so much more to say and not enough time to say it. I wanted to say it all: wanted to give her all the history that is hers. This past. This family. I wanted her to know, wanted her to understand what it meant that she was being stretched beyond the walls of her parents' house, that she was of that house, certainly, but also of others—the one across the river, and the one down the road that almost became a museum but didn't because Elizabeth burned it to the ground so that all that remained was the charred, burnt wood of the story that is hers.

At the end of the hallway, before I turned the corner to leave through the locked doors, I glanced back at her. She still sat with her legs tucked under her, her hoodie up, and then she raised her arm and gave me a wave, a goodbye, a see ya never.

27

It wasn't until the next day—almost 5:00 am—that I remembered I'd completely forgotten about Louise and her clothes and bedding I'd put in the wash for her. After I left the treatment center, I went to the bar and talked with Bobby, told him how it went—"Jesus," he had said, "she tried to kill you? She must really hate your guts"—and after I brought him home, I drove home and had a strong urge for apple pie. I drove out to Jim's Corner and the whole way I had my high beams on and when I got there all he had were packaged Hostess Fruit Pies, which I still bought, and at home I ate them outside on the cold steps and drank coffee and smoked until I couldn't take the chill anymore. I went to bed, meaning I lay there restless on the couch until morning, until I remembered what I'd forgotten about: my mother.

The sun was bright off the white hard snow when I left my house to go to Louise's. I wanted to stop and get her a coffee and toast and eggs, but I'd left her for far too long to stop off and figured I'd make her some when I got to her house. I didn't have much gas left, but it was enough to get me there and I figured I'd go fill up after.

The neighbor was outside when I pulled in and parked my truck. He was jabbing an ice chopper into the ice that covered his driveway. I said, "How you doing?" and he stopped and in the bright sunlight looked up and squinted and said, "Fine," and went back to cracking the ice. With a limp, I walked up the steps to Louise's and the neighbor yelled to me.

"You still owe me money," he said. "For the car seat."

I was halfway up the stairs and said back to him, "I know. I'll get it for you the next time. Is that OK?"

He said he could use it today, and so I said I'd get it today.

"Let me see Louise for a bit and then I'll go to the bank," I told him.

He didn't say anything and went back to chipping the ice.

I went inside, and before climbing the steps up to Louise's apartment, I went downstairs to the washer and dryer in the basement that smelled like oil. They were both empty. I thought maybe someone had taken her sheets out and put them somewhere so they could use the washer, but I couldn't find anything. I left and went up the steps to the first floor and then climbed the stairs to Louise's apartment. The doorknob turned, but the door didn't move. She had the dead bolt turned, the dead bolt she'd said so very long ago was broken, and so I knocked a few times. Nothing, and so then a few times more.

"Louise?" I said loudly. "You sleeping?"

Nothing.

"Louise?" I said again. I could hear her TV on, could hear that show with Dr. Something.

"Louise!" I knocked again, harder and louder. "You gotta undo the dead bolt!"

But she didn't answer.

I thought maybe I could get her attention by going outside and yelling at her through the window high above, even though it was closed. I yelled her name a few times before I started picking up chunks of hard snow and throwing them at her window, hitting the glass.

"Louise!" I said, and then I paused, trying to think who I should say I was. The doctor? The nurse? Fredrick? Her son? I decided against them all.

"It's me!" I yelled. "It's me! Go open the door!"

The window opened and the woman who lived next to Louise stuck her head out.

"What the fuck do you want?" she said, and I realized I was at the wrong window.

I apologized and told her what I was doing.

"Well, her window's over there," she said. I went to that one and started again, throwing the chunks of hard snow and ice at the window. I would have kept going but from behind me, the neighbor spoke.

"What's the matter?" he said.

"Louise locked the damn dead bolt," I said.

"I got a key for it," he said.

"Why do you have a key for my mother's door?"

"She gave it to me," he said. "A long time ago."

I waited outside with my hands on my hips, looking up at the window and my cold breath rising. A cloud had passed by and the sun sneaked out and blinded me, so I looked down and blinked a few times and walked to the front of the building where the neighbor was with the key.

"Here," he said. "Just give it back when you're done."

"You're not getting the fucking key back," I said, "and you're not getting any fucking money for that fucking car seat neither. Now fucking get."

I climbed the narrow steps to the top floor. At her door, I slid the dead-bolt key into the keyhole and turned. The door swung open, and then I shut it behind me. I banged my shoes on the mat and then took them off.

The TV was blaring, the narrator of Dr. Something's show talking about that standard Y incision.

"Louise," I said, walking to her bedroom. "Why the hell did you give that neighbor a key to—"

With the sheets I forgot to dry, Louise's bed was made so neatly, the corners and sides tucked in tightly, and in the middle of the bed lay my mother, her hands gripping the blanket and holding it up to her neck, and right beside her was that elephant, equally tucked in and equally still.

"Louise?" I said.

She didn't move.

". . . and this finding confirms that the attack on Matthew's face was not by . . ."

I turned the TV off, and in the quiet I walked to the side of her bed.

"Mumma?" I said, and I put my finger on her stiff neck.

I sat in the recliner I always sat in and smoked a cigarette. Louise's phone rang in the kitchen, and then it stopped. I turned the TV back on but put the volume down to three. Before I sat down again, I took the elephant away from her body, and I held it, rolled it over in my hands and rubbed its fur. And then I set it next to me in the recliner, closed my eyes, and took a deep breath, and when I opened them, she was still the way she had been, lifeless, and so I just started talking, told her body the truth of every story I had ever been part of, beginning with who that elephant belonged to.

28

I cremated her. The ground was too hard for any burials, and so I held on to her ashes until the earth softened. There was a part of me that didn't want to put her all in the ground, and so I bought one large urn and then two small ones. I kept one and I gave the other to Bobby, who was so torn up about Louise. He stopped drinking at the bar and started drinking at my house, almost every single night, from late January to May, when we could finally put my mother to rest next to Fredrick. I don't know how many drunken toasts Bobby gave my mother during those months. "To the best woman this earth has seen," "To the mom I wish I had," "She didn't give a fuck about nothin'," and "Why'd she have to go like this?" When he was particularly drunk, he would open the tiny urn and speak French: "Vous nous manquerez et on se souviendra d'eux," "Une vie trop tranquille est une mer morte," and "Après la pluie, le beau temps."

And after the rain, the good weather did come.

*

The only other person besides Bobby—and Gizos—to know my mother died was Mary, because I went through her to buy the plot next to my father. And so it had to have been Mary who told the others on the reservation that Fredrick's wife had passed away, because who else would have said something?

On the day we buried Louise—on the day I got down on my knees, my leg and body still hurting, and lowered her large urn into a square hole in front of a headstone that read "Loving Mother & Loving Wife"—a small group of people gathered to watch. I recognized a few of them, but mostly they were random people stopping by to give their condolences. I didn't know why, but I expected Gizos to show up. He didn't, although he did send flowers and make a donation in her name to that treatment center that looked like a spider. I stayed longer than I wanted to—Bobby was inconsolable and drunk—but I suppose it was good because Mary showed up, and she wasn't alone. Elizabeth was with her, as was Roger, and all three came over to me.

The first thing Mary said to me wasn't about my mother but instead was about Bobby. "Who is that?" she asked. "He's freaking people out."

I didn't know it until Mary said it, but Bobby was going around showing people Louise's ashes, and so I went up to him and told him to quit it or get in the fucking car, that Mary and my daughter had shown up, that Louise's granddaughter was here, and he looked so, so very sorry and went and sat down against the chain-link fence of the cemetery.

"He's done," I said to Mary. "Thanks for coming."

"I am sorry she's gone," Mary said.

A moment later she said, "I always liked her," and then she grabbed Roger gently by the arm and pulled him away so it was only me and Elizabeth standing there.

"You would have gotten a kick out of your grandmother," I said to her. "She was a lot like you in so many ways."

"I thought she was funny when we used to wait together for our ECTs," Elizabeth said.

"You look good, by the way," I said. She did. She had on a flower-patterned dress, and her hair was braided. "How are you feeling?"

"You should stop worrying about me and start worrying about yourself," she said.

She was probably right. I looked terrible. I hadn't been taking care of myself. My nails were dirty, and if you lifted my pant leg, you'd see my wound had gotten infected again. I imagine both of my eyes looked like they'd been punched.

It got too quiet, and Elizabeth went to speak, but I cut her off.

"I have something for you," I said. "If you want it."

I said I'd be right back. A few people stopped me and said they were sorry. Bobby was asleep against the fence.

In the back seat of my truck, I grabbed the elephant, and

in the front seat I dug around for the small urn I'd meant to keep. I took them with me and went back to Louise's grave, where Elizabeth stood waiting.

"Here," I said, and I handed her the elephant and the urn.

"Isn't that your mom's baby?"

"It is," I said. "And if Louise knew everything, she would have wanted you to have it. The elephant is actually yours, anyway."

"Mine?" Elizabeth asked.

"Yours," I said. "I can tell you about it, if you want. I can tell you about her." I got down on my knees one more time, and with my hands I pulled the pile of moist dirt next to the headstone and dragged it and dumped it into the hole, covering my mother in her urn. The wind blew and rippled the trees, their pale green underbellies showing. I thought I was alone then, just me and my mother, but before I could pull the last bit of dirt that was there, Louise's granddaughter told me to move, and she got on her hands and knees and with her arm she pushed the rest of the earth, our sweet, sweet earth, over our shared blood that was now turned to ash.

Dear readers,

As a publisher of shamelessly literary books, in addition to bookshop sales, we rely on subscriptions from people like you in order to publish in line with our values.

All of our subscribers:

- receive a first edition copy of each of the books they subscribe to
- are thanked by name at the end of our subscriber-supported books

BECOME A SUBSCRIBER, OR GIVE A SUBSCRIPTION TO A FRIEND

Visit andotherstories.org/subscribe to help make our books happen. You can subscribe to a selection of the books we're in the process of making. To purchase books we have already published, we urge you to support your local or favourite bookshop and order directly from them – the often unsung heroes of publishing.

OTHER WAYS TO GET INVOLVED

If you'd like to know about our upcoming books and events, please follow us via:

- our monthly newsletter, sign up here: andotherstories.org
- Facebook: facebook.com/AndOtherStoriesBooks
- Instagram: @andotherpics
- TikTok: @andotherbooktok
- X: @andothertweets
- Our blog: andotherstories.org/ampersand

OUR SERIES DESIGN

The inside text is set in Albertan Pro and Linotype Syntax. Albertan was created by Jim Rimmer in 1982. It was originally made for use in hand-setting limited edition books at Jim Rimmer's own Pie Tree Press. Syntax was created by Hans Eduard Meier in 1968.

Our jacket design is by Elisa von Randow, Alles Blau Studio, who said: 'Choosing simplicity and bringing the author's work to the cover was the starting point suggested by the editors. The next step was to choose a typeface that would convey the contemporary and bold spirit of the publisher's catalogue. After many studies, the simplest and most radical idea was chosen.' The jacket's typeface is Stellage, designed by Mark Niemeijer and released in 2020 by SM Foundry.

OUR MATERIALS

And Other Stories books are printed and bound in the UK using FSC-certified paper from the most ecological paper mills, stamped with a bio-degradable foil. In a North of England collaboration, our jacket's card stock is Vanguard, a paper manufactured by James Cropper. Nestled among the Lake District fells, papermaking craftsmanship and stewardship of the natural environment are integral to all operations at the James Cropper mill. As a specialist in upcycling fibre, James Cropper created the world's first recycling process dedicated to upcycling take-away coffee cups into fine papers. The cover fibres of the book you're reading had a previous life holding espresso.

THE DOUBLE-CURVE ARTWORK ON THE COVER

Artist Maya Tihtiyas Attean explains her process: 'This design features elements of a traditional double curve motif, which can symbolise events, people, or ideas. I drew inspiration from archival drawings of double curves created by other Penobscots in the 1800s. In my design, the curved lines represent our river, flowing separately on both sides of a flame. The flame, a powerful and sustaining symbol, represents our humanity and survival. Above the flame, I included a drop of blood to symbolize the blood quantum system imposed on Indigenous people since colonial times. Creating this piece has been deeply meaningful to me, as it allows me to contribute to the narrative of my people by contextualizing traditional patterns with contemporary ideas and symbolism.'

THIS BOOK WAS MADE POSSIBLE
THANKS TO THE SUPPORT OF

Aaron McEnery
Aaron Schneider
Abigail Walton
Adam Lenson
Adriel Levine
Aija Kanbergs
Ajay Sharma
Al Ullman
Alasdair Cross
Albert Puente
Alex Fleming
Alex Ramsey
Alex (Anna) Turner
Alexandra German
Alexandra Stewart
Alexandria Levitt
Ali Boston
Ali Ersahin
Ali Smith
Ali Usman
Alice Carrick-Smith
Alice Wilkinson
Aliki Giakou
Alison Hardy
Allan & Mo Tennant
Alyssa Rinaldi
Amado Floresca
Amaia Gabantxo
Amanda Milanetti
Amanda
Amber Casiot
Amber Da
Amelia Dowe
Amitav Hajra
Amos Hintermann
Amy Hatch
Amy Lloyd
Amy Sousa
Amy Tabb
Ana Novak
Andrea Barlien
Andrea Larsen

Andrea Oyarzabal
  Koppes
Andreas Zbinden
Andrew Burns
Andrew Marston
Andrew Martino
Andrew McCallum
Andrew Milam
Andrew Place
Andrew Place
Andrew Reece
Andrew Rego
Andrew Wright
Angus Walker
Anna French
Anna Gibson
Anna Hawthorne
Anna Holmes
Anna Kornilova
Anna Milsom
Anne Edyvean
Anne Germanacos
Anne Ryden
Anne Willborn
Anne-Marie Renshaw
Annette Hamilton
Annie McDermott
Anonymous
Ant Cotton
Anthony Fortenberry
Antony Pearce
April Hernandez
Archie Davies
Aron Trauring
Asako Serizawa
Audrey Holmes
Audrey Small
Avi Blinder
Barbara Mellor
Barbara Spicer
Barry Norton
Becky Matthewson

Ben Buchwald
Ben Schofield
Ben Thornton
Ben Walter
Benjamin Heanue
Benjamin Judge
Benjamin Pester
Benjamin Winfield
Beth Heim de Bera
Bianca Winter
Bill Fletcher
Billy-Ray Belcourt
Björn Dade
Blazej Jedras
Brandon Clar
Brendan Dunne
Brett Parker
Brian Anderson
Brian Byrne
Brian Isabelle
Brian Smith
Bridget Prentice
Briony Hey
Brittany Redgate
Brooks Williams
Buck Johnston &
  Camp Bosworth
Burkhard Fehsenfeld
Buzz Poole
Caitlin Farr Hurst
Caitlin Halpern
Caleb Bedford
Cameron Adams
Camilla Imperiali
Carla Ballin
Carmen Smith
Carole Parkhouse
Carolina Pineiro
Caroline Kim
Caroline Montanari
Caroline Musgrove
Caroline West

Carrie Brogoitti
Caryn Cochran
Catharine Braithwaite
Catherine Connell
Catherine Fisher
Catherine Jacobs
Catherine Lambert
Catherine McBeth
Catherine Williamson
Catherine Tandy
Cathryn Siegal-
  Bergman
Cathy Leow
Cecilia Rossi
Cecilia Uribe
Ceri Lumley-Sim
Cerileigh Guichelaar
Chandler Sanchez
Charles Dee Mitchell
Charles Fernyhough
Charles Heiner
Charles Rowe
Charlie Mitchell
Charlie Small
Charlotte Coulthard
Charlotte Holtam
Charlotte Whittle
Chelsey Blankenship
Chenxin Jiang
Cherilyn Elston
China Miéville
Chris Blackmore
Chris Clamp
Chris Johnstone
Chris McCann
Chris Potts
Chris Senior
Chris Stevenson
Christina Sarver
Christine Bartels
Christopher Fox
Christopher Lin
Christopher Scott
Christopher Stout

Cian McAulay
Ciara Callaghan
Claire Brooksby
Claire Mackintosh
Claire Williams
Clare Wilkins
Clare Young
Claudia Mazzoncini
Cliona Quigley
Colin Denyer
Colin Matthews
Collin Brooke
Conor McMeel
Courtney Lilly
Craig Kennedy
Cynthia De La Torre
Cyrus Massoudi
Daina Chiu
Daisy Savage
Dale Wisely
Dalia Cavazos
Daniel Cossai
Daniel Hahn
Daniel Sanford
Daniel Syrovy
Daniela Steierberg
Darcie Vigliano
Darren Boyling
Darren Gillen
Darryll Rogers
Darya Lisouskaya
Dave Appleby
Dave Lander
David Alderson
David Anderson
David Ball
David Eales
David Gould
David Gray
David Greenlaw
David Hebblethwaite
David Higgins
David Johnson-Davies
David Kaus

David F Long
David Morris
David Richardson
David Shriver
David Smith
David Toft
David Wacks
Dean Taucher
Deb Unferth
Debbie Enever
Debbie Pinfold
Deborah Gardner
Deborah Green
Debra Manskey
Declan O'Driscoll
Denis Larose
Denis Stillewagt &
  Anca Fronescu
Denise Brown
Derek Meins
Diane Hamilton
Diane Josefowicz
Diane Salisbury
Diarmuid Hickey
Dinesh Prasad
Dominic Bailey
Dominic Nolan
Dominick Santa
  Cattarina
Dominique Brocard
Dominique Hudson
Doris Duhennois
Dorothy Bottrell
Dugald Mackie
Duncan Chambers
Duncan Clubb
Duncan Macgregor
Dyanne Prinsen
Ebba Tornérhielm
Ed Smith
Ekaterina Beliakova
Eleanor Maier
Eleanor Updegraff
Elif Kolcuoglu

Elina Zicmane
Eliza Mood
Elizabeth Atkinson
Elizabeth Balmain
Elizabeth Braswell
Elizabeth Draper
Elizabeth Franz
Elizabeth Guss
Elizabeth Eva Leach
Elizabeth Rice
Elizabeth Seals
Elizabeth Sieminski
Ella Sabiduría
Ellen Agnew
Ellie Goddard
Emma Louise Grove
Emma Morgan
Emma Post
Emma Wakefield
Eric Anderson
Erin Cameron Allen
Ethan White
Ethan Wood
Evelyn Reis
Ewan Tant
Fawzia Kane
Fay Barrett
Felicity Le Quesne
Felix Valdivieso
Finbarr Farragher
Fiona Mozley
Fiona Wilson
Forrest Pelsue
Fran Sanderson
Frances Gillon
Frances Harvey
Frank Pearson
Frank Rodrigues
Frank van Orsouw
Gabriel Garcia
Gabriella Roncone
Garland Gardner
Gavin Aitchison
Gavin Collins

Gawain Espley
Gemma Alexander
Gemma Hopkins
Geoff Thrower
Geoffrey Urland
George Stanbury
George Wilkinson
Gerry Craddock
Gillian Grant
Gillian Spencer
Gina Filo
Glen Bornais
Glenn Russell
Gloria Gunn
Gordon Cameron
Graham Blenkinsop
Graham R Foster
Grainne Otoole
Grant Ray-Howett
Hadil Balzan
Halina Schiffman-
   Shilo
Hannah Harford-
   Wright
Hannah Levinson
Hannah Jane
   Lownsbrough
Hannah Madonia
Hannah Rapley
Hans Lazda
Harriet Stiles
Haydon Spenceley
Heidi Gilhooly
Helen Alexander
Helen Mort
Henrike Laehnemann
Howard Norman
Howard Robinson
Hugh Shipley
HumDrumPress Amy
   Gowen
Hyoung-Won Park
Iain Forsyth
Ian Betteridge

Ian McMillan
Ian Mond
Ian Randall
Ian Whiteley
Ida Grochowska
Ilya Markov
Inbar Haramati
Ines Alfano
Inga Gaile
Irene Mansfield
Irina Tzanova
Isabella Weibrecht
J Shmotkina
Jack Brown
Jaclyn Schultz
Jacob Musser
Jacqueline Haskell
Jacqueline Lademann
Jake Baldwinson
James Avery
James Beck
James Crossley
James Cubbon
James Kinsley
James Lehmann
James Leonard
James Portlock
James Richards
James Ruland
James Saunders
James Scudamore
James Silvestro
James Thomson
Jan Hicks
Jane Dolman
Jane Leuchter
Jane Roberts
Jane Roberts
Jane Woollard
Janet Digby
Janis Carpenter
Jason Montano
Jason Sim
Jason Timermanis

JE Crispin
Jeanne Guyon
Jeff Collins
Jen Hardwicke
Jennifer Fain
Jennifer Fosket
Jennifer Frost
Jennifer Mills
Jennifer Yanoschak
Jenny Huth
Jeremy Koenig
Jeremy Sabol
Jess Decamps
Jess Wood
Jessica Gately
Jessica Queree
Jessica Weetch
Jethro Soutar
Jill Harrison
Jo Clarke
Jo Heinrich
Jo Lateu
Joanna Trachtenberg
Joao Pedro Bragatti
 Winckler
Jodie Adams
Joel Hulseman
Joelle Young
Johannah May Black
Johannes Holmqvist
Johannes Menzel
Johannes Georg Zipp
John Betteridge
John Bogg
John Carnahan
John Conway
John Gent
John Hodgson
John Kelly
John Miller
John Purser
John Reid
John Shaw
John Steigerwald

John Walsh
John Whiteside
John Winkelman
John Wyatt
Jon McGregor
Jon Riches
Jonah Benton
Jonathan Blaney
Jonathan Busser
Jonathan Leaver
Jonathan Paterson
Jonathan Woollen
Jonny Anderson
Jonny Kiehlmann
Jordana Carlin
José Echeverría Vega
Joseph Camilleri
Joseph Thomas
Josh Glitz
Josh Ramos
Joshua Briggs
Joshua Davis
Judith Gruet-Kaye
Julia Rochester
Júlia Révay
Julia Von Dem
 Knesebeck
Julie Atherton
Juliet Willsher
Juliette Loesch
Junius Hoffman
Jupiter Jones
Juraj Janik
Kaarina Hollo
Kalina Rose
Karen Gilbert
Karen Mahinski
Karl Chwe
Karl Kleinknecht &
 Monika Motylinska
Katarzyna
 Bartoszynska
Kate Beswick
Katharine Robbins

Katherine Sotejeff-
 Wilson
Kathryn Edwards
Kathryn Williams
Kati Hallikainen
Katie Freeman
Katie Zegar
Katrina Mayson
Keith Walker
Kelly Hydrick
Kenneth Blythe
Keno Jüchems
Kent McKernan
Kerry Broderick
Kieran Cutting
Kieran Rollin
Kieron James
Kirsten Benites
Kitty Golden
KL Ee
Kris Fernandez-
 Everett
Kris Ann Trimis
Kris Ann Trimis
Kristen Tcherneshoff
Kristen Tracey
Krystale Tremblay-
 Moll
Krystine Phelps
Kurt Navratil
Kyle Pienaar
Lana Selby
Laura Ling
Laura Zlatos
Lauren Pout
Lauren Trestler
Laurence Laluyaux
Leah Binns
Leda Brittenham
Lee Harbour
Leona Iosifidou
Lex Orgera
Liliana Lobato
Lilie Weaver

Linda Jones
Lindsay Attree
Lindsay Brammer
Lindsey Harbour
Lisa Hess
Liz Clifford
Liz Ladd
Lorna Bleach
Louis Lewarne
Louise Aitken
Louise Evans
Louise Jolliffe
Lucinda Smith
Lucy Moffatt
Luise von Flotow
Luiz Cesar Peres
Luke Healey
Luke Murphy
Lydia Syson
Lynda Graham
Lyndia Thomas
Lynn Fung
Lynn Grant
Lynn Martin
Mack McKenna
Madalyn Marcus
Maeve Lambe
Maggie Humm
Maggie Livesey
Marco Magini
Margaret Dillow
Mari-Liis Calloway
Marian Zelman
Mariann Wang
Marijana Rimac
Marina Castledine
Mark Grainger
Mark Reynolds
Mark Sargent
Mark Sheets
Mark Sztyber
Mark Tronco
Mark Troop
Martha Wakenshaw

Martin Haller
Martin Price
Martin Eric Rodgers
Mary Addonizio
Mary Clarke
Mary Ann Dulcich
Mary Tinebinal
Matt Davies
Matthew Cooke
Matthew Crawford
Matthew Crossan
Matthew Eatough
Matthew Francis
Matthew Lowe
Matthew Woodman
Matthias Rosenberg
Maxwell Mankoff
Meaghan Delahunt
Meg Lovelock
Megan Wittling
Mel Pryor
Melissa Quignon-
   Finch
Michael Aguilar
Michael Bichko
Michael Boog
Michael James
   Eastwood
Michael Gavin
Michael Parsons
Michaela Anchan
Michele Whitfeld
Michelle Mercaldo
Michelle Mirabella
Miguel Head
Mike Abram
Mike Barrie
Mike James
Mike Schneider
Miles Smith-Morris
Mim Lucy
Mohamed Tonsy
Molly Foster
Molly Schneider

Mona Arshi
Monica Tanouye
Morayma Jimenez
Moriah Haefner
Myza Gouthro
Nancy Chen
Nancy Cohen
Nancy Jacobson
Nancy Oakes
Naomi Morauf
Nasiera Foflonker
Natalie Middleton
Nathalia Robbins-
   Cherry
Nathan McNamara
Nathan Weida
Nichola Smalley
Nicholas Brown
Nicholas Jowett
Nicholas Rutherford
Nick James
Nick Marshall
Nick Nelson & Rachel
   Eley
Nick Rushworth
Nick Sidwell
Nick Twemlow
Nico Parfitt
Nicola Hart
Nicolas Sampson
Nicole Matteini
Nicoletta Asciuto
Niharika Jain
Niki Sammut
Nikola Ristovski
Nina Aron
Nina Laddon
Nina Todorova
Norman Batchelor
Odilia Corneth
Ohan Hominis
Owen Williams
Pankaj Mishra
Pat Winslow

Patrick Hawley
Patrick Hoare
Patrick Liptak
Patrick McGee
Patrick Pagni
Paul Bangert
Paul Cray
Paul Ewing
Paul Gibson
Paul Jones
Paul Jordan
Paul Milhofer
Paul Munday
Paul Nightingale
Paul Scott
Paul Stuart
Paul Tran-Hoang
Paula McGrath
Paula Melendez
Pavlos Stavropoulos
Pawel Szeliga
Pedro Ponce
Perry
Pete Clough
Pete Keeley
Peter Edwards
Peter Goulborn
Peter Hayden
Peter Rowland
Peter Wells
Petra Hendrickson
Petra Stapp
Philip Herbert
Philip Leichauer
Philip Warren
Phillipa Clements
Phoebe McKenzie
Phoebe Millerwhite
Phyllis Reeve
Piet Van Bockstal
Prakash Nayak
Rachael de Moravia
Rachael Williams
Rachel Beddow

Rachel Belt
Rachel Gaughan
Rachel Rothe
Rachel Van Riel
Rahul Kanakia
Rajni Aldridge
Rebecca Caldwell
Rebecca Maddox
Rebecca Marriott
Rebecca Michel
Rebecca Milne
Rebecca Moss
Rebecca Peer
Rebecca Roadman
Rebecca Rushforth
Rebecca Servadio
Rebecca Shaak
Rebekah Lattin-
  Rawstrone
Renee Thomas
Rezart Bajraktari
Rhea Pokorny
Rich Sutherland
Richard Clesham
Richard Ellis
Richard Ley-Hamilton
Richard Mansell
Richard Smith
Richard Soundy
Richard Stubbings
Richard Village
Risheeta Joshi
Rishi Dastidar
Rita Kaar
Rita Marrinson
Rita O'Brien
Robbie Matlock
Robert Gillett
Robert Sliman
Roberto Hull
Robin McLean
Robin Taylor
Robina Frank
Roger Ramsden

Ronan O'Shea
Rory Williamson
Rosabella Reeves
Rosalind Ramsay
Rosanna Foster
Rosemary Horsewood
Ross Beaton
Royston Tester
Roz Simpson
Ruth Curry
Ryan Bestford
Ryan Day
Ryan Pierce
Sabine Griffiths
Sally Ayhan
Sally Baker
Sally Warner
Sam Gordon
Samuel Crosby
Samuel Wright
Sara Kittleson
Sara Unwin
Sarah Arboleda
Sarah Arkle
Sarah Brewer
Sarah Lucas
Sarah Manvel
Sarah Stevns
Sasha Dugdale
Scott Adams
Scott Baxter
Scott Chiddister
Sean Johnston
Sean Kottke
Sean McGivern
Sean Myers
Selina Guinness
Severijn Hagemeijer
Shamala Gallagher
Shannon Knapp
Sharon Levy
Sharon White Gilson
Sienna Kang
Silje Bergum Kinsten

Simak Ali
Simon Clark
Simon Pitney
Simon Robertson
Simone Martelossi
SK Grout
Stacy Rodgers
Stefano Mula
Stella Rieck
Stephan Eggum
Stephanie Miller
Stephanie Smee
Stephanie Wasek
Stephen Fuller
Stephen Pearsall
Stephen Wilson
Stephen Yates
Steve Clough
Steve Dearden
Steven Diggin
Steven Hess
Steven Norton
Steven Williams
Stewart Eastham
Stuart Allen
Stuart Wilkinson
Summer Migliori Soto
Susan Edsall
Susan Jaken
Susan Morgan
Susan Wachowski

Susan Winter
Suzanne Kirkham
Suzanne Wiggins
Tamar Drukker
Tania Hershman
Tania Marlowe
Tara Roman
Tatjana Soli
Tatyana Reshetnik
Taylor Ball
Terry Bone
Tess Lewis
The Mighty Douche
    Softball Team
Theresa Kelsay
Thomas Alt
Thomas Campbell
Thomas Fritz
Thomas Noone
Thomas van den
    Bout
Thuy Dinh
Tiffany Lehr
Timothy Baker
Timothy Cummins
Tina Juul Møller
Toby Ryan
Tom Darby
Tom Doyle
Tom Franklin
Tom Gray

Tom Stafford
Tom Whatmore
Trevor Brent Marta
    Berto
Trevor Latimer
Trevor Wald
Tricia Durdey
Tulta Behm
Tyler Giesen
Val & Tom Flechtner
Valerie Carroll
Vanessa Baird
Vanessa Dodd
Vanessa Heggie
Vanessa Nolan
Vanessa Rush
Veronica Barnsley
Victor Meadowcroft
Victoria Goodbody
Vijay Pattisapu
Vilma Nikolaidou
Wendy Langridge
William
    Brockenborough
William Mackenzie
William Richard
William Schwaber
William Wilson
Yoora Yi Tenen
Zachary Maricondia
Zoe Taylor